MIYA T. BECK

THE

PEARL

HUNTER

BALZER + BRAY
An Imprint of HarperCollins*Publishers*

Balzer + Bray is an imprint of HarperCollins Publishers.

The Pearl Hunter
Copyright © 2023 by Miya T. Beck
Map art © 2023 by Sveta Dorosheva

Library of Congress Cataloging-in-Publication Data

Names: Beck, Miya T., author.
Title: The pearl hunter / Miya T. Beck.
Description: First edition. | New York : Balzer + Bray, [2023] |
   Audience: Ages 8-12. | Audience: Grades 4-6. | Summary:
   "When Kai's twin sister, Kishi, is stolen and killed by the
   legendary Ghost Whale, Kai sets out on a long and dangerous
   adventure to bring her back to life"— Provided by publisher.
Identifiers: LCCN 2022021832 | ISBN 9780063238190 (hardcover)
Subjects: CYAC: Twins—Fiction. | Sisters—Fiction. | Sea
   monsters—Fiction. | Fantasy. | LCGFT: Fantasy fiction. | Novels.
Classification: LCC PZ7.1.B434739 Pe 2023 | DDC [Fic]—dc23
LC record available at https://lccn.loc.gov/2022021832

Typography by Molly Fehr
22 23 24 25 26 LBC 5 4 3 2 1

First Edition

๑๑๑

For Howard and Talia,
my land and my sea

๑๑๑

*Nothing
in the world
is usual today.
This is
the first morning.*

–IZUMI SHIKIBU

Hovering deep underwater with her black hair fanning out all around her like squid ink, Kai stretched her hands toward her twin sister. Kishi was her mirror reflection. They shared the same chestnut-brown eyes and lightly freckled noses. They shared the same broad shoulders and long legs that rippled with muscle from a lifetime spent swimming. But people could tell them apart if they knew where to look. Kishi's right ear stuck out like an anemone flower while Kai's did on the left. Kishi's belly button was an innie while Kai's was an outie. Kai was also a lefty. But in this moment beneath the sea, the only difference that mattered to Kai was that Kishi was wearing her white diving headscarf. Kai hadn't earned hers yet.

The current ruffled the triangular point of Kishi's headscarf and the hem of her white diving skirt. As Kishi extended her arms, Kai expected to feel the pressure of their palms meeting. Instead her hands met a slick, invisible membrane. The gap between her hands and her sister's hands was about the length of a chopstick. Kai frowned and pushed against the clear barrier. It didn't give. She tried again. Impossible. Only then did Kai notice the fear and desperation in her sister's eyes.

"Kai," Kishi said, her voice muffled and air bubbles streaming from her mouth. "Stay away from the ghost wall."

Kishi's eyes went glassy. Her hands slipped off the membrane. Kai jolted awake.

Her heart was pounding. In the blur between sleeping and waking, she didn't know where she was. But then she inhaled the warm tart breath of her sister. The gray and white contours that at first seemed like a distant hilly landscape turned out to be the side of Kishi's head and the bedroom wall behind her. They lay on the futon facing each other, their noses almost touching. Her sister was fine. It had just been a dream. As her heart rate went back to normal, Kai rolled onto her back and stared up at the thatched ceiling. What was a ghost wall? Jellyfish were transparent. Did that mean they were going to encounter a giant jellyfish today? Or was she simply nervous about diving solo for the first time? Some villagers thought being identical twins meant that they shared special powers like the blind shamanesses who communicated with the gods and the dead. Though Kai and Kishi could finish each other's sentences, they weren't psychic. She didn't have a clue what the dream might mean.

As the sky pinked and purpled through the latticed window, her eyes fell on Aunt Hamako's tool belt, which had been hanging limply from its peg across the room since she died six pearl seasons ago. The knife. This was her chance, while Kishi was asleep. Mama had the blunt diving knife specially made as a birthday gift for Hamako, with freshwater pearls embedded where the blade met the base. Kai had always admired it. Slipping out of bed, she grabbed her own knife from her tool belt. Then she tiptoed across the room and swapped it for her aunt's, running her index finger over the luminescent sea-green pearls, shaped like baby teeth and glimmering in the low light. An ache rose in her throat that she quickly pushed down. *Crying is for gentlemen writing poetry in the capital,* Hamako used to say, pretending to sob uncontrollably into her sleeve. *We pearl divers don't have time for tears.*

She'd been more like a big sister than an aunt, regaling the twins with bedtime stories and village gossip and taking them out on boating and hiking adventures. She was the one who taught them the names of trees and flowers and picked out the constellations in the night sky. Hamako found joy in everything she did, and Kai wanted something of hers on this important day.

"Kai, what are you doing?"

She whirled around, hiding the knife behind her back. Kishi sat up on the futon, her hair disheveled and her plain wide-sleeved top falling off one shoulder.

"Nothing," Kai said. "Just thinking about Hamako and wishing she could be here today."

Kishi crossed her arms and narrowed her eyes. "Put it back," she said.

Kai tucked the knife inside the waistband of her trouser skirt and held up her empty hands. "Put what back?"

Snorting with disbelief, Kishi marched across the room. Kai slid between her and the tool belt. When Kishi grabbed her arm, Kai jerked free and danced away. But Kai realized her tactical mistake as Kishi grabbed Hamako's tool belt from the peg.

"I knew it," Kishi said, pulling out the plain-handled knife. "Put it back."

"Hamako would want me to have it," Kai said.

Kishi raised her left eyebrow. "Right, because you were her favorite."

"Why do you care if I use her knife?" Kai snapped. "You already had your day, Miss Perfect."

They were both supposed to graduate to solo dives last month after passing the final test, where they had to hold their breath underwater while Mama counted to fifty and then dive down to the seafloor thirty times in a row without a break. But on her last trip, Kai scooped up three mussels, breaking Mama's rule that they only bring up one mussel at a time. Like Hamako, Kai liked to grab as many as she could. These didn't even need to be pried off the rocks. It seemed like a waste, to leave behind mussels that begged to be taken.

How many times have I told you not to do that? Mama said when she surfaced.

Pearl diving is risky, Mama—you've said it yourself, Kai argued.

We don't need to make a risky thing even riskier, she retorted. *You swim one stroke at a time, and you take one mussel at a time.*

We could also be possessed by foxes when we go to the cemetery, Kai countered, since spirit-possessing foxes were said to lurk near burial grounds. *That doesn't stop us from visiting Hamako.*

That's not the same, Mama said. *Why do you have to be so stubborn?*

I'm not being stubborn, Kai shot back. *You're being stupid.*

She hadn't really believed that Mama would punish her. But that's exactly what happened. Kishi did her ceremonial first solo dive while Kai seethed in the boat. Ever since then, Kai had been the meek, obedient daughter, bringing up only one mussel at a time.

Kishi puffed up her chest with righteousness. "It's going to set Mama off if she sees you with that knife," she said.

"She's only going to know if you tell her," Kai said.

Kishi clucked her tongue. As she marched toward the bedroom door, Kai grabbed her by the sleeve and said the worst thing she could think of: "If you tell her about the knife, I'm going to tell her about the village chief's son."

Kishi gasped and wrenched her sleeve away. "You only think about yourself," she said. "That's why nobody likes you."

Blinded by a rage that only her sister could provoke, Kai pinched Kishi hard on the fleshy part of her underarm. When Kishi shrieked, she felt a twinge of guilt. She loved her sister yet sometimes hated her with the intensity of the deepest, darkest point in the sea. There was no in-between. Kishi dropped Kai's knife and came at her with both hands raised, shoving her hard in the chest. Kai stumbled into the wall with a sharp scream. Pushing off the wall, she charged at Kishi. Suddenly the bedroom door slid open.

"Girls, what is going on?" Their mother stood in the doorway with a wide stance, her fists on her hips and her elbows out. She was already dressed for the boat in a white linen swim skirt and a padded indigo jacket to ward off the early morning chill.

Alarmed at the prospect of losing her solo dive, Kai jerked her body to a halt as if she had puppet rods and strings attached to her limbs. Kishi stepped in front of Kai's knife on the floor, blocking it from their mother's view.

"Nothing, Mama," Kai said as Mama's gaze shifted to Kishi, the one who could be counted on to tell the truth. Kai held her breath and waited to see what would win out, anger or solidarity.

Kishi's shoulders slumped. "Nothing, Mama," she said.

Their mother gave them each a warning look, then slid the door shut. Kishi picked up Kai's knife from the floor and tossed it on the futon. Then she turned her back to Kai and started to get ready, banding her hair at the nape of her neck. Kai kept Hamako's knife to spite her.

Usually Kai was the sluggish one in the mornings, the last one in the boat. But today she couldn't get away from Kishi fast enough. Kai threw on her diving skirt and jacket, then opened the bedroom door with a bang and crossed the living room, where Mama kneeled by the hearth in the middle of the floor packing jars of dried mussels and wineberries into a lunch basket. In the entryway, Kai stepped into a pair of woven sandals. The front door of the thatched cottage faced a small cove where their fishing boat and a small rowboat rested on the pebbly beach. Standing on the veranda, she gazed at the Freshwater Sea, a rosy mirror beneath the breaking sun.

Trays and buckets had been left scattered along the veranda where they shucked their catches. They used every part of the mussel, scraping out the meat and laying each piece out to dry in the sun, setting aside the half shells to be sold to artisans. Any pearls that they found, they cleaned and stored in jars hidden beneath the pantry floor. Twice a season, they sold the pearls, which came in a rainbow of colors, to the noble houses in Chowa, the capital of the Heiwadai Empire.

Last autumn, at the end of pearl season, Kai and Kishi accompanied Papa to the capital for the first time so that they would know what to do when their parents grew too old to make the journey. The trip took a full day, traveling to the southern end of Biwa Province by boat to Nishi Port, and then by oxcart on bumpy roads over a mountain pass. Their pearls had been in high demand because of the emperor's coronation ceremony, which meant the ladies and gentlemen of the court all had special wardrobes made. Chancellor Fujiwara had named the reign of the new emperor—who'd just had his coming-of-age ceremony—the Era of Everlasting Peace. This made everyone laugh, since the emperor would probably still be a young man when his era ended. Once the emperor had a crown prince come of age, the chancellor would force him to retire and put his son on the throne. That was how the chancellor had stayed in control for three decades.

Kai had mixed feelings about her first trip to the capital. She'd been in awe of the grand villas with their beautiful gardens, and loved the bustling streets where gentlemen in tall black lacquered hats rode sleek horses while ladies traveled in palm leaf carriages with the hems of their silk robes dangling beneath the doors. At the same time, she'd never been made more aware of her family's commoner status. The attendants in the great houses had looked at them with distaste, as if they were rats who had come to eat up all the rice.

Kai grabbed two empty buckets from the veranda and placed them in the fishing boat. Then she went to the shed, which stood to the right of their cottage and was surrounded by wineberry bushes. Opening the door, she picked up a stack of shallow round baskets and a pail of coal. The coals went into a little heater in the middle of the boat. Kai always thought about Hamako while she did chores because she and Kishi used to pass the time as they shucked mussels or picked wineberries repeating the fairy tales that their aunt had told them. One would start with "Once upon a time," and then the other would follow with the next line. Sometimes they changed the stories to make them better, like the tale about the virtuous Princess Hase, whose poetry once soothed a roaring river. The princess's jealous stepmother ordered a servant to take Hase to the mountains and kill her. But the servant disobeyed and hid Hase in a mountain cottage. And that's where Kai and her sister departed from the real story. Instead of the emperor coming to rescue the princess, they decided that a band of tiny house fairies, samurai with toothpick-sized swords, trained her every night in the art of the sword, and that a blind shamaness taught her how to control the river using her poetry. Princess Hase then conquered the empire and got her revenge by sending a flood of river water to the capital that carried her evil stepmother out to sea.

As Kai poked the hot coals with a stick, her throat felt raw. It had been a long time, maybe a year or more, since she and Kishi had told a story together. The last time she tried, Kishi had shrugged and said, *Aren't we too old for fairy tales?*

Hamako wasn't too old for fairy tales, Kai pointed out. But after that Kai gave up, and she wasn't sure what hurt more, that they'd stopped honoring Hamako's memory or that she'd lost this connection with her twin.

Tossing the stick to the sand, Kai held her chapped hands over the coals for warmth. Out of the corner of her eye, she saw Kishi and Mama emerge from the house arm in arm. Kai and Kishi had been so excited last summer when they shot past their mother in height. They were now a head taller. But that was also when things began to change between them. Kishi used to despise the village boys just as much as Kai did. There was an old superstition that twins were monsters, a curse from the gods. When they were born, the midwife told Mama and Papa to pretend they only had one baby and keep Kishi, the oldest, and get rid of Kai. Mama told the midwife that girls were revered in pearl diving families and therefore she saw twin girls as a double blessing. These boys had treated them like lepers, and for as long as Kai could remember, the boys would shout, "Go away, dirty mermaids!" and throw rocks at them.

Lately these same boys kept trying to get Kishi's attention. Sometimes on the walk to town to trade dried mussels for millet, a boy would grab the bag from Kishi's hands and try to get her to chase him. Sometimes the boys wrestled each other to the ground and called out to her to watch. Last week, the village chief's son fell into step with them and began bragging about the pheasant he'd shot from a thousand paces away. Judging from his soft cheeks and hands, Kai doubted he could shoot a bird if it flew in front of his face. He'd always been smug, which was surprising given that he was short and stout and had buckteeth. As he walked with them, Kai realized he'd slimmed down and caught up to them in height. His teeth no longer seemed too big for his face, and his voice cracked as he boasted about how he was sure to win the archery contest at the summer festival. When Kishi giggled, Kai rolled her eyes. But whenever Kai made fun of her sister for encouraging the boys, Kishi accused her of being jealous. Maybe she was. They were identical twins, yet the boys liked Kishi better.

Kai hadn't been sure if she'd started walking faster or if Kishi and the chief's son started walking slower. By the time she reached the rock they called the sleeping cat rock, just past the grove of ginkgo trees where they used to play games of hide-and-seek, her sister and the boy had lagged far behind. Kai sat on the cat's back to wait. Suddenly they veered off the path. Wondering what could have caught their attention, Kai went to look. As she neared the spot where they left the path, she heard the chief's son speaking in a low teasing voice and her sister giggling. Kai stepped around a ginkgo tree and found Kishi in his arms. She gasped, and Kishi jumped away from him, her face beet red. When Kai warned her later that she was deluding herself if she thought the chief would allow his son to get involved with a pearl diving family, Kishi stormed off and didn't speak to her for two days. Kai wasn't being mean, just truthful. She didn't see the chief's son rowing their boat.

"Mama, look," Kishi exclaimed. "Kai must have been possessed by an industrious spirit. She's done all the chores."

"Yes, I like this new Kai," Mama said, her dark brown eyes crinkling into crescent moons and a smile playing on her full lips. "No need to call the exorcist."

Kai glowered at her sister. "Your jokes are almost as dumb as a certain boy in town," she said.

Kishi stuck out her tongue, and when she sat down on the bench, Kai noted that she left a significant gap between them. Mama climbed in and stored the lunch basket beneath her seat across from Kishi. They always sat in the same spots. The place next to their mother and across from Kai remained empty.

The sky was on fire now and the sea glowed a deep shade of pink. Mama held her hands over the heater, nine strong slender fingers and one mangled pinkie that had been caught in the rocks years ago, when she reached her teens and started to dive on her own. She'd managed to rip the tip of her finger off and surface while she still had air. Rocks didn't have teeth or nails or any other kind of weapon. Yet they were a pearl diver's most dangerous enemy.

On the day Hamako died, Kai and Kishi had been in the boat moving mussels from the baskets into the buckets. Suddenly their father threw off his tunic and dove into the water. Their mother, who had just surfaced, immediately went back down. Kai had used an oar to pull Mama's basket toward the boat and Kishi had leaned over to pick it up. Then they stepped up on the bench, held hands, and waited. Kai knew that Kishi was counting the seconds like she was. When they reached twenty, Kai looked at Kishi and they wordlessly agreed that it was time to jump in. As they bent their knees and leaned forward, Mama broke through the water. Papa came up seconds later holding Hamako, her eyes unseeing, her hand torn and bloody from the rocks. Ever since then, Mama had a one-mussel rule. Even though Kai could hold her breath longer than anyone in the family, Mama argued that she'd need that extra time if something went wrong. Kai understood her fear, but she didn't have the patience to do it her mother's way. Diving for mussels was boring and repetitive. Hunting for the giant crinkly octopus in the rocks or the spotted flatfish camouflaged in the sand was what made being underwater worthwhile. Then she would scoop up as many mussels as she could to make up for lost time.

But ultimately Mama held the power over whether Kai could dive alone. So she swallowed her pride and played by her mother's rules. Now that her day had come, she could not figure out why Papa was taking his sweet time getting ready. Tired of waiting, Kai jumped out of the boat and ran back to the house. When she stuck her head inside the door, he was clamping his broad-brimmed straw hat on his head. The hat was too small for him, leaving a red welt on his forehead by the end of each day. Kai and Kishi spent a lot of time debating whether his hat was too small or his head was too big. But Papa insisted that it was a fine hat, and that the snug fit kept him from napping while they were on the boat.

"Papa, come on," Kai said. "It's time to go."

"Quick, hurry," he said with a broad grin that showed off his squat square teeth. "Before the mussels run away."

"Before Mama changes her mind," she said darkly.

He palmed her head with his large calloused hand. "Go easy on her," he said. "She's trying to keep you safe."

"We don't even know for sure that Hamako tried to take extra mussels," she groused. Hamako would not only bring up two mussels in each hand, but she'd even tuck a fifth one in her tool belt.

Papa sighed. "When terrible things happen, sometimes we have to find a reason, something to blame, in order to keep on going," he said. "If it makes your mother feel better, then what's the harm? The fate of the Heiwadai Empire doesn't rest on whether you bring up one mussel or four."

Kai nodded and looked down at her feet as they walked to the boat, wishing she could be more considerate like her sister. Once she took her seat, Papa pushed the boat into the water. Then he leaped in and walked on the benches to get to the front, his lean calf brushing her elbow. Papa liked to joke that the gods had made him out of spare parts. He was built like an ox in his upper body but had skinny bamboo poles for legs. His exceptional arm strength made him the fastest rower among the fishing villages that dotted this part of the Freshwater Sea. Every year he won the speed contest at the summer festival in honor of the sea gods. Even so, it was no secret that some villagers called him half a man for marrying a pearl diver. Papa said he'd rather be a half man than a monkey's bottom.

As the boat glided toward the horizon, the sea breeze prickled Kai's exposed thighs and she hunched over for warmth. Her stomach clenched and she felt a nervous buzz. But when she looked at Kishi for reassurance, her sister turned her soft gaze to the sea. She had the same dreamy look that she got when she was practicing the Dance of the Blue Waves for the summer festival, or when she was organizing her shell collection by color and size. But what was giving her that look now? The village chief's son? Kai could not understand how her sister could like him at all.

She wished they could go back to being kids again. She didn't like that their bodies were changing, their hips and breasts filling out their swimsuits. She didn't like that the village matchmaker had started to approach families with girls their own age. And she especially didn't like that Kishi would rather giggle and whisper with the chief's son than with her. She wanted to go back to lazy afternoons on the beach when they played with their shell collections like dolls and built little driftwood houses and gave the shells ridiculously literal names like Spotty and Stripey. Back then if they had a fight, Mama and Hamako would separate them. Kishi would go inside and help Mama cook while Kai tended the vegetable garden with her aunt. But within minutes they'd be sending hand signals to each other, and soon they'd slip off together to spy on Papa in his hammock. They'd pretend that he was an ogre, and they'd clutch each other and shriek with laughter every time he turned to look at them.

These days they fought more and made up less. Kai wasn't sure why.

When Papa stopped rowing, Mama rummaged in her

knapsack. Then she stood up, holding out a white diving scarf with purple crosshatch marks. The scarf was folded into a neat triangle.

"O mighty sea gods," she said, "I humbly present to you my daughter Kai, who carries on our family's pearl diving tradition. We thank you for your protection and generosity."

Kai felt a lump rise in her throat as she bowed and took the scarf from her mother. "I accept this honor and give thanks to Benzaiten," she said, referring to the female sea deity whom all pearl divers revered.

Kai tied the scarf around her head, knotting the ends at the nape of her neck, and cast off her jacket. Then Kishi handed her a collection basket and attached the tether to the back of her tool belt. Hugging the basket to her chest, Kai stood poised at the edge of the boat. The dawn dives were always the hardest because that was when the sea seemed to be the most alive and the most strange. Pinks and yellows spiraled in the water like something out of a dream, and some part of her feared that once she dove in, she would be lost in that mad swirl forever.

Kai usually entered the water the same way Mama did, turning her back to the sea and falling in bottom first. Sometimes she copied Kishi, leaping sideways and scissor-kicking her legs. Poised at the edge, she decided from that day on she would go in the same brave way Hamako did, looking straight at the sea. Kai tossed out her basket and jumped into the water like a chopstick, arms at her sides and toes pointed.

The icy shock of the water was quickly followed by familiarity, comfort, and relief that what lay below was a cool cloudy blue. Once she broke through the surface, she treaded water near her floating basket and took in a slow deep breath, her lungs expanding until there was no more room in her rib cage. Then she plunged into the depths. After a few strokes, her muscles loosened and warmed. She thought she might feel lonely without her mother trailing her, but she didn't. A school of minnows flitted past. A silvery fish blew kisses at her. Reaching the ocean floor, she swept her hands across the gravel, startling a crusty flatfish.

When she found a dark blue oval, she pulled a half mussel shell from her tool belt and placed it with its rainbow interior faceup, to mark the area so that she could find the bed again. Then she used Hamako's knife to pry off the mussel. Arcing her body, she rose toward the surface, following her tether to the black orb of her basket. As she neared the top, she let out her breath in a long slow whistle until her head breached the water. Wiping her eyes with her free hand, she dropped the mussel into the basket while her family clapped. She hugged the basket to her chest and grinned. She was officially a pearl diver now.

Kishi and Mama jumped in, swimming away from the boat with their baskets until the three of them formed a triangle. Then they went to work, plunging to the depths. On Kai's third trip down, Kishi passed holding up four fingers, meaning she was swimming up with her fourth mussel. Had Kai not been underwater, she would have gasped. Kishi was throwing a silent challenge to see who could collect the most mussels. Even though Kai could hold her breath longer, Kishi was the faster swimmer. Kai knew she should ignore her sister. That would bother Kishi more than losing. But Kai was fiercely competitive, and the truth was she wanted to get back at Kishi. Not for the knife, but for sneaking off the path with the chief's son.

To beat Kishi, she either had to swim fast or bring up more mussels on each trip. However, if their parents noticed, she'd be in trouble and they'd halt the morning dive. She decided to keep pace with Kishi as best she could and then grab as many mussels as possible on the last dive to beat her. Each time she and her sister passed each other, they flashed numbers. By the time Kai had reached nineteen, Kishi had twenty-one. Her muscles felt like overcooked noodles. With the water growing choppy, Papa was going to call them back to the boat at any moment.

Kai pried off a mussel with too much force, and it popped out of her hand into a patch of feathery seaweed. As Kai searched frantically for the lost mussel, Kishi puffed out her chest and arced toward the surface. She held up her index and middle finger twice. Twenty-two. *No time*, Kai thought. Whenever she chastised herself, she heard her aunt's excitable voice in her head. *Get a new one*. Glancing up, Kai saw her mother's silhouette pushing her basket toward the boat. She was done for the day. Kai darted to the spot where she'd plucked her first mussel that morning and scooped up four, two in each hand. Her lungs burned as she powered herself to the top with one last kick. When Kai broke through the surface, Kishi was bobbing next to her basket with a triumphant smile. Kai dropped all four mussels into her basket with a dramatic clatter.

"Twenty-three," she announced.

Kishi's smile faded. Mama stood up in the boat, hands on her hips. "Kai," she said. "I can't believe you. How do you expect me to trust you?"

Papa picked up the bamboo pole that he used to help them climb back in the boat. Before he could extend it to her, Kishi took a deep breath and disappeared underwater. Since she was a rule follower, she'd only bring up one more for the tie. All Kai needed was one to win.

"Kishi, Kai," Mama shouted. "Get back in the—"

Kai dove, drowning out the rest of her sentence. She raced to the bottom, her strokes sloppy with fatigue. Kishi was already there, her black hair fanning out behind her scarf and the soles of her feet fluttering. Her hands brushed left and then right. She was having a hard time finding another mussel. Kai swam faster. She'd almost reached the bottom when a cold pocket washed over her and the seafloor went dark. She flipped around to look up. Whatever was passing overhead was massive. The moment the shadow passed, she hurried back to the boat.

"There's something down there," she said, out of breath. "Something big."

Suddenly Kishi's basket jerked and whizzed across the water. Kai's heart jumped into her throat. Papa threw off his jacket and dove into the sea.

"Kai, get back in the boat," Mama shouted, extending the bamboo pole.

But she had to go help her sister. Detaching the line from her tool belt, Kai followed her father. Papa was about two-thirds of the way down, holding the snapped end of Kishi's tether and spinning in a frantic circle. Her own insides went loose and frayed at the sight of that rope. A high-pitched ringing filled her ears. No, this could not be happening. No, no, no. Kishi could not be gone.

A cold current rippled through her. A ghastly white claw—no, a giant beak—no, the skeleton of a whale—came between Kai and her father. But how could a whale carcass move so quickly? Then she saw Kishi was caught inside its rib cage, banging her fists in front of her face. She seemed stuck. Kai swam to her without considering whether it was wise. When she reached for Kishi, all she felt was slick fishy skin beneath her hands. That's when the dream came back to her—the ghost wall. For a moment they mirrored each other, their noses and palms pressed against the clear surface. Kai realized Kishi hadn't said "ghost wall" at all. She'd said, "Stay away from the ghost *whale*."

Hamako had told them the story of the ghost whale, the bakekujira, a thousand times. How could she have forgotten? Kai pulled out the knife, the one that had sparked their fight, and stabbed the invisible skin. But the dull blade squeaked and slipped right off. Then she tried to grab on to the whale as it slithered by. But there was nothing to hold on to. All she could do was watch as the bakekujira flicked its bony tail and sped away, taking her sister with it.

2

Kai broke through the surface, wheezing and coughing. Papa was climbing into the boat. With water dripping from his ashen face, he reached over the side and hauled her in. Mama had curled into a ball between two benches. Kai turned her back. She couldn't stand to see her mother like this.

"It went that way," Kai said, pointing farther out to sea.

As Papa rowed hard in one direction and then another in pursuit of shadows on the dappled water, Kai berated herself for not knowing what the dream had meant. Whenever Hamako had told the story of the bakekujira, she lit candles all around the bedroom. In the flickering glow, she'd drape a white robe over her head and extend her arms to play the white whale rescuing a fishing boat caught in a terrible storm. Instead of being grateful to the whale for bringing the boat safely back to port, the village chief ordered the fishermen to kill it, since one whale could feed the village all winter long. The fishermen refused.

When Hamako reached the part where the village chief harpooned the whale himself, she swooned and fell to the floor, lying still and silent beneath the white robe until Kai and Kishi tiptoed up to her and lifted the fabric. Then she would leap to her feet and the girls would scream. Whirling around in the robe, she played the whale's skeleton, haunting the shore, scaring away the fish and attacking the fishing boats until the villagers finally appeased the bakekujira by throwing his murderer into the sea. To this day, a ghost whale sighting was considered bad luck and meant that the sea gods were angry. But Kishi didn't deserve to be punished. *I'm the one who breaks the rules*, Kai thought. *I'm the bad twin.* What if the ghost whale had come for her but took her sister by mistake?

They rowed for what felt like an eternity, changing course every time Kai thought she saw a plume in the distance. By the time the sun was directly overhead, her eyes burned and Papa's arms shook from the strain of rowing. Meanwhile Mama continued to rock and keen, a wild sound that pierced Kai through and through.

"We need to go back and get the other men to help look," Papa said, wiping beads of sweat from his brow.

"No," Kai said, her voice shrill. "We'll lose too much time."

"Kai, we'll all be stranded at sea if I row for much longer," he said.

"Then let me row," she said, trying to wrest the oars from him. "Papa, please."

The oars didn't budge from his grasp no matter how hard she yanked. Letting go, she clutched her head and screamed at the sea.

"I'm sorry, Kai," he said, tears brimming in his eyes as he turned the boat around.

When Hamako died, Mama had wrapped her in a towel and hugged her for the entire boat ride home. Kai couldn't stop staring into her aunt's vacant eyes. She didn't feel sad, just cold and empty inside. She couldn't believe Hamako was dead. She had to be pretending, like she did when she performed the bakekujira's death scene. Kai was sure Hamako was going to pop up with a mischievous smile and exclaim, "Fooled you!" That numbness never went away, no matter how many pearl seasons passed with her aunt's tool belt hanging unused on the wall.

Now Kai felt only pain, worse than a thousand jellyfish stings, as if one of the soldiers who came to collect goods from their village had carved her stomach out with a sword, which was what they were told would happen if they failed to give their share.

When they reached their cove and the boat coasted toward the sand, Papa jumped out. But he was so exhausted that his knees buckled and he fell, scraping his hands and knees on the pebbly rocks. With great effort, he dragged their boat up onto the beach. Mama continued to wail. The wild, lost sound set Kai's teeth on edge. She had to get away from her mother.

Kai grabbed two sloshing buckets of mussels and carried them to the veranda. Leaving them by the door, she went inside to change. Her chest began to heave as she stepped into their bedroom. First Hamako, now Kishi. Kai balled up her diver's headscarf and tossed it in the corner. Then she pulled Hamako's knife from her tool belt and hurled it against the wall, leaving a divot. Breathing heavily, she slumped on the futon with her head between her hands. Cold horror seeped from the earthen floor through the soles of her feet, radiating through her chest and out to her calloused fingertips. She'd picked a fight with her sister before a dive. How could she have been so stupid? After Hamako, she knew an accident could happen at any time. Hearing her parents come into the house, she quickly changed into a wide-sleeved white blouse that she tucked into a tan trouser skirt. She should have stayed on the veranda to shuck the mussels, to do at least one helpful thing. Kishi would have. But she didn't. She couldn't. Instead she went back to the fishing boat.

Her indigo jacket lay on the bench and she put it on, shivering in the harsh sun. A few minutes later, Papa dashed out the door and headed down the path toward the village. He would go find the other fishermen by the docks, and when he returned she would go with him to look. Her sister was out there somewhere. If Kishi were dead, she would feel it. Wouldn't she?

The front door slid open and Mama walked toward the boat. She was clad in a teal silk robe with a seashell pattern that she once received as a gift from a noble house in exchange for their pearls. Even the village chief's wife didn't have a robe as beautiful as this one.

"I'm going to the temple to pray," Mama said, her eyes puffy and red. "You should come with me."

Kai shook her head. "I want to go back out with Papa."

Mama's face twisted into her pickled-radish look, cheeks sucked in and brow furrowed. "Let the men do what they need to do," she said. "Come with me to the temple."

"But I can help," Kai said.

"They know how to do a search," she said.

"I want to stay with Papa," Kai said.

Mama looked down at the sand, her face roiling with emotion. "You know how it is for our family here," she said. "If you're in the boat crying, you'll make the men uncomfortable. I'm telling you—your presence will make it harder, not easier."

Kai crossed her arms and set her mouth in a defiant line. Mama's eyes flashed.

"Why do you have to be so stubborn?" she scolded. "Why can't you listen? This wouldn't even have happened if you two hadn't been playing that stupid game." Mama covered her mouth with her hand. But it was too late.

Kai felt her stomach lurch as if she'd fallen through a sheet of ice into the freezing water below. Kishi would still be here if she'd let her win. That's what Mama was saying.

"Don't say that!" Kai shouted, even though she knew it

was true. She climbed out of the fishing boat and pushed the two-person rowboat that Papa made them as a New Year's gift last year into the water.

"I'm sorry," Mama said. "Come inside and let's both calm down. Kai, please."

"No!" she yelled, hopping into the rowboat and rowing as hard as she could against the current. "I'm going to find Kishi."

Mama sloshed into the water up to her knees. "Kai," she called out, bereft.

Tears streamed from her eyes, turning Mama and the shore into a blur. Kai rowed until their cottage became a speck. Until her shoulders ached and the oars tore open blisters on her palms. When she could no longer take the pain, she pulled the oars into the boat and wiped the sweat and tears from her face with her sleeve. Bamboo Island bobbed to her left, rising from the sea like a frightened turtle shell. She looked in the direction of the village for boats but saw no signs of a search party. She could wait here for her father and the other men. Papa would say that what happened wasn't her fault. But she wouldn't believe him, and that would feel worse than Mama saying it was.

She took a jagged breath and wiped her face again with her sleeve. Her head ached from crying. Hamako used to take her to Bamboo Island to explore the lava caves. Between the beach and cliffs, she remembered passing a large burial mound. Hamako said the spot marked the grave of a monstrous carp who foolishly went to battle against the Dragon King, the sea god who lived in a coral palace deep in the Freshwater Sea. Other less imaginative villagers said a creature that big must have been a whale. Maybe the bakekujira would be drawn to it.

Kai rowed to the island. When she reached the shallows, she jumped out and lugged the rowboat onto the beach. The breeze whispered through the feathery-tipped bamboo on the hill while white clouds formed a mackerel pattern in the stark blue sky. The day was so shockingly ordinary and beautiful, she thought she must have dreamed the ghost whale. Any moment now, Kishi would say, "Wake up, sleepyhead. You're going to miss your first solo dive."

Kai's last trip to the island had been just weeks before Hamako died. With the wind ruffling her shoulder-length hair into a lion's mane, her aunt had charged ahead. *Slow down*, Kai had said. *But low tide is the best time to go into the caves*, Hamako had exclaimed. *Don't you want to save the snails? One of them could be a princess who will take you to visit the Dragon King.* Kai had rolled her eyes because at least three pearl seasons had passed since she'd last rescued snails. *I'm not a baby anymore, Aunt Hamako*, she'd said. Now she wished she'd been nicer. A lump rose in her throat.

Kai set off along the beach toward the cliffs. Within minutes she reached the burial mound, an unremarkable heap of rocks and shells that was smaller than she remembered. On the other side, closest to the cliffs, she kicked off her sandals and stripped down to her wide-sleeved white under-shirt and waded into the ocean. Wearing white in the water was supposed to bring good luck, though that hadn't helped Kishi today. The tops of the caves in the cliffs peeked above the waterline. She swam along the perimeter, diving down every so often to check for the ghost whale inside each cave. No sign of it. By the time she'd gone far enough around that she could no longer see the burial mound, she was tired and feeling as foolish as the stonecutter who wasted wish upon magical wish until he was a rock at the mercy of another stonecutter. The sea was vast and the ghost whale could be anywhere.

She decided to go around one more bend, frog kicking past a protruding rock where a group of white herons hopped and fluttered. Probably the sunlight was playing tricks, but there did seem to be something glimmering beneath the sur-face. Kai took a deep breath before she dove and swam closer to what appeared to be a submerged rock, a white rock, a white rock with a large circular indentation. It was the ghost whale's eye socket. Flailing upward, she took in a mouthful of water. Despite her coughing and sputtering, the monster remained still. Maybe it was sleeping.

She slipped underwater again without a splash, passing four long fingers that had to be a fin and following along the curved slabs that formed its rib cage. Below one of its middle ribs, she spotted Kishi, lying on her side with her eyes closed, as if suspended in the water. Her heart twisted. *Please don't let her be dead*, she thought. A sob worked its way up her throat, forcing her above the water to collect herself. She treaded in place, uncertain of what to do next. Even if Kishi was dead, she couldn't leave her inside the whale.

Swimming stealthily toward the ghost whale's head, Kai examined its maw underwater, which from the side looked like a duck's bill. Its top jaw, almost level with the surface, was smooth. But the bottom, long and narrow, was like a giant saw. Before she could change her mind, she dove and swam through the gap, over spiky teeth that looked like stalagmites in a cave. She swam with her arms extended, until her hands touched a spongy surface. Then she crawled toward the back of its mouth and stood up, knee-high in water. Craning her neck, she saw a sky-blue circle overhead that had to be its blowhole. Toward the tail end, she made out a white wishbone, the start of the rib cage. She took a tentative step, feeling for resistance with her foot. She was on a slant, though, and on her third step she slipped and tumbled down. It was a strange sensation, seeing water all around yet not feeling wet. She swayed as she got back on her feet, gagging at the stench of rotting seaweed.

Spreading her arms, she felt a soft membrane beneath her fingers, which she hoped meant she was in the tube leading to its stomach. Far below her and on either side flashed silvery specks, schools of fish passing by. As the invisible tube leveled off, fish fins and shell bits cracked beneath her bare feet. The rotting stench grew stronger. Her eyes burned and she started to gag again. Pinching her nose closed, she breathed through her mouth to keep herself from vomiting. Kai used to roll her eyes whenever Mama told her to swim one stroke at a time, but she followed that advice now. She only thought about taking one step, one step, one step. The gleaming rib bones curved toward her like dragon claws reaching for a golden egg, an image that she'd seen painted on a temple ceiling in the capital. Those claws had belonged to the Dragon King, probably the only creature more terrifying than the bakekujira.

"One, one, one," she whispered as she put one foot in front of the other. Her skin looked papery inside the whale, a bluish white. Up ahead she saw a shadowy pool. As she drew closer, the shadow became more distinct and a triangle of white—Kishi's headscarf—came into view. She rushed forward with a strangled cry and dropped to her knees, lifting Kishi's head into her lap. Her face had a blue tint. She seemed to be taking shallow breaths.

"Kishi," she said, slapping her sister's face lightly. "I'm here. Wake up."

A rumble ran through the whale. They needed to get out before it moved. If it dove and swam far out to sea, they'd be stranded. Kai hooked her elbows beneath Kishi's armpits and walked backward, dragging her in the direction of the whale's mouth. Flecks of fin and shell gathered behind Kishi's heels.

"You're going to owe me after this, Kishi," she said to distract herself. "You'll have to go on all of the trips with Papa to the capital without me."

At the incline that led to the ghost whale's mouth, she slowed down to make sure her foot held with each step. Sweat trickled down her forehead and behind her knees. "Do you remember when we went to the home of the lady who used to be in the empress's entourage? And she said that she was going to add the pearl seller's twin daughters to her list of 'squalid things'?"

This old woman, famous for writing about court life, had been speaking in a loud, quarrelsome voice behind an ornamental folding screen, clearly intending for them to hear, and she said she'd rank them between the inside of a cat's ear and an unlined fur robe. The head servant apparently liked the lady of the house even less than she liked commoners, because she'd shaken her head and said, "Don't mind her. Nobody cares about her lists anymore."

Despite their luxurious lives, Kai wouldn't trade places with the ladies in the capital for all the jewels in the world. Papa called them catfish in silk robes. He said they could hardly walk or see because they were forced to stay inside dark gloomy rooms all the time. They would never know the joy of floating on the water with the sun warming their faces.

"You have to stay with me, so that one day when the warlords overthrow the capital, we can shower the lady of the lists with cats' ears and unlined fur robes," Kai said.

When she reached the whale's throat, where the air was less swampy, she stopped to catch her breath. Somewhere above was the bakekujira's invisible brain. Did ghost whales dream, and was that the cause of the rumbling? Or did it feel her feet sinking into its insides? She hoisted Kishi higher on her chest and pulled her along the tapering plank of its jaw. The water quickly rose from her ankles to her knees to the tops of her thighs. To slip out, Kai realized they'd have to go underwater for several seconds. She swam on her back and held Kishi to her chest, watching the bakekujira's top jaw grow skinnier and skinnier. Just as they went fully underwater, Kai pinched her sister's nose shut with her fingers. When they passed over its sharp teeth, Kishi's body suddenly jerked. Kai tugged, then realized that her sister's ankle had caught in the ridge of a tooth. Curses ran through her head as she awkwardly tried to angle Kishi's leg while still covering her nose and mouth. Somewhere above, Kai heard water spray through the blowhole. The monster was awake.

She yanked one more time and Kishi's foot came free. Swimming hard, Kai broke through the surface. As she gasped for air, she pulled Kishi's body closer to her chest. She didn't have time to check if her sister was still breathing. She pulled Kishi along as fast as she could. The bakekujira lurched forward. Time slowed down. The long pointy jaws opened wide. With each kick, she felt the force of the current dragging them closer and closer to the ghost whale. As the sky turned into white bone, she let out a shriek of frustration and despair. The jaws closed in. Then she heard a loud thud and the world went sideways.

The sky and the sea flipped over. A wave pummeled her, ripping Kishi from her arms. Shadows as thick as a monsoon cloud swirled all around. Floundering underwater, she couldn't tell up from down. Her lungs screamed for air. She clamped both hands over her mouth, but her body no longer listened to her brain. Just as the water pushed its way between her lips, something in the shadowy churn scooped her up.

3

Facedown, arms and legs splayed, she slid over something coarse and scaly. Whatever had caught hold of her moved underwater at an alarming speed, so fast that her ears tingled. Next she felt a pulling sensation, as if two people were yanking her earlobes in opposite directions. Her lips and nostrils stretched open. As water gushed down her throat, she thought this must be the feeling of drowning. But then the pressure dissipated and she realized she was still breathing. Reaching up with one hand, she touched her ear and found a long slit. Did she have gills? How was that possible?

You brainless bag of bones, begone, hissed a deep, primitive voice that sounded like it was inside her head. A lightning bolt crackled through the water, turning everything a hot white. As the white faded, she saw the ghost whale in silhouette flick its tail and flee. Before she could decide whether she was safer holding on to this creature or letting go, they shot upward. Kai squeezed her eyelids shut as they broke through the surface into the dazzling sun. The sides of her face tingled and puckered as she coughed up water. When she touched her hands to the sides of her head, she had ears again. She was sitting on top of the creature, on a scaly gold expanse in the agitated water. Her sister lay sprawled on her side not far from her. She scrambled over to Kishi, lifting her head and cradling her in her arms. Kishi's warm brown eyes stared blankly at the sky. Her body was heavy like a sack of rice.

"Kishi," she said. "Kishi, no."

A smoky blast followed by a deafening roar almost knocked her over. She looked up to find the head of a snarling sea dragon hovering above them. It had a long brittle face with black fins between its horned ears and hard amber eyes. Sharp yellow fangs protruded from its jaws. She flinched as the dragon bellowed, its hot sulfury breath singeing her skin. A small startled scream escaped her lips as she clasped Kishi tighter.

Suddenly, they plunged underwater again. Kishi's hair flew in her face. Her ears tingled and stretched, the pressure building until she thought her eyeballs might pop. As swiftly as they started moving, they jerked to a halt. She touched her face and felt the long slits beneath her fingers. But Kishi's face hadn't changed at all. She didn't have gills. The dragon curved its sinewy neck to look at them, its nostrils flaring. Its black wings billowed on either side like ship sails. The rest of its serpentine body coiled below, ending in a pointy tail covered with black spikes. They seemed to have traded the ghost whale for a dragon, neither of which was supposed to exist outside of stories.

I exist, mortal, the craggy ancient voice said inside her head.

Wait, was the dragon talking to her? Was it reading her mind?

I am not just any dragon, the voice said. *I am Ryujin, the Dragon King.*

She must have drowned trying to escape the bakekujira. She had to be imagining this. There was no other explanation for a talking dragon. In myths and fairy tales, the Dragon King was the god in charge of the tides and he was as changeable as the ocean, sometimes benevolent, sometimes thin-skinned and malicious. Every year at the summer festival, the villagers honored him with a procession. Fifty men inside a dragon costume danced down the steps of the temple, through the village, and into the surf. Kai began to giggle uncontrollably and then sobbed, which made a chuffing noise in her gills and sent some water down her throat. Maybe this was part of her spirit journey to the Underworld. She pulled a silvery piece of fish fin from Kishi's billowing hair and caressed her pale cheek.

You are not dead, pearl diver, the voice said. *I rescued you. But you cannot hear my words above water, so I brought you back into the sea.*

Kai squeezed her eyes shut for a moment and shook her head back and forth to knock out the voice. It was eerie and frightening, to hear these thoughts that were not her own.

These are my words, not my thoughts, he said. *If you heard my thoughts, you would not behave in such an ungrateful manner. You would be on your knees, thanking me for my divine intervention.*

What? Divine intervention? A truly divine intervention would have saved her sister, not her. Why did a god care about a pair of lowly pearl divers anyway? None of this made sense.

The Dragon King's ears flattened with displeasure and a stream of fire shot from his mouth in an arc above her head, causing the water to boil and bubble. She cowered and hugged Kishi. She knew she should compliment him, say something to appease him, but she couldn't control the flow of her thoughts. Every part of her being was begging, screaming, *Please bring my sister back.* Her chest heaved, and with each ragged breath she swallowed water because her gills did not work when she cried. *Please.*

I govern the ebb and flow of the sea, not the life force, the Dragon King said. *I have no influence in the spirit realm.*

The Dragon King moved in a lazy spiral. Kai curled around her sister and sobbed into her shoulder. She probably could have stayed that way forever. She wished he had let her die, too. They had come into the world together like a double-yolked egg. One could not be without the other.

I will take you back to your boat on Bamboo Island, the Dragon King said.

But his words didn't register. All she could think was that their mother had given birth to them in the sea with Hamako helping the midwife, and it was only fitting that they died there as well. *Take away my gills,* she thought back. *Leave me here with her.*

Mortals never cease to amaze, the Dragon King said in a deep, raspy voice. *Always dissatisfied with what is given to them. My son-in-law, the fisherman Urashima Taro, was the same. My daughter brought him to our home in the Freshwater Sea and gave him immortality, and he rejected this most precious gift.*

She closed her eyes and felt the water cradling her. Hamako had told them the tale many times. Urashima Taro rescued a turtle from a group of boys tugging on the poor creature's legs and beating its shell with a stick. That turtle turned out to be the Dragon King's daughter. The sea princess brought him to the coral palace and married him. But after three days, Urashima Taro missed his parents and decided to return to land. When he arrived at his village, he discovered three hundred years had passed and everyone he knew was dead. Kai wept every time her aunt told the story because it seemed very real. In the sea, time felt languid and devoid of meaning.

I'm sorry, Dragon King. I don't deserve a second chance. My sister is the one who should live. Just ask Benzaiten. Benzaiten was the protector of pearl divers everywhere, in the Freshwater Sea and the Saltwater Sea. They'd been praying to her their whole lives.

Yes.

Kai opened her eyes and was startled to find his ancient face just inches from hers, his nostrils flaring.

Let us go see Benzaiten, he said. *She will decide if you will live or die.*

She nodded through her tears, feeling a spark of hope. The Dragon King had no power in the spirit world, but maybe Benzaiten did. Her brother was Enma, the lord of the Underworld. She would know how good Kishi was, that Kishi was dependable and responsible, the twin who always made the right choice—well, except for wandering off the path with the chief's son. That had been foolish. Not even Kishi was perfect.

The Dragon King uncoiled his massive body, raised his powerful black wings toward his ears, and flapped them toward his tail. As they shot forward, Kai held on tight to Kishi with one arm and gripped one of the Dragon King's scales with her other hand.

She wondered how Benzaiten would appear, if she would take the form of a sea serpent as she was sometimes shown in paintings, or a human form with eight arms, like the statue at their temple. When Kai was little, she used to pray for extra arms so that she could swim faster than Kishi. She also loved that Benzaiten's eight arms allowed her to do so many things. She was the master of the sword and also of the lute. Sometimes she held a key for prosperity, and she also inspired poets and dancers who wanted their words and movements to flow like water.

Does one day in your realm really equal one hundred years on land? Kai asked the Dragon King, thinking about how the tale of Urashima Taro ended. Bringing Kishi back from the dead wouldn't do much good if they went home only to find a century had passed.

Urashima Taro was a kind but foolish lad, the Dragon King said. *In human time, only a few hours had passed. He returned when he normally would from fishing. Those village boys who beat my daughter with a stick wanted revenge because he had interfered. First they came up with a false story to get his parents to leave their house for the day. Then one boy put on a disguise. When he saw Urashima Taro approach the house, he exited through the front door as if he lived there. At first, Urashima Taro insisted it was his home. But the boy pretended it was his. Then Urashima Taro asked where his parents had gone and how such a thing could come to pass when he had been in the underwater palace for only three days. Taking advantage of Urashima Taro's confusion, the boy said no family by that name had lived there in three hundred years and that the fisherman must be a ghost who had come to visit his ancestral home. How the boys laughed when he ran away crying. It was all a trick.*

So his parents had not been dead after all. Kai suddenly felt sick at the thought of how her parents must feel right now. Papa was probably still out searching with the other fishermen. But Mama would be all alone. The women in the village would not rally around her. They hadn't when Hamako died. A century ago, seven pearl diving families lived in their village. But a stretch of poor mussel harvests caused some to move away. The others switched to fishing when they had only boys and couldn't find any girls willing to marry in and take up pearl diving. Once Kai asked why no other girls wanted to dive for pearls. Hamako said most girls didn't have the strength and stamina since they hadn't been training their whole lives like Kai and Kishi had. It didn't help that the village elders bad-mouthed pearl divers for being "unfeminine."

What they really don't like is that we're independent, Hamako said.

As Kai and the Dragon King hurtled through the sea, the blues deepened and darkened. Aqua, teal, peacock, sapphire, indigo. Soon a white dot in the distance caught her eye. The dot grew into a blur. Then the edges became more defined, elongating into a castle with towers that tapered at the top like ink brushes. The strange thing was, she couldn't see the seafloor. The castle appeared to float, and the towers seemed to move. As they approached the diamond-encrusted gate, Kai realized the castle wasn't moving so much as writhing. The walls looked crinkled and leathery, like a sea snake. She shuddered. The castle was made out of sea snakes.

They passed through the gate into a courtyard lined with

round bushes sprouting pale, delicate coral flowers and sea whips with pearly beads along their stalks. Jeweled squid and red cucumber-shaped jellies sparkled and glowed in and around the floating sea plants. The Dragon King halted in the middle of the courtyard. Kai lifted Kishi up so that her head lolled against Kai's chest, in case she was aware of what was happening. Her spirit might still be inside her body. That was why it was customary to let the deceased rest for several days, to make sure their spirits had truly departed.

Kai was about to ask the Dragon King if Benzaiten would appear as a sea snake when a soft hiss filled her head. The shushing grew louder. Two snakes, each about six paces long, slithered toward them carrying a dais that they then placed in the courtyard. Next came a procession of six snakes. *All hail Benzaiten*, they said.

The hissing faded, replaced by atonal flute music. The white castle stopped writhing. A massive white snake, twenty or thirty paces long, with diamond-shaped black eyes, undulated through the arched castle door. As the giant snake spiraled onto the dais, the flute rose to a high-pitched shriek. The snake lifted its head, and its body crinkled and hardened around the edges. Beneath the translucent layer, its body contracted in some places and bulged in others. The snake's head shriveled, replaced by curly gray hair. From the crackling snakeskin stepped an old woman with eight arms spoking from her robe, which was a patchwork of embroidered silks in shades of green and blue. A glittery white snake wrapped around her head like a crown. Kai wondered why Benzaiten chose to be old when a goddess could probably appear to be any age she wanted. But Kai was also relieved. Benzaiten seemed less scary this way.

The flute music dwindled. Two snakes carried away the molted snakeskin. Then Benzaiten kneeled on the floating dais with all eight hands in her lap. Her snake attendants slinked around her, their bodies entwining.

How now, noble Benzaiten, the Dragon King said.

Ryujin, she said in a voice as sweet as red bean jam. *How nice of you to visit. Would you like some tea? I have a lovely vitality blend, originally from India, you know.* She rummaged in the pockets of her gown, pulling out a pestle, an axe, a rope, a flute, and a spear. *Whatever did I do with that teapot?* she said irritably. *It was here yesterday.*

Kai bit the inside of her cheek to keep herself from giggling, which she did when she was scared or nervous. She also remembered to straighten her shoulders and lift her head, the way her mother taught them to do if a villager gave them a dirty look or a pack of boys called them sea witches. The Dragon King cleared his throat.

That's quite all right, he said. *Next time we'll have tea. I have a most vexing problem.*

Oh? Benzaiten stretched her pliant neck toward them. *I see you've brought humans.*

These young ladies are pearl divers.

Her elongated neck snapped back to her body. *The good*

kind of mermaid, as I call them. What seems to be the trouble?

The Dragon King's eyes smoldered as he spoke. *The tides did report to me that the bakekujira escaped from the deep, dark trench where I had banished it. I set out to bring all of my wrath and fury upon that bag of bones and discovered this brave pearl diver pulling her sister out of the jaws of the beast.*

Benzaiten sighed. *That bakekujira is so stupid, it would eat its own mother. Ryujin, can't you drown it or set it on fire?*

Alas, it can't be killed, the Dragon King said. *It's a terrible design flaw. Now this mortal says that I should have let her die with her sister. Such arrogance must be punished. I say she must accept her fate and live. What say you, Benzaiten?*

But, Kai said, desperate to break in and make her case before Benzaiten made a decision.

The Dragon King whipped his neck around, bellowed, and directed a stream of fire over her head. Kai yelped and crouched over her sister.

Well, she is impudent, Benzaiten said. *You've shown remarkable restraint, Ryujin. I would have gladly let her die. Tell me, young pearl diver, how dare you reject a gift from the gods?*

Great Goddess, Kai said, her voice sounding small. It took effort to think of what she wanted to say without any other thoughts crowding in. *The women in my family for generations have prayed to you and worshipped you. It was very kind of the Dragon King to save me from the bakekujira. But you see, Kishi isn't just my sister. She's my twin. We grew in our mother's belly together and we've spent every moment of our lives together.*

We're two halves of a whole. That's why I'm begging you. Please bring her back. I can't live without her at my side.

Benzaiten's snake attendants hissed their disapproval. The Dragon King swished his spiky tail.

Benzaiten raised her eight hands and held out her palms. The hissing immediately stopped. *I am only considering your request because the pearl divers have been loyal to me, while other mortals who live by the sea have turned their backs and prayed to the land gods. But let me ask. Do you think it is wise to alter the course of a human life? That kind of interference is like tossing a stone into the water, rippling outward and encompassing others in ways we can't predict.*

Bolstered by the fact that she hadn't said no yet, Kai pressed on. *I don't know if it's wise or not. But I promise you, any ripple effect would only extend to my parents and me. We are the last of our kind in our province. Kishi is probably our only chance to continue the family line. You see that I'm blunt, and if you asked my mother she'd add stubborn and impatient. But Kishi is kind and sweet and smart. Even the village matchmaker likes her, and that's saying something.*

The creases around Benzaiten's eyes deepened and she pursed her lips. *Let's have a look at her,* she said.

Two snakes came forward with a stretcher on their backs made of a patchwork of embroidered silks similar to the goddess's robe. As Kishi started to drift toward them, Kai held on fiercely, unwilling to let her go.

My dear, I'm trying to help you, Benzaiten said.

Reluctantly Kai released her and Kishi floated to the stretcher, which the snakes carried to Benzaiten. The sea goddess laid one hand on Kishi's chest and another over her forehead. Then she pulled a conch shell from her pocket and held the tapering end to Kishi's lips.

Her spirit has already left her body and is making the journey to the Underworld, Benzaiten said. *It's too late.*

Forgetting her fear of sea snakes, Kai pushed off the Dragon King and tried to swim toward the dais. Two sea snakes blocked her path.

Please, she said. *It was a mistake, a mix-up. The ghost whale should have taken me, not my sister. Kishi is good. She deserves to live. I'm the one who should be punished. Please. Can't you ask Enma to send her spirit back from the Underworld and take mine in her place?*

Kai lowered her eyes and braced for a sea snake to strike, or for the Dragon King to burn her to a crisp.

My brother passes judgment on the newly dead. He is the one who decides who will be reborn and who will go to the Eight Great Hells. Unlike me, he is not easily swayed, Benzaiten said. *What do you have to barter with? He'll want something in exchange.*

Kai cast around for an answer, for something worthy of a deity. *I have freshwater pearls at home,* she said. *As many as you want.*

Something out of the ordinary, Benzaiten said. *This is no small favor.*

I don't have anything else, Kai admitted, devastated to come so close to saving Kishi only to fall short. She felt pressure build around her eyes from tears that could not force their way out into the water.

Surely a girl brave enough to go inside the bakekujira must be able to find something that Enma wants, said the Dragon King, his gold scales stark against the dark blue sea.

Benzaiten brought all her hands together in prayer position. *There is one thing that I can think of*, she said. *But getting it will require more than courage. I'm not even sure that the great warrior Tawara Toda could handle this.*

I'll do anything, Kai said.

Benzaiten's dark infinite eyes threatened to swallow her. *Have you heard of Dakini?*

Kai nodded. Dakini was the Fox Queen, a powerful nine-tailed fox and the leader of all kitsune, the supernatural foxes who could shape-shift or take over a human body through spirit possession. Unless the fox had more than one tail, a person couldn't tell the difference between a regular fox and a supernatural one. So Kai and the other children in the village had been taught from a young age to stay away from all foxes.

She has a magic jewel. A pearl. Like this. Benzaiten pulled the teapot out of her pocket and tossed it over her shoulder with annoyance. *I mean, like this.*

She held out a jewel unlike any Kai had seen before, oblong with the facets of a diamond but the sheen of a pearl.

It barely fit in her hand and sparkled like the sea beneath the sun. Kai was so dazzled that every word she'd ever known flew out of her head.

Take it from her and bring it to me, Benzaiten said.

You speak of stones and ripples, noble Benzaiten, the Dragon King said, his voice a steamy growl. *Control of a magic jewel is far more complicated than whether one mortal lives or dies.*

Kai looked anxiously from the Dragon King to Benzaiten. She knew from the old stories that many of the gods had special gems, including the Dragon King, who used two to control the tides. She didn't understand exactly what would happen if Benzaiten or Enma had the Fox Queen's pearl. But what did Benzaiten's motives matter as long as she got Kishi back?

Why should the land gods have such undue influence in the affairs of mortals? Benzaiten said. *When did we sea gods become the lesser gods? We can use the foxes to bring the balance back. The bull should not be revered above the dragon.*

Tenjin, the Dragon King said, almost spitting the name. *A false god if there ever was one.*

A century ago, Tenjin had been a courtier named Michizane. After his death, his political rivals started dying one by one and people thought his angry spirit was getting revenge. In order to appease him, he was elevated to god status and given the name Tenjin. Kai could see why the other gods might not respect him.

I'll do it, she said. *Where can I find Dakini?*

Excellent, Benzaiten said. *The foxes gather at Sky Mountain every month when the moon is full. You'll have two weeks to get there.*

She'd never heard of Sky Mountain. *How far is it from the Freshwater Sea?* she asked.

Sky Mountain rises to the east, near the shore of the Saltwater Sea, Benzaiten said. *First you must pass over the Seven Silent Mountains. Then you will reach the Perpetual Plain of Eternal Afflictions, where you will cross the Three-Pronged River. From there, you will travel through the Valley of the Windswept Pine. Finally you must find your way through Laughingstock Forest to reach the base of Sky Mountain.*

That sounds far, Kai said. She'd been to the Saltwater Sea once on a family trip, which had required them to travel by oxcart. It had taken a long time, maybe a week. *Can I walk there?*

Of course you can, she said, with a sharp wave of her eight hands. *Or did the bakekujira eat your feet?*

There is another way, the Dragon King said. *The Cloak of a Thousand Feathers would save her a great deal of walking.*

The Cloak of a Thousand Feathers sounded like the kind of thing a mountain hermit would wear. *What does the cloak do?* Kai asked.

Anyone who wears the cloak can fly, the Dragon King said. *It hangs at the top of a tall fir tree on the other side of the Great Ridge of the Fourfold Repudiations. The path can be found at Driftwood Beach, on the coast north of Bamboo Island. I will take you.*

Someday, when the revolution came, as Papa said it would, Kai wanted to be in charge of renaming. There would be no more place names longer than it took for a monkey to fall out of a tree.

The cloak is guarded by the Crows of the Eternal Night, Benzaiten said. *You'll have to get past them.*

How do I do that? Kai asked.

You're a resourceful girl, she said. *You'll figure it out.*

Once I get to Sky Mountain, how do I get to Dakini without being possessed by a fox? Kai wondered. When a fox had possessed the grandfather of the village basket weaver, the old man used to wander the streets naked.

Momotaro the Peach Boy never asked so many questions when he set out to defeat the demons on Devil's Island, Benzaiten said.

Kai annoyed her own family with constant questions, too. Why did she have to sweep the floor when it would just be dirty again tomorrow? Why was the village chief always a man? And why limit herself to one mussel when she could easily bring up two?

But that's just a— She caught herself before she said "fairy tale." *Even Momotaro had help from the dog, the monkey, and the pheasant,* she pointed out.

Noble Benzaiten, perhaps you can give the girl something to assist her with this undertaking, the Dragon King said. *There must be something in those pockets of yours.*

Ryujin, do you mock me? Benzaiten said mildly. *Very well.*

Benzaiten reached into her mysterious pockets. Out of one came a silver bow. Out of another she pulled a quiver full of arrows. Both objects floated away from Benzaiten and hovered in front of Kai at chest height.

She grasped the bow and gazed at the sparkling silver arrows in the quiver. *What does this do?* she asked. There had to be something special about it, like maybe the shooter would never miss their mark.

It shoots arrows, Benzaiten said.

Kai tried again. *What I meant is, does the bow have any magical powers?*

Oh, goodness no. It shoots arrows, that's all, she said, her whole body shaking with mirth. The snakes laughed along with her in a whispery hiss. Kai didn't know why they were laughing. What was the point of receiving a gift from the gods if it didn't do anything special?

Am I supposed to kill Dakini? Papa had a bow and sometimes she and Kishi played around with it, setting empty mussel shells on top of rocks and logs and trying to hit them. But she had never shot at a living thing.

Benzaiten's eyes turned cold and reptilian, and Kai shivered. Maybe that was why the goddess appeared as an old woman. She fooled the other gods into thinking she was harmless.

You'll do whatever is necessary, Benzaiten said, *to save your sister.*

The strange flute music filled the air again. Benzaiten's

eight arms merged into a white scaly trunk. Her curly silver hair shriveled and disappeared. Her face broadened and flattened. Flicking her forked black tongue, she swayed her head, as if hypnotizing prey. Then she and her snakes slithered into the castle, taking Kishi on the stretcher with them. Kai bit the knuckle of her index finger to keep from crying out. She was terrified for her sister and didn't want to leave her here, even though Benzaiten had said her spirit was already gone.

She slung the bow and quiver over her shoulder, then swam to the Dragon King's back. Once she grabbed his scales, he flapped his powerful wings and they sailed through the castle gate. Looking over her shoulder, she watched the castle shrink into a white smudge, leaving only a trace against the indigo sea, like the afterglow of a firefly.

How am I going to find my way to Sky Mountain? I've hardly traveled outside of Shionoma Village, and never alone. She hadn't meant to speak to the Dragon King. That was simply the anxious thought running through her head.

Fear not, valiant pearl diver, the Dragon King said. *I, too, have gifts.*

The water turned bright blue as they neared the shore. Schools of fish gave the Dragon King a wide berth and crabs rushed to bury themselves in the sand. Halting in a bed of seagrass, the Dragon King turned his scaly head to look at her. Out of nowhere, a silver chain appeared around her neck with a pendant made of pink sea coral.

Tell the compass where you wish to go and it will always point you in the right direction, he said. *You must address it as O Wandering One.*

She held the pendant in her hand. *O Wandering One, which way is Sky Mountain?*

A silver needle quivered and spun around until it became a silvery blur. Then it slowed until the sharp tip pointed in a southeasterly direction. Next a plain wood bowl that fit in her palm floated in front of her face.

This bowl will provide you with food on your journey, the Dragon King said. *This you must call O Great Source of Bounty.*

O Source of Great Bounty, she said.

O Great Source of Bounty, the Dragon King said. *All bounty is great, but not all sources are.*

Thank you, Dragon King, Kai said. Despite his generosity, doubt gnawed at her. She felt tired and scared. She needed Kishi more than ever right now. Whenever their parents gave them a task to do, Kai's impulse was to dive in. Kishi wanted to talk through the steps first. Kai used to tease her that she needed steps for getting up in the morning. One: Open eyes. Two: Sit up in bed. Three: Put feet on floor. But now, Kai needed a plan. She didn't have the faintest idea of how to go about taking the pearl.

About this cloak, Kai said. *Is it one thousand feathers from the same kind of bird, or one feather each from a thousand different birds?*

For the first time, the Dragon King seemed flummoxed. *I*

do not know, he said. *I have never seen the cloak.*

What if I get there and it's gone? she asked.

His horned ears drooped. *Then you will have to walk to Sky Mountain,* he growled. *I am a god of the sea, not of the land.*

You've been extremely generous and kind, she added hastily, remembering that the jellyfish no longer had bones because one had made the Dragon King angry. Still, she couldn't quiet her mind. She had so many questions. *Does Dakini keep her pearl in her pocket, too? What if her pockets are as full of junk as Benzaiten's?*

Every fox has a pearl, the Dragon King said. *It's the source of their magic. They carry the pearls in their tails. Dakini's is the biggest and most powerful.*

Suddenly she remembered how on their trip to the capital they'd seen a strange concentrated glow in the distance from the oxcart. Papa had said it was fox fire, from a gathering of foxes. Now she realized that the glow came from their pearls.

If Dakini is an immortal fox, an arrow won't kill her, she said.

Every time you shoot her, she will lose a tail, the Dragon King said. *Once she is a one-tailed fox, she is mortal again.*

Kai could barely hit a tree with a bow and arrow. *How am I going to shoot a supernatural fox nine times in a row without getting killed or possessed?*

The Dragon King sighed and walked toward the shore. The familiar rolling motion of the waves washed over her.

Mortal, you are a pearl hunter, he said. *Trust the pearl to tell you what to do.*

Maybe supernatural pearls gave directions. But freshwater pearls did not. She didn't dare contradict him, though. The Dragon King's head broke through the surface. As they emerged from the ocean, her gills tightened and puckered into ears. The pressure didn't bother her as much this time, which made her worry that the skin around her jaw had stretched out and would now sag like a deflated puffer fish. Looking down, she realized she was wearing the clothes that she'd left on Bamboo Island, her indigo jacket over her plain wide-sleeved undershirt, a hemp trouser skirt, and straw sandals. The Dragon King had conjured them somehow. She tucked the magic food bowl into one of the two secret pockets that their mother had sewn inside their jackets so that they could hide pouches filled with pearls when they traveled to the capital.

Gazing over the Dragon King's craggy head, Kai took in the driftwood snaking along the beach, the sand dunes pinking in the sunset, and the black ridge jutting like a grave marker into the bruised sky. Tomorrow she would be on the other side of that void and anything could happen. But tomorrow her sister would not die, and that meant tomorrow could not be worse than today.

When they reached the damp sand, the Dragon King swung his tail around so that she could slide down. "Thank you for everything, Dragon King," she said, bowing to him.

The Dragon King gave a ferocious roar, which Kai took to mean farewell. Turning back to the sea, he dove beneath a breaking wave, his spiny tail arcing above the foam. As Kai watched him disappear, the sun finally set on the longest day of her life.

4

Kai tried to wring the water from her sleeves and trouser skirt, then looked around. Except for the rustling waves and the driftwood, the beach was silent and empty. Where was she? How far from home was this? She wrapped her arms around herself even though she wasn't cold. Until today, Kai had never been away from her family. *Oh, my parents*, she thought as her heart tightened. By this hour, they'd be in a panic. They'd already lost one daughter and now Kai was adding to their grief. She should have asked the Dragon King to send a messenger. He might have said no, but she should have at least tried.

It was too late now. All she could do was get the pearl as quickly as possible and go home. She couldn't imagine facing her mother again unless she brought Kishi back. Holding up the pendant, she turned toward the mountains.

"O Wandering One," she said. "Please show me the way to the Great Ridge of the Fourfold Repudiations."

The needle blurred into a circle and then stopped, pointing straight ahead at the flat-topped ridge. She zigzagged around the driftwood and shuffled over sandy dunes. At the trailhead, she paused, wary of the things that might be lurking in the dark—bandits, ogres, foxes, cute monstrous mice that were said to explode if the mountain spirits grew angry. If Hamako were here, she'd punch her fist in the air, say, "Let's go," and sing songs at the top of her lungs to let all those menacing creatures know that she wasn't scared.

Kai thought she had a terrible singing voice. But she could tell stories, the stories that her aunt told and that she and Kishi repeated to each other.

"Once upon a time," she said to the keening crickets and the cicadas as she moved along the dark path, "there was a military officer waiting for his wife to come home. When she finally arrived, there was not one but two of her. The officer knew that one of them had to be a fox. Taking out his sword, he threatened them each with the blade. The first woman begged for her life: 'Please, please don't kill me. I'm your real wife.' The second woman snapped, 'Put that away. Have you lost your mind?' That's how he knew that the second woman was his wife. The impostor returned to fox form, peed on the officer's leg, and ran away."

The last part always sent her and Kishi into peals of laughter, but thinking about that now made her choke up with tears. She tried to tell another story, but all she could think was that she'd never get to make up new endings with Kishi, and that made her cry harder. Kai was glad that nobody was around to hear her blubber besides the crickets and the cicadas. When she ran out of tears, she forced herself to sprint up the trail. The harder she pushed her body, the less she felt, and she didn't want to feel anything ever again. The last part of the trail was so steep that she crawled on her hands and knees to the top, where she collapsed on the ground. When her breath evened out, she staggered to her feet and wiped away the dirt and gravel stuck to the side of her face. On the ocean side of the ridge, a thin sliver of moon scratched the sky. When she turned around to the valley, dark trees blotted the hill and clawed around a pond in the distance. She couldn't pick out the fir tree or the murder of crows in the dark. Exhausted, she climbed a broad-branched tree and settled where the trunk forked. Then she took the magic bowl out of her jacket pocket. She wasn't hungry. But it was something to do, something to occupy her so that she didn't dwell on what her mother had said. This was all her fault.

"O Great Source of Bounty," she said. "Please give me porridge."

Even though she was bone weary and thought nothing could surprise her after all she'd seen that day, she flinched and nearly dropped the bowl when a white plume rose from the middle. The skinny wisp of steam grew strength until it looked like a geyser spilling over. Steam spread across the surface until it covered the bowl rim to rim. Her index finger hovered over the cloud. She was tempted to plunge her finger through the surface to see the magic below as it happened. But she was afraid that the cloud might burn or turn her finger into porridge, too. The steam lingered and then began to roll up in the opposite direction, from the rim back to the center, revealing porridge beneath. When the last dot of cloud disappeared, she eyed the porridge warily. Bringing the rim to her lips, she took a small swallow to make sure it was real. Warm but not too hot, and the perfect consistency—not too thin or too gloppy. To have whatever food she wanted at any time was astonishing. In the years when they had poor pearl harvests, her family had squeaked by on dried mussels, fish that Papa caught, and vegetables from the garden. Now she could ask for delicacies that she'd only heard about from visiting the capital, jellyfish salad and grilled fish stuffed with nuts and seaweed and shaved ice drenched in syrup. Yet all she wanted right now was porridge, something plain and comforting.

Once she finished, she folded her jacket to make a pillow and closed her eyes. She didn't expect to sleep, not without the sea's gentle rhythm and Kishi breathing next to her. She was sure she'd have nightmares about the ghost whale and about the slithering sea snakes. Yet when she next opened her eyes, she was shocked to find morning sun glimmering through the leaves. First, because she couldn't believe she'd slept. Second, because she couldn't believe that she was in a tree and not in her own bed. Everything that had happened, from the ghost whale to the Dragon King to Benzaiten, had to have been a fever dream. She touched the scratchy bark beneath her fingers and felt the pressure in her bladder from having to pee. This was real. It hit her with a sickening thud that Kishi had died.

Kai balled up her hands and dug her nails into her palms. She wanted to scream until the sky shattered and then burrow into the ground. Instead she took a deep breath, a diving breath, and pushed the sadness and the horror down, squeezed them into a mochi-sized ball that she shoved into a box, a wooden puzzle box with secret sliding panels like the ones the village woodworker made. Kishi could come back, maybe. But Kai had a long way to go for that to happen. She stood up on the branch and climbed higher until she could look out at the valley. In the distance, an ominous black cloud swirled around a tapering tree that towered high above the rest. It was like seeing a storm on the horizon, only instead of waiting for the storm to barrel into the shore, she was going into its heart.

As she hiked down the path in the summer heat, sweat dripped into her eyes and made her feet slide inside her sandals. She hated the damp prickly feeling of her clothes sticking to her skin. She wasn't used to dealing with heat. At home she could always go jump in the sea. Stopping in a strip of shade, she asked the magic bowl for water. But nothing happened. She asked again. Nothing. Had she dreamed that it made porridge last night? Or could it already be broken? To test it, she asked for tea. The bowl immediately clouded over and a light brown liquid appeared. She took a tentative sip. It was in fact hot tea.

"O Great Source of Bounty, please give me water," she asked for the third time. Again nothing happened. This seemed like a major oversight on the magic maker's part. She wondered if there was a bureau for repairs in the Dragon King's palace. It would be in the basement, run by a samebito, a black shark with human arms and legs who had been sent to work there as a punishment for once making the Dragon King angry. Each broken thing would bring the samebito to tears because it would remind him of his mistake, when he accidentally stepped on the Dragon King's seashell horn. If Kishi were here, she'd jump in to continue the story. She'd say that the samebito would examine the magic bowl and start to cry, filling it to the rim with his tears. And then they'd have water. The samebito would be rewarded for his good deed and allowed back into the Dragon King's service. Everyone would live happily ever after. That's what would happen if Kishi were here.

The trek down to the valley took the entire morning. By the time the path leveled off, the sun was high overhead. Kai came to a bramble that walled in both sides of the path. Beyond the bramble, the Crows of the Eternal Night swarmed in a perfect disk near the top of the fir tree. She could see the cloak hanging from the tip. It was a long way to climb. Would the branches hold her weight? Worried thoughts circled around and around like the crows. Getting the cloak without falling out of the tree seemed difficult but not impossible. But taking a magical pearl from a supernatural fox? To distract herself as she followed the twisting path through the bramble, Kai tried to remember more fox stories. Maybe one would have a clue that could help her.

"Once upon a time," she said, "there was a foolish man who went for a walk on a desolate country road and came across a beautiful woman. They returned to the village together and he walked her home, to the finest house he had ever seen. Since the village wasn't that big, he thought it was strange that he'd never noticed the house or this woman before. But she was so beautiful that he dismissed this thought. Head over heels in love, he followed her inside and didn't leave. A year went by and they had a son. The man had never been happier. Meanwhile, his two brothers searched for him all over the village. They finally found him in a crawl space beneath a shabby warehouse. When they pulled him out, the man said his wife and son were still inside. But all the brothers saw were two foxes running away. A shape-shifting fox had bewitched the man, and though he thought he had spent a year with her, it had only been a day. As my aunt liked to say, there is no moral to this story, only that foolish men who fall for beautiful women in unlikely places get what they deserve."

The last time Hamako had told this story, Kai asked her

afterward if that's why she wasn't married, because so many men were stupid. *Kai*, Kishi had said, her face turning red from embarrassment because she thought the question was rude. But Kai didn't see why. She wasn't suggesting there was something wrong with Hamako. Their aunt laughed and said, *It's fine. There are plenty of good men like your father. In fact, a very nice man, a boatbuilder up the coast, asked me to marry him. But your mother said something that always stuck with me. She said when she kissed your father for the first time, she felt radiant, like how a pearl must feel when the shell has been cracked open and it's brought into the light. The boatbuilder didn't make me feel that way. Remember, girls, we pearl divers can provide for ourselves. You can marry for love or not marry at all.*

Kai liked the idea of remaining single the way her aunt had. But she realized now that she'd envisioned Kishi always being with her, and that if Kishi married she'd choose someone like Papa. Someone hardworking and smart and funny. Someone who Kai approved of and wouldn't mind living in the same house with. That was why Kishi flirting with the village chief's son upset her so much. For the first time, Kai realized that a future husband wasn't an add-on to their lives, but a force that might change everything.

The eerie caws grew louder. Around the next bend, the bramble opened up to a clearing. Kai felt like she'd stumbled upon the gate to the Underworld. The Crows of the Eternal Night flew in a tight pack, blotting out the sun overhead. The band of birds was so thick that she could no longer see the cloak dangling from the top of the tree. When she stood sideways with half her body in the bramble and half in the clearing, she was divided down the middle by shadow and sunlight. The air was cold on the tree side, like being inside a deep cave.

Squatting at the edge of the clearing in the sun, Kai studied the knotted trunk. If her family linked hands, they still would not form a complete circle around it. The lowest branch appeared to be well over her head, which meant she'd have to use the knots as foot- and handholds. If she spent too much time thinking, she'd lose her nerve. Kai set her bow and quiver on the ground, then marched toward the tree, pulling her jacket tight around her to ward off the chill. She hadn't taken more than five steps when the crows' caws went from eerie to angry. She ran toward the trunk as a black blizzard descended, their wings battering her, their beaks pecking her head, their shrieks ringing in her ears. Flailing her arms overhead, she managed to shake them off and retreat to the perimeter. Threat averted, the birds returned to circling high above. Blood streamed down her arms from the shallow cuts. This was going to be harder than she thought.

Taking out the magic bowl, Kai considered what the crows might like to eat. First she asked for raw millet. When she tossed the grain on the ground, a few birds came down to investigate, not the stream she hoped to see. At home she sometimes saw birds pecking at chestnuts on the ground.

She asked the bowl for chestnuts, but they came roasted. She threw them into the clearing anyway. Once again, a few came to investigate and then returned to the flock. She got the sense that these birds were coming down to make sure there was no danger, not because they were hungry. Next she tried walnuts, which garnered the same tepid response. Maybe magical crows didn't eat.

Kai gave up and ran to the tree again, cloaking her head with her jacket this time. She made it a few steps farther before the birds brought her to her knees. They clawed at her jacket, yanking it off her body. She grabbed the sleeve and swung around wildly in a circle. When the crows let go, she stumbled backward and fell. Scrambling to her feet, she ran back into the bramble. One crow kept attacking her head. She flicked her jacket to shoo it away. When the crow came at her face, she smacked it with her fist, lost her balance, and fell to the ground next to her bow. Without thinking, she loaded an arrow and shot at the squawking bird. Even at close range, she missed and the arrow clattered to the ground. But to her amazement, the crow went after it. Then a dozen more descended on the arrow and they started fighting. Of course. Crows liked shiny things.

She grabbed another arrow and shot it in a high arc away from the tree. More crows chased after it. She shot off another and another, getting more height and distance with each one, until all the crows had gone in pursuit of the arrows. Looking up to the top of the tree, she glimpsed the cloak, a fantastic hodgepodge of browns, blues, yellows, reds, and greens. Dropping the bow, she dashed to the tree and scaled the trunk, digging her fingertips into the crevices and grimacing as the rough bark scraped her forearms and calves. Once she reached the branches, the climb became easier. Keeping her eyes trained up so that she didn't get dizzy and fall, she listened for the crows. They still sounded far away. Through the branches, she saw the cloak fluttering. She climbed faster.

As Kai neared the top, the branches began to bend and sway under her weight. With each step, she held her breath. Up close, the hooded cloak had a strange hideous beauty, with feathers in different shapes, sizes, and colors all mixed together. When the hem was eye level, she tugged on it. The second her fingers grazed the cloak, the birds screeched. Turning her head, she saw them rise from the ground into a single black cloud. In a panic, she stepped one branch higher, grabbed the cloak, and tried to yank it down. But the branch snapped beneath her feet and she slipped. As she hugged the trunk for dear life, her feet scrabbled to find a hold.

Her left foot found the stub of the broken branch. Using it for leverage, she grabbed at the cloak again. Blackness closed in as the crows raked her head with their talons and pecked at her back and legs. Somehow she managed to unhook the hood from the treetop. Clinging to the trunk with her right arm, she held the cloak in her left hand and tried to use it to shield herself from the birds. She was not going to be able to climb down with the crows attacking. If she could get the cloak on, at least that would give her a protective layer. She managed to thrust her left arm into the sleeve. The cloak began to tug and pull skyward. Was it trying to fly? The last thing she wanted to do was test the cloak from the top of a tree and plunge to her death.

The crows grew even fiercer, going for her eyes. Screaming, she hooked her leg around the trunk and batted at them with her right arm. There was no choice. She was going to have to trust that the cloak did what the Dragon King said it did. She shoved her other arm into the sleeve and the cloak shot up in the air. Terrified, she clasped the treetop between her feet. The birds backed off, circling warily. Then she let go of the tree and spun in a slow circle, spiraling upward like a sky lantern. A giddy laugh escaped her lips.

"I'm flying," she called out to the crows.

Kai kept laughing, from fear as much as from wonder, as she levitated higher and higher, until the revolving disk of crows shrank to the size of an inkblot.

Her first impulse was to fly to Sky Mountain as fast as her new wings could go. But flying didn't turn out to be as easy as it looked. When she tried to make her body horizontal and move forward, she pitched into a somersault. Her stomach lurched into her throat as she tumbled toward the earth. Punching her arms over her head, she managed to pull out of the death spiral just as she reached the tree line.

She hovered until her heart stopped hammering. Then she tried again. She discovered that if she thrust her wings down with a slight rolling motion, she moved forward. Every so often, she wobbled in the air currents. But she managed to keep her balance. When she saw a pond glimmering in a ring of trees, she glided in careful circles, tilting one wing down and the other up, descending bit by bit. When she neared the ground, she fluttered her wings just enough to soften the landing. She still hit the ground too hard, stumbling forward with her hands out, eating dirt as she slid to a stop. Her acrobatics disturbed a pair of swans, who puffed out their wings and honked at her for invading their space. Since she'd had her fill of angry birds for one day, she showered them with pebbles and shooed them away.

When she stood up, the cloak tried to make her fly again and she had to bring her arms straight down by her sides to make it stop. Carefully, she slipped one arm out, then the other. The cloak dropped to the ground. She nudged it with her foot and it didn't move. Satisfied that the cloak couldn't fly off on its own, she stripped off her clothes and waded into the pond. The tiny pockmarks from the crows' beaks stung all over again as she washed off the dried blood. To dry herself, she sat on a rock in the sun. Only now that she had a moment to collect her thoughts, she realized she'd left the bow back at the fir tree. Would the bow really help her against the foxes, though? She was such a poor shot. She also didn't want to see the crows again. That made the decision for her. When she was dry and warm, she threw on her clothes, making sure the magic bowl was still secure in her jacket pocket. Then she put on the feather cloak, which dragged on the ground and swallowed up her hands. Hamako would have loved it. She loved costumes. But Kishi would hate it. She only liked to wear things that made her look pretty. Kai didn't care what she wore as long as she was comfortable. Though the cloak looked heavy, it felt light and shimmery on her body.

"O Wandering One," she said, holding up the coral pendant, "please show me the way to Sky Mountain."

The needle quivered and spun until it pointed southeast. How far in that direction did she have to go? A day? A week? The gods were maddeningly vague, not only with their instructions but also with the tools they gave.

Holding her arms out at shoulder height, she levitated and beat her wings vigorously, ascending until the trees looked like a blanket of moss. In the distance she saw mountains— the Seven Silent Mountains, she hoped. To pass the time, whenever she saw a mysterious dot moving, she swooped down to see if it was a deer, or a bear, or an ox pulling a cart. She also practiced gliding like a hawk, circling in one direction and then another. When a flock of geese flew straight at her, she assumed her bigger size would trump their numbers. But they didn't change their path, and at the last moment she had to dive out of their way.

When she reached the base of the first mountain at

sundown, she settled in a ropy ginkgo with large sturdy branches. Her arms ached from holding them out. But it was good to hurt, because otherwise she'd think about Kishi. She hoped Benzaiten's message got to Enma before Kishi faced judgment in the first of the Eight Great Hells, which was for the sin of killing. That meant any living thing, down to a mosquito. How much would the deaths of thousands of mussels weigh against Kishi? If Kai let herself think about that, then she'd also have to think about where Hamako's spirit had gone. Mama had assured them that Hamako went to heaven to be reborn. But they were young then. Mama had to say that.

When she fell asleep, she dreamed about flying. She soared over a lake, her reflection showing more bird than girl. In the dream, she kept confusing the surface with the sky and wound up crashing into the lake. Beneath the surface she found an upside-down world. She stood on the sky, her feet in puddles of clouds. The trees formed frilly skirts overhead, and mud rained from the earth, followed by bones that reassembled themselves after they fell from their graves. The bones became baku, dream-eating creatures made up of tiger legs and elephant heads and bear bodies. The baku knew she had a magic bowl and they asked her for orange slices. Then they sucked out the juice and smiled at her with the rinds in their mouths.

5

Kai woke feeling calmer and more confident. Twelve days. She had twelve days to reach Sky Mountain. She still didn't know how she would take the pearl. But she'd bested the birds and the cloak was hers. Maybe she could do this after all. That morning she flew between two of the Seven Silent Mountains. The mountains were in fact so quiet that she swore she could hear the furry mountain goats chewing leaves. Around midday, she came to a silvery lake that reminded her of her dream, of the dream eaters. When they were little, Hamako painted a baku on a cloth scrap to hang over their futon and keep the nightmares away. Any time a dream became too scary, Kai would think, *But wait, I have a baku*, and whatever scary thing was happening in her dream would stop. It had been a powerful feeling, to control her dreams that way. Eventually Kishi decided they were too old to believe in the baku and took down the picture. Kai would have kept it there, even though she knew dream eaters didn't exist.

As she flew over the lake, she was so deep in memory that she didn't register what the three streaks winking in the sunlight might be until it was too late. An arrow whizzed past her ear. Another grazed her hip. Then pain seared her right shoulder. Thrown off-balance, she tumbled head over heels and hit the water, landing on her back. As she plunged into the depths, there was no beautiful mirror world waiting for her, only murk. Her shoulder screamed in agony. The lake was not deep. But the arrow had pinned the cloak's sleeve to her right shoulder, and beneath the weight of the wet feathers, she struggled to stand up. After all those arguments with Mama about taking too many chances in the ocean depths, she was going to drown in shallow water.

Suddenly a swimmer with a shock of dark hair appeared, a teenage boy clothed in a loose tunic and trousers that billowed in the water. He wrapped an arm around her midsection and hauled her closer to shore where she could stand. As she doubled over coughing, hot pain shot through her arm. He waited patiently, holding the soggy cloak so that the arrow didn't pull on her shoulder. Water dripped from his raggedy mop of black hair and down his long gaunt face. When she stopped wheezing, he propelled her to the beach, where she fell to her knees. Out of the corner of her eye, she could see the arrow shaft sticking out of the fleshy part of her arm like a giant pin. He draped the cloak across her back so that it didn't tug on the arrow and placed one hand on her shoulder blade.

"I'm going to pull it out on three," he said in a cool, calm voice. "One, two, three."

A lightning shock flashed through her body. She cried out and collapsed on the ground, the hood of the cloak falling across her face. She turned on her side and curled into a ball, gripping her right shoulder with her left hand. Four hairy ankles in rough dirty trousers appeared on the damp sand and she froze.

"What is it, Ren?" said a gruff voice that came from the man on the left.

"I'm not sure, but there's a girl inside," said Ren, the one who had rescued her. His tone was clipped, devoid of judgment or emotion. "The feathers are some kind of coat."

"A girl who flies like a bird," said the other man in a smooth silvery tone. "Impossible."

He bent over and shoved the hood away from her face. Kai whimpered and squinted in the sunlight.

"She's got to be some kind of witch," the gruff one said, spitting on the ground. "We should put an arrow through her head before she casts a spell on us."

"Hold on now, Doi. Don't be hasty. Could she be a phoenix? The feather pattern is unusual. Let's have a look at her. Ren, hold her up."

"She's in a lot of pain," Ren said.

"Shut up, boy," the one called Doi said. "Nobody asked for your opinion. You heard Goto. Stand her up."

Ren hoisted her up and set her on her feet. Her legs shook from the weight of the wet cloak and her shoulder throbbed. They were standing in a cove edged on either side by maroon reeds. Doi, the one to her left, had a scraggly beard flecked with gray, a nose shaped like a garlic bulb, and dry fleshy lips. Goto had a soft, pudgy face at odds with his flinty brown eyes. They both looked to be about her father's age and wore shabby hunting cloaks. With a sinking feeling, she realized they were probably not villagers out on an afternoon hunt, but bandits.

"The colorful feathers are like a phoenix," Goto said. "Don't you remember there was a painting of one on that jewelry box?"

"I've never seen a picture of a phoenix with a girl inside," Doi said. "I still say we shoot it. Better safe than sorry."

"Think what a phoenix would be worth," Goto said. "We could sell her to one of the generals. We'd have sake for months."

This couldn't be happening. She couldn't be captured and sold. She had to rescue her sister. Why hadn't she been more careful? Maybe if they thought she'd been possessed by a fox, that might scare them into letting her go. But why would a girl possessed by a fox wear a feather coat? She racked her brain for supernatural creatures in bird form.

"I'm a tennyo," Kai said. "If you let me go, I'll repay you with treasure."

Doi cackled. "If you're a celestial nymph, then I'm the Shining Prince," he said, referring to Genji, the handsome, brilliant courtier in an epic tale that was wildly popular in the capital.

Goto eyed her with suspicion. "Tennyos are supposed to have white feathers," he said.

In the fairy tale that Hamako had told, a group of tennyos stopped to bathe in a lake, leaving on the shore their white feather coats, which allowed them to fly. A man spotted them and stole one of the coats. When the rest of the tennyos flew back to heaven, the one whose coat had been stolen was stranded on earth. The man, feigning ignorance, asked her what was wrong and then convinced her to marry him. Years later, she found her coat hidden in a cupboard and flew away, abandoning her husband and two children. That was one of the stories that she and Kishi had changed. In their version, the mother cut off a strip from the bottom of her coat and made two smaller coats for her children to wear. Then they all flew off to the heavens, leaving the sneaky husband behind.

"That's just in the stories," she said. "I can bring you pearls. Pearls that are worth a fortune in the capital."

Doi's furry eyebrows shot up. A crafty smile spread across Goto's face. "Pearls," he said. "How many?"

"Jars filled with them," she said.

The two men turned away to confer. "If we let her go, we can't trust her to come back," she heard Doi say.

Their voices dropped. Ren removed the soaked feather

cloak from her shoulders and squeezed the water out. He was tall and painfully thin, his collarbone and hip bones jutting beneath his damp clothes. After folding the cloak, he removed her jacket and examined her shoulder through the ripped fabric of her undershirt. She clenched her jaw to keep from crying out. She could see bright red blood seeping through the fabric, but she couldn't see the underside of her arm. His dark eyebrows seemed locked together in a perpetual frown.

"How bad is it?" she asked.

"You got lucky," he said. "It missed the bone. It looks like a large puncture wound."

"I'm not feeling so lucky right now," she said, doubling over from a wave of pain. Bile rose in her throat. She couldn't believe this might be the end for her and her sister.

"Ren, tie her up," Goto called out. "We're going to General Takagi's compound. We'll camp at the falls."

Ren placed a hand on her good shoulder. "I want to clean the wound out first. Can you walk to that log over there?"

She nodded and straightened up with effort. Goto and Doi walked ahead toward the trees, where four mangy horses waited. Ren guided her to the fallen log, where she sat down and put her head between her knees, hoping the nausea would pass. He rested his bow against the log near her leg and walked over to the horse with a pack on its back. Goto and Doi also had bows slung over their shoulders. She wondered which one of them had hit her. Ren returned with a saddlebag that he set down by her feet. Then he rolled up her sleeve and poured water from a canteen over the wound. It felt like fireflies exploding.

"What are all these cuts from?" he asked, pointing to the round scabs that dotted her arm.

"I got in a fight with a murder of crows," she said.

The corner of his mouth ticked upward ever so slightly. "Yeah? Who won?"

"I thought I did," she said. "But now I'm here."

The stinging subsided. From the saddlebag, Ren pulled a square cloth used to wrap and tote things and cut off a strip with a pocketknife. She had the feeling he'd done this before. He had an air of competence that made him seem almost like an adult, though she guessed he was not much older than her. "What are you? Bandits?" she asked.

He smirked. "Bandits by day," he said. "Traveling circus by night."

"What does that mean?" Kai winced as he wrapped the cloth bandage around her arm.

"You'll see," he said. "Have you ever been on a horse before?"

She shook her head. She'd only seen horses from a distance in the capital. Nobody in her village had a horse. The farmers used oxen to plow fields and pull carts.

Ren studied the packhorse and frowned. "I guess you better ride with me, then," he said.

He threaded her left arm into her jacket sleeve and draped

the other side over her injured shoulder. Then he used a rope to bind her hands in front of her. The bonds were tight, but not so tight that they cut into her wrists.

"Is this General Takagi the head of one of the military clans?" she asked.

The chancellor appointed noblemen to serve as governors of each province. But in reality, military clans controlled everything. Papa said the imperial court had put too much power in the hands of the generals because the nobles would rather spend their days drinking sake and writing poetry. If the generals ever stopped fighting each other and attacked the capital, the noble houses would be in trouble.

"Yep," he said, tying another length of rope around the middle of the rolled cloak.

Kai waited for him to elaborate, but he didn't. "So their plan is to sell me to General Takagi like some kind of exotic pet?"

"That's a good guess," he said, adding the bound-up cloak to the brown packhorse. Then he guided her to a black horse with a white star on its forehead, which was attached to the packhorse by a lead line. The black horse pawed the ground with a hoof that looked iron hard and tossed its head. Kai dug her feet in the ground, afraid to get too close.

"She's not going to hurt you," Ren said. "Come on. You don't want to make Doi wait."

The two men had already mounted, Goto on a tawny brown horse and Doi on a dark brown horse with a white splotch on its hindquarters. The men's horses and the pack-horse had saddles. But Ren's horse didn't have anything on its back.

Ren laced his fingers together near the horse's belly. "I'll boost you up. Step into my hands with your left foot."

"What if it moves?" she asked, fearful that she was going to sail over its back, slip off the other side, and have those very hard hooves crush her.

"She won't," he said.

"How do you know?"

Annoyance rolled across his face. "You think I want you to fall off? Look, if you don't get on this horse, Doi's going to get angry. And trust me, you don't want him angry."

No, she probably didn't want that. She did as Ren said and stepped into his laced hands with her foot. He pushed her up high enough that she could grab the horse's mane between her fingers and swing her other leg over the horse's back. The horse gave off a strong earthy odor. When it shifted its weight, she sensed an unpredictable, coiled-up energy.

Ren jumped on behind her. Kai had never been this close to a boy or a man before, other than her father. Hot with embarrassment, she tried to lean forward so that her back didn't touch his chest. He smelled like horse, but also like charred wood and sweat. He picked up the reins in his left hand, his wiry arm forming a semicircle around her waist. The sleeve of his faded indigo tunic rested on her thigh. When he clucked, the horse began to walk and the packhorse followed. They fell in line behind Doi and Goto, riding away from the pond into a heat-smothered forest.

The colors seemed muted, either by the pain in her arm or by the damp heavy air. The wilted trees were a dull shade of green against the dull gray sky. Moss ravaged tree trunks and devoured rocks. She shook her head to ward off the flies that buzzed her ears. One bit the top of her ankle so hard that she thought she'd been stung by a bee. Tears filled her eyes. Kai had never been so miserable. Where were the gods now that she needed them? She had crashed back to earth, into a world without magic. But this was not the real world of her village, where the worst thing that ever happened was an unkind look or word. This was the world that she only knew about from the news passed on by the fishermen and the shopkeepers, of warlords and pirates and bandits, rough men who made innocent people suffer in ways that she didn't want to think about right now. At sea, she would have had a chance. She could out-dive and out-swim these men. But on land, the cloak was her only source of power, and it was strapped to the saddle of the packhorse.

"Do you have a name?" Ren asked, quietly enough that Goto and Doi couldn't hear.

She tried to remember the name of the tennyo whose coat was stolen. Maybe this was a trick question.

"I won't tell them," he added.

"Kai," she said.

"Well, Kai," he said, "once your shoulder feels better, I'm

going to put you on the packhorse. But for now, you're stuck with me. If you keep leaning forward like that and we start moving faster, you're going to fall."

She tried to sit up straight without touching him. Her shoulder throbbed. The sway of the horse at least was soothing, like bobbing in the sea.

"Isn't it easier to ride with a saddle?" she asked.

"It's a crutch," he said. "A saddle and stirrups give you a sense of safety that isn't real."

"Is that why you don't use one?" she asked.

"I don't use one because we only have three," he said.

The gap between them and the other bandits widened. When Doi glared over his shoulder, Ren moved the horse into a trot to catch up. Kai gripped the horse's coarse mane. Each bouncing step made her grimace with pain.

The flies grew thicker. The horse kept tossing its mane and flicking its ears. The sun broke through the clouds and the leaves trembled and shimmered. Kai was ready to cut her arm off. She couldn't remember another time when she had been in so much pain. Up until now, her injuries had been pretty ordinary, considering their dangerous line of work. A scraped knee. A nicked finger. A jellyfish sting. Relief from the flies finally came when they emerged from the forest and climbed a rocky path next to a gorge with a river far down below. She considered pitching herself off the horse and over the cliff. Suicide was probably the honorable thing. But she couldn't bring herself to do it, because that was not just giving up on her own life. That was giving up on Kishi. And even though it shouldn't have mattered, she didn't want to risk hurting the horse. Ren, on the other hand, was a bandit and probably deserved to die.

When they hit a steep stretch of trail, he told her to lift her seat and lean forward. "You said I'd fall if I did that," she said irritably.

"When we go up, you lean forward," he said. "When we go down, you lean back. The rest of the time, you sit straight. That helps the horse."

She shifted forward. It wasn't the horse's fault that it had to work for bandits. "What's your horse's name?" she asked.

"Encumbrance," he said.

She rolled her eyes. "Fine, don't tell me."

"That's her name. I swear." Kai detected amusement in his voice.

"I can see you have great affection for her," she said.

"I needed a horse to ride and Goto told me to pick one, but I wanted to keep both," Ren explained. "He said having two more horses to feed was a burden and an encumbrance. So that's what I named them."

Kai glanced back at Burden plodding along behind them up the narrow path. "Heartwarming," she said. "Are you related to Goto or Doi?"

"Nope."

"Why are you with them, then?"

"Why were you flying over a lake in a bird suit?"

She didn't answer. As long as Goto and Doi thought she

might be a tennyo, she had some value, and maybe General Takagi would let her go.

"How long is it going to take us to get to General Takagi's compound?" She tensed as she waited for the answer, even though that information wouldn't tell her anything useful. She didn't know where they were in relation to Sky Mountain, anyway.

"Two days," he said.

"Have you ever heard of Sky Mountain?" she asked.

He took so long to answer that she started to wonder if he was ignoring her question or hard of hearing. "Can't say that I have," he said. "What's there?"

"Dakini, the Fox Queen," she said. "I'm supposed to find her."

He guffawed. "Don't foxes eat birds?"

"I can fly," she said. "I wasn't planning on getting that close."

He gave a short but appreciative laugh and she felt a jolt of pride that immediately set off a warning drum in her head. Ren was a bandit who robbed people and probably worse. How could she enjoy talking to him? There had to be something very wrong with her.

As the sun dipped behind the trees, they dismounted near the base of a waterfall that cascaded in a soft whisper. Ren sat her down next to a willow tree and bound her to the trunk. Then he set about taking care of the horses, removing their saddles and bridles. Meanwhile, Doi and Goto went to a flat sun-warmed rock at the edge of the falls and stripped off their clothes. Kai pulled her knees into her chest and trained her eyes on the ground until they dove into the water. How had she gone from diving for pearls to this? Nothing that had happened since the moment she saw the ghost whale seemed real.

When Ren led the horses to the river to drink, she studied the knots on the rope that bound her hands to see if she might be able to get loose overnight. But no matter how she twisted her wrists, she couldn't slip one hand out. When he finished with the horses, Ren came over and untied her.

"Come on," he said, walking in the direction of the woods.

Kai eyed him warily. "Where are you taking me?"

"If you'd rather stay here, feel free," he said with a shrug.

Her shoulder thrummed with pain. She was dizzy with exhaustion. But it was true that she'd rather stick close to Ren than be left alone with Goto and Doi. She got up and followed him. He almost glided as he walked, making no noise, while dried leaves crunched beneath her feet. He seemed at ease in the forest on his own and she wondered what bound him to these men.

"So what's the hardest part about flying?" he asked as he collected twigs.

"Landing in a tree," she said. "You need to come in with the right speed at the right angle. I still haven't figured out what that is. And of course I don't have talons to grip the branch."

"You said you were heading to Sky Mountain," he said. "How are you navigating when you're in the air?"

He was testing out her story, putting pieces together. She realized she'd already given away that she hadn't been flying long. The pain in her shoulder was clouding her head and making her careless. She felt a dull ache around her temples.

"You need to rest?" Ren asked.

She nodded and leaned against a tree trunk. He set the firewood that he'd gathered next to her feet and continued to collect sticks while she watched him work. Gold light filtered through the trees. Her gaze wandered to a brown rabbit hopping near a shrub. She watched the bunny sniff around, looking for something to nibble on. Out of the corner of her eye, she saw a metallic flash. The rabbit jerked to the side and fell over, an arrow through its neck. Kai gasped. Ren put the bow back on his shoulder and went to collect the rabbit. She wasn't upset by the killing so much as the fact that she hadn't seen it coming. She had a feeling he was the one who'd shot her.

When they returned, Goto and Doi were lounging on the rocks by the waterfall, passing a flask back and forth. Ren tied her to the willow tree again and built a campfire. After skinning the rabbit, he threaded it on a stick and cooked it over the flames. When it was ready, Goto and Doi sat by the fire and tore into it. They continued to pass the flask, their voices growing rowdier. Ren brought her some water and a few morsels of rabbit meat. It was stringy and gamy, but she didn't want to seem ungrateful, so she ate it anyway. She wasn't sure if she could take the magic bowl out of her inner jacket pocket during the night with her hands bound, and she didn't want to risk having one of the bandits see her with it. Once she ate the few bites of meat, Ren cleaned her wound again, which burned as he poured water over it. Then he took her into the woods to relieve herself.

"If you run, I'll put an arrow in your leg and you'll die slowly," he said. After seeing him kill the rabbit, Kai knew he'd have no trouble hitting her, even in the dark.

When they returned, Doi was standing on the large flat boulder by the falls juggling a half dozen seedpods. He threw them high in the air, spinning around and catching some behind his back. Meanwhile Goto had put on a lady's silk robe and was powdering his face white. Kai gaped at them. Every few years a traveling theater group performed in her village. The men had played the women's parts in those shows.

"I thought you were kidding about the circus," she said to Ren.

"They used to be actors," Ren said. "Being a bandit pays better. Now they just perform for captive audiences."

"Lucky me," Kai said.

Goto rushed over and grabbed her sleeve.

"The best seat in the house has been reserved for you," he said, leading her to a log facing the boulder, with the campfire at her back. Confused, Kai looked over at Ren, who sat down on a rock nearby, took out his pocketknife, and whittled a stick as if nothing out of the ordinary was going on.

Doi let the pods fall one by one. Then he put on a gentleman's black lacquered cap. Goto, carrying a child's parasol, joined Doi on top of the boulder. It occurred to Kai that all these props had belonged to the people whom they'd robbed.

"Ren," Goto said in a loud whisper.

Ren looked up, his eyelids heavy with indifference. "Scene," he said flatly.

Goto thrust out a hip. "You called, my lord?" he said in a shrill falsetto.

"Yes, my lady," Doi said in a loud pompous voice. "I need you to call the doctor. I'm under the weather."

"Under the weather, you say? You don't need a doctor for that, dear. You can borrow my parasol." Goto swung around and smacked Doi in the forehead with it. He stumbled backward.

"Now can you call the doctor?" he said, grabbing the handle. "I have a headache." Doi bent over, clutching his belly and erupting in laughter.

Disconcerted, Kai glanced over at Ren, who kept his eyes fixed on his whittled stick.

Suddenly Doi stopped laughing and glared at her. She lowered her eyes to the ground.

"You're supposed to laugh," he said as something small and hard bounced off her head. Doi was throwing seedpods at her. Another zinged her shoulder, her bad shoulder, and she yelped. Turning her body away from him, she protected her head with her left arm.

"What's the matter with you, tennyo?" he roared. "You think you're too good for us?"

Kai whimpered. Doi scared her more than the Dragon King shooting fire. She couldn't even pretend to laugh.

Goto placed a heavy hand on Doi's shoulder. "It's because she's part bird," he said. "Birds don't laugh. They don't play tricks. In the old stories, the fox plays tricks, the monkey plays tricks, even the crab. But you never hear about the bird."

Doi spat on the ground. "What about the tongue-cut sparrow? That bird played a trick on the old woman."

"The sparrow taught the greedy woman a lesson," Goto said. "It's not meant to be funny. I'm telling you, Doi. Birds don't laugh. But I know what will help."

Goto hopped down from the boulder and broke into a warbling song in a deep baritone: "The moon is rising, so round and full."

It was a song Kai had learned as a child. But with Goto lumbering toward her, the song was alarming instead of comforting. He opened a flask and held it up to her lips. She turned her head and knocked the flask away with her bound hands, almost spilling the liquor.

"Naughty bird," he said, grabbing her by the hair, his pudgy face so close that she could see his jumbled teeth and smell his sour breath. "I should cut your tongue out like the sparrow. Ren, give me your knife."

He wouldn't. Would he? She'd taken Goto to be the schemer and Doi to be the violent one. In a panic, she tried to smack Goto's chest with her bound hands and push him away, which sent a shock wave through her shoulder.

"You don't want to do that," she heard Ren say. "You'll regret it in the morning. She's worth more in one piece."

For a second, Goto's hand gripped her hair more tightly. She bit her lip and prayed that he would listen to reason. Breaking into another song, he let go and staggered away. Kai fell in a heap on the ground, her breath coming in sharp gasps. Goto and Doi both stumbled into the woods. As soon as they disappeared, Ren hopped to his feet.

"Come on," he said, grabbing her elbow and helping her up.

He led her back to the willow, where he bound her feet and looped a length of rope around her waist to tether her to the tree. Kai was filled with anger and humiliation at her own powerlessness. She hated not being able to defend herself. If she ever got away from them, she was going to learn how to use a weapon. Maybe she'd take up archery. You didn't have to be bigger than your enemy to use a bow and arrow.

Ren worked quickly and quietly, and Kai didn't say anything, sensing that he wanted to be finished by the time Goto and Doi came back. Once she was secured to the tree, he went back to where he'd been sitting and kept whittling the stick as if he'd never moved. A few minutes later, Goto and Doi flopped on the ground next to the campfire. Kai made herself as small as she could against the tree. But out of sight seemed to be out of mind.

In the dying light of the campfire, she watched Ren watch them. Once they started snoring, he tossed the stick aside and lay down, using a saddlebag as a pillow. Beneath his impassive mask, she sensed deep undercurrents. Every move he made was calculated. He seemed almost as much a captive as she was.

6

All night long her shoulder throbbed in time to the men's snores and the horses' grunts. Kai kept shifting around, trying to get comfortable on the bumpy roots and small rocks. Her bound feet and hands kept going numb, and every so often she had to wiggle her fingers and toes until they tingled. She was lightheaded, too, which probably meant she needed food. Unless it meant she'd lost too much blood.

While she wiggled and shifted, she also prayed for Hamako's spirit to protect her. But mid-prayer, she stopped. If their ancestors' spirits had the power to help them, then why hadn't they intervened? How could the bakekujira swallow up Kishi if their aunt and their grandparents and their great-grandparents were guarding them? Where had they been when the bandits shot arrows at her over the lake? Kishi would probably say that they hadn't done enough during the Festival of the Dead to show devotion to their ancestral spirits. Kishi was always quick to find fault in herself. But Kai thought they'd done their best, scrubbing the graves clean, leaving offerings of fruit and flowers, and lighting lanterns in front of their cottage so that the spirits could find their way home. Then, three days later, Kai and her family released their lanterns to float away on the sea. The whole ritual was a fairy tale, she realized now. A way of pretending that they could keep bad things from happening. She felt a dark formless despair, like a shadow that had been ripped from its physical body.

When owl hoots finally gave way to bird chatter at dawn, Ren got up. He tied a dark blue bandanna around his forehead, causing his coarse, unruly hair to stand up like hijiki seaweed. After taking out a brush from a saddlebag, he groomed the horses with steady, even strokes. Even at this early hour, the horses' coats already had dark sweat stains. He spoke to them in a low gentle voice, and one of them, the packhorse, Burden, wrapped its neck around his lean torso as if giving him a hug. When he finished grooming, he walked toward Kai. She hadn't really noticed his eyes yesterday, which were a dark brown like tree bark after a rainstorm. Without greeting her, he untied her hands and started to roll up her sleeve.

She jerked her arm away from him even though the movement sent a sharp pain through her shoulder. "I'm not a horse," she said. "You can't just grab me like that."

He let go and raised his hands. "You know what, Kai? You're one more thing I have to take care of. But if you want that wound to get infected, that's fine with me."

"Oh, well, I'm so sorry to add to your list of chores," she said. "It's not like I asked to be kidnapped. All I meant is you could at least tell me what you're going to do before you do it."

"Fine, I'm trying to change that bandage so that you don't die," he said. "Is that better?"

"Much," she said, wincing as he pulled off the blood-crusted cloth. "Thanks for what you did last night."

He grunted and continued to work, pouring water from the canteen over the wound and wrapping it again. His silence nettled her, even though she shouldn't have cared. He probably came to her defense because it was less work for him. If Goto had cut her tongue, Ren would've had to fix her. He was just as despicable as the other two were. He was dirt. No, worse than dirt, since beautiful things like flowers came from dirt. He was the green scum on a stagnant pool. Nothing good came from that. When he finished bandaging her up, he went back to the campfire and repacked the saddlebags, shifting items around. Goto and Doi groaned as they stumbled to their feet.

"Ren, tack up the horses," Goto said. Then he and Doi went off into the woods.

Ren saddled and bridled their horses. When the two men returned, they hopped on and rode off. Kai was still tethered to the tree.

"Where did they go?" she asked when Ren walked over to take down the two remaining bridles from a branch. Maybe this was her chance to escape. He tried to protect her last night, so he had to feel sorry for her, at least a little.

"To check for travelers coming through the pass up ahead," he said.

"You mean to rob people," she said.

He ignored her, going to Burden and pulling the bridle over her face and working the bit into her mouth.

"I was telling the truth when I said I could bring back pearls," she called out.

"It's not up to me," he said, adjusting a buckle on the horse's cheek.

"If you let me go, I'll bring you treasure," she said. "I promise."

"If I let you go, they'll kill me," he said.

He really was a prisoner to these men. A heavy fatigue washed over her. Other than bribing him, Kai didn't know how to persuade him. She sensed that tears would only make him uncomfortable. When he had the packhorse tacked up, he came back and untied her. She could make a run for it and bolt into the forest. But even as she had those thoughts, she knew she wouldn't run. With every stride, she'd be bracing for an arrow between her shoulder blades, and when it hit, as it inevitably would, she'd see the tip come out through her breastbone. Now that she knew real pain, she was afraid of it.

"I want to teach you a couple of things before you ride Burden today," he said.

Kai followed him to the packhorse, walking stiffly. Her inner thighs were tight and sore. She could barely turn her neck. And the entire area around her right shoulder ached. As they approached, Burden flicked her ears forward and looked at them with eager, anxious eyes.

"When you meet a horse for the first time, close your hand and let her smell you," he said, holding out his fist.

Kai did what he said, extending her left hand toward the horse's velvety snout. Burden snuffled her, and Kai patted her wide forehead. Her stomach fluttered at the prospect of riding alone. She didn't want to fall. Like he had yesterday, Ren went to the horse's side and laced his fingers. Kai stepped into his hands and he boosted her onto Burden's bare back. The packhorse was shorter and stouter than Encumbrance.

"You want to keep your shoulders, hips, and heels in a line," he said. "Sit up straight, but don't tense up."

"Right," she said. "What do I possibly have to be tense about?"

Out of the corner of her eye, she thought she saw a faint smile, which both pleased and confused her. *He's nicer to animals than he is to people*, she thought. *He'd kill me if he had to.* Holding the reins, he led Burden along the path until they reached a flat section. He told her to cluck to tell Burden to walk, and to sit back and say "whoa" to stop. As they went back and forth along the same stretch of trail, Kai tried to meld into the horse's swaying gait.

Absorbed in the lesson, she forgot about her shoulder

until Ren made Burden trot, and that bouncy gait sent shock waves up and down her arm. But Kai discovered that if she relaxed into Burden's back, she didn't bounce quite so much.

"Don't look down at her," he said as he jogged alongside. "Keep your eyes up and look where you want her to go."

After a few minutes, he let go of the reins. When Burden picked up speed and Kai started to bounce around, she panicked and jerked on the reins to stop the horse. Ren, who was still running beside them, said, "Whoa," and slowed her to a walk.

"Don't yank on her," he said. "She's not going to run away with you. Encumbrance might, but not this girl."

Kai took a few deep breaths to clear her head and tried to use her fear to fuel herself into action, the way she had when she'd had one arm in the feather cloak and had to let go of the tree in order to get the other arm in. She trotted Burden up and down the path a few more times and didn't need Ren to slow her down. For someone who didn't talk much, he was a good teacher and he seemed genuinely happy with her progress.

"You're getting it," he said with an excitement that opened up his whole face.

Kai felt a rush of delight. She was riding a horse! She couldn't wait to tell Kishi. The thought of her sister made her yank on the reins again.

"Sorry, sorry," she said to Ren before he could say anything.

She patted Burden on the neck in apology. "I didn't mean to do that."

Kai didn't understand how she could feel joy in anything. She'd been kidnapped and was about to be bartered like an ox while her sister's body was trapped in a sea snake purgatory. All she should be thinking about was how to escape and how to get the pearl.

When Goto and Doi returned, Ren was attaching feathers to an arrow shaft next to the dead campfire and Kai was tied to the tree again. Doi tossed a small bundle to Ren to add to the saddlebags—whatever they'd stolen in their heist. Then Ren untied her and put her on Burden. He'd divided the packs between the horses this time so she had a saddle. With her feet firm against the stirrups, she felt more secure. Since Burden was still tethered to Encumbrance, she didn't have to steer or worry about her horse running away. All she had to do was not fall off.

The harsh sun beat down on the dry brush as they climbed toward the summit. Wondering if this was the pass where Goto and Doi had come earlier, she looked around for evidence of an ambush. Something fluttered at the base of a rock just off the path. She squinted at it as they passed by. It might have been a handkerchief or a sash. But she couldn't be sure. After everything she'd seen lately, she didn't trust her eyes anymore.

From there the trail went mostly downhill. Ren gave her the occasional riding tip when Goto and Doi were far enough ahead not to overhear. She practiced moving Burden to the right by kicking with her left foot, and moving to the left by kicking with her right foot. Burden seemed happy to have a rider instead of a bunch of saddlebags. She had more spring in her stride. Kai found it fascinating that she could communicate what she wanted through her legs and that the horse wanted to comply.

They reached a grassy meadow dotted with wildflowers. With the Seven Silent Mountains behind them, Kai wondered if they had reached the Perpetual Plain of Eternal Afflictions. Goto and Doi shot ahead. Her body tightened and Burden skipped sideways.

"When you get nervous, she gets nervous," Ren said. "You're making her think there's a predator waiting to pounce."

"I can't go that fast," Kai said.

"You'll be fine," he said. "The canter's smoother than the trot. The worst thing that could happen is you fall into the grass."

"True, and that would only be the fourth worst thing that's happened to me this week," she said.

Wanting to grasp something sturdier than the reins, she grabbed Burden's mane with her left hand for extra security and they took off, Burden bounding forward so that she was running almost side by side with Encumbrance. Ren was right. Cantering was smooth. It was like becoming one with a wave in the sea, surging forward in a rolling motion. They swished through the tall grass and all the terrible things that had happened fell away as she moved to the hypnotic rhythm—three quick hoofbeats and a pause. *One-two-three-soar.* Every so often, Ren gave her pointers. Don't let her leg slide so far back. Try to keep her hands quiet. Kai loved the challenge of learning something new, of moving her body in a different way. When Burden began to snort with each step, Ren slowed them to a walk to give the horses a breather.

"That was fun," she said. "Can we gallop next?"

He grinned and then sucked in the corner of his mouth. "One thing at a time," he said.

The biggest dragonflies she'd ever seen, armored flutes with glittery eyes, darted over the wildflowers. One hovered in place and then launched straight up in the air. Another one flew at her head, causing her to flinch.

"They're huge," she said with awe. "I've never seen dragon-flies that big."

"I can't stand them," Ren said. "They're mean. One got caught inside my sleeve last week and bit me."

"Is that why this is called the Perpetual Plain of Eternal Afflictions?" she asked.

He snorted. "You sound like a one-hundred-year-old nun. Nobody calls it that anymore. We call it the Flatlands. The only things that will afflict you are the bugs."

"Dragonflies eat mosquitoes," she pointed out. "They're a force for good."

"Dragonflies eat each other, too," he said. "Which makes

them not all that different from people."

"That's a dark view of the world," she said.

"You obviously haven't seen much of the world."

Kai didn't doubt that he'd seen much worse than she had, but she was tired of his superior tone. "My sister just got killed by a sea monster," she said. "And one of you shot me. So I think I've seen plenty of the world."

Her eyes stung with tears. Even when she wasn't aware of them, they were always there now, lurking just below the surface. The tall grass shushed as the horses moved through the meadow. A dragonfly hovered by Encumbrance's ear and she startled, hopping to the side and bucking. Kai thought she would have screamed, but Ren didn't react to the bucking at all.

"I'm the one who hit you—sorry about that," he said. "Your sister was attacked by a sea monster?"

Kai nodded. "She was swimming," she said. "We live in a village called Shionoma in Biwa Province."

The words caught in her throat. Home seemed so far away. Her earliest memory was of the sea, sitting with Kishi on the wet sand and giggling while the surf washed over them. The thought of that simple happy time made her homesick and heartsick and every other kind of sick.

"So do you and the other tennyos get along with the mermaids, or are there turf wars?"

She didn't have to see his face to know that he was smirking. "Nobody in my village likes mermaids," she said.

"They're bad luck. If you do something stupid, that's called 'catching a mermaid.'"

He laughed and his frown lines vanished, giving her a glimpse of who he might have been if he weren't a bandit, and she found herself wishing that they were just regular kids out for a ride. "How did you wind up at Mirror Lake?" he asked.

How much should she tell him? He seemed to know that she was an ordinary girl. But if he hadn't figured it out, she didn't want to make him feel stupid. "You won't tell them, right?"

Though they rode side by side, Encumbrance always liked to stay slightly ahead of Burden. Ren glanced over his shoulder at her. "You haven't figured out how this works yet?" he said. "They tell me what to do. I don't tell them anything."

"I can bring my sister back if I can take something from Dakini," she said.

He gave her a skeptical sidelong glance. "You think you can bring your sister back from the dead?"

"I can't, but Benzaiten can," she said.

His eyebrows dipped in a frown. He probably thought grief had turned her mind into porridge. "Why would a sea goddess want to help a tennyo?" he asked.

It was a fair question, and probably one that General Takagi would ask too, if he was smart. "We're pearl divers. That's why," she said. She took a deep breath, but she couldn't hold the words inside. They bubbled up her throat and spilled from her mouth. "And we're twins. We have a deep bond, deeper than other siblings. Even though our bodies aren't physically connected, we always feel connected. I don't know if that makes sense. I told Benzaiten that we couldn't be separated. We need to be together, whether we're alive or dead."

She probably should not have admitted to being a twin, a freak of nature. But instead of disgust, she caught a strange excitement in his voice.

"You're a twin," he said. "I'm a twin, too. Do you know what she's thinking and feeling all the time?"

Kai was stunned. She'd never met another twin. "We'll say the exact same thing at the exact same time, word for word," she said. "Some people find that eerie."

"When you're apart, do you ever have a feeling—anger, or sadness, or excitement—that's not connected to what's happening to you? It's happening to her, but you feel it?"

She started to say yes. But the truth was that she and Kishi had rarely been apart. "Before her accident, I had a premonition," she said. "But I didn't know that's what it was until it was too late."

Her right rein dipped down farther than her left and she adjusted the strap. Up ahead, she could hear Goto singing a ballad in a jokey baritone.

"Wait, how do you know you're a twin? When's the last time you saw him?" Kai regretted her words almost immediately, since nothing good could have happened. She and Kishi might be the only twins in the Heiwadai Empire who had grown up together.

"I've never met him," Ren said. "I don't even know his name. I lived with the owner of a boardinghouse when I was little. She's the one who told me. My mother was staying there when she had us. She couldn't bring herself to kill her baby monsters. Instead, she disappeared with my brother and left me behind."

Kai already felt like a mirror that had shattered into an infinite number of pieces, like she was carrying those slivers around inside and pretending that they weren't there. She couldn't imagine never knowing Kishi. "Is that how it is for you, like maybe you're feeling what he's feeling?"

"Yeah, it's hard to explain," he said, his mouth puckering as he fell into a brooding silence. "Sometimes I'll feel angry for no reason at all and I'll wonder if it's him. And then I'll think, *What do you have to complain about? You got our mother.* Last summer, I had this incredibly vivid dream that I was being attacked by a fox. It felt so real. Since then, there's been nothing. Maybe that really happened. Maybe a fox killed him and he's gone."

Kai was about to tell Ren that her premonition came in a dream. But Doi had stopped his horse and turned to watch them. Ren moved the horses to a trot to catch up, ending their conversation. As the sun went down, Goto and Doi stopped by a sedate river, which she guessed was the first tine of the Three-Pronged River. This was her fourth night away from home, but it felt like she'd been away for months. Papa was probably going out in the boat and searching for her every day. Had he found the rowboat on Bamboo Island? Mama probably spent her days in bed crying, just as she had after Hamako died. Kai took her pain and imagined doubling it. She would either be bedridden or moving as fast as a blur, because anything in between would be unbearable.

Ren took her to the river and checked her wound. The pain was less intense this time as he poured clean water from a cup over her shoulder. While he worked, she gazed up at the moon. Each night it gained another sliver. Each night she lost ground. Tomorrow they would arrive at the general's compound and that would seal her fate. She couldn't think of another time in her life when the future seemed so uncertain.

"It's scabbing over," Ren said as he wrapped a clean bandage around her arm. "That's good."

She nodded. She already knew the wound was healing because the skin had started to feel tight when she moved her arm. Ren opened a pouch filled with dried taro root and offered it to her.

"You should eat," he said. "Riding will take it out of you."

Kai wasn't hungry. But he was right. She needed to keep up her strength in case she had a chance to escape. She felt bad taking what little food he had away from him, though. If she showed him the magic bowl, would he keep her secret or take it from her? He didn't have to teach her how to ride a horse or share his measly rations. She knew he liked her. But he was also a survivor. Kai took a piece of the taro root and studied his face, the long narrow nose, the high cheekbones, the stray wispy hairs along his stark jawline.

"How long have you been with them?" she asked, motioning downriver, where Goto and Doi were soaking their feet.

"I'm not sure," he said. "Nine winters, I think. I started eating more and the woman at the boardinghouse didn't have enough to go around. Goto and Doi needed a servant."

"I'm sorry," she said. "It must be hard, not having a real family." How would it feel to grow up as a blank slate, to not know where you came from? She and Kishi were defined by the Freshwater Sea. Sometimes she felt smothered by that history. But she also knew she belonged.

"Don't be," he said. "It doesn't bother me."

"I'm sorry because I know what you missed," she said.

He scowled. "I've seen fathers sell their daughters for a cup of rice and brothers try to kill each other over some prank that one of them pulled when they were six. So I'm not so sure that I missed anything."

Kai should have stopped talking and not risked upsetting him. But she was also running out of time. "Do you ever think of leaving them?"

His mouth hardened into a thin line as he bound her wrists together, pulling on the ends until the rope dug into her skin.

"That hurts," she said, wincing. "It's too tight."

"I know what you're doing and it's not going to work," he said, standing up.

Kai got to her feet and held her wrists out to him. "Ren, please. You just seem like you'd be happier on your own. You don't need them, so I'm wondering why you stay."

He shoved her forward. "You're not sweet-talking me into letting you go," he said. "Even if I was stupid enough to take off with you, you want to know what would happen? Doi would track us, and he'd find us, and he'd make sure we died in the slowest, most painful way he could think up. So get it out of your head. You're better off pleading your case with General Takagi."

He tethered her to an oak, where a colony of large black ants crawled over her feet faster than she could brush them off. Then he stalked over to the campfire and poked at the flames with a stick. Kishi would have known how to say all that in a way that softened him. Kai knew she was too blunt. At home, her lack of delicacy hadn't mattered since she always had her sister. Kai had never needed a friend. Until now.

7

All evening, she kept trying to shake off the ants as they crawled up her legs. Like the dragonflies, they were large, with sleek bodies the length of a sewing needle, and even though they didn't seem to bite, she couldn't stand the ticklish feel of their legs on her skin. Meanwhile Goto and Doi drank by the campfire. Instead of boisterous, tonight they seemed cranky, and she worried it was only a matter of time before they dragged her over to serve as their captive audience. First Goto chastised Ren for taking too much time on the horses while Doi groused that he hadn't done a thorough enough job. Then Doi complained that the pheasant was overcooked while Goto said it was undercooked. They also bickered over how to sell her to General Takagi.

"We'll tell him that the general in the northern province

has offered us her weight in jewels," Goto said, jabbing his finger in the air.

"He'd have to be a fool to fall for that," Doi said, stroking his gnarled beard. "She's built like a farm girl."

"Once he sees her fly, he'll forget all about that," Goto said. "Or we'll tell him that the chancellor himself has made an offer."

"Why stop there?" Doi said. "You might as well say the emperor is giving up his throne for her."

Doi held the flask upside down over his mouth and cursed. It was empty. Kai tensed. But the amount of alcohol turned out to be just enough to make them sleepy, not enough to fuel the night circus. They lay on their backs looking up at the stars and talking about all the riches they would have once they sold her. As soon as they started snoring, Ren glided over and loosened the tie around her wrists, which had made her skin red and raw.

"Thank you," she said, her voice sounding small and miserable. But he didn't answer.

Unable to sleep, all she could think about was her bed at home. She missed Kishi pulling the covers off every time she rolled and hearing Papa do his funny whistle-snore through the wall. Kai especially missed how Mama used to hold her and rock her to sleep whenever she was sick and how soothing that was. She'd give anything for the chance to ask Mama for forgiveness. Toward dawn, Kai fell into a half sleep, where she was aware that the sun was rising but she was too groggy and headachy to open her eyes. The sound of running water near her head snapped her awake. Doi was relieving himself against the tree, her tree, and a stream of urine was running down the bark into the dirt near her face. She screamed and lurched away.

"Excuse me for sullying your pristine dreams, tennyo," he said, laughing uproariously.

Her heart pounded like a pellet drum. Her chest heaving, she turned to face the tree trunk so that he wouldn't see her cry. It hit her that if General Takagi didn't buy her today, she'd be their prisoner until they found someone who would. But she didn't know if that was what she should wish for. What if General Takagi turned out to be more savage than the bandits?

When Ren untied her a few minutes later, he was stone-faced. "They want me to clean you up," he said, clamping his hand on her left shoulder and guiding her to the river.

He was still angry. But what did she care? Sitting on a rock at the water's edge, she watched the morning sun dance across the surface and tiny fish flit around a small pool by her feet. On the opposite bank, a doe grazed beneath a tree. Ren checked her shoulder. This time he didn't put on a bandage.

"A tennyo probably wouldn't have leaves in her hair," he said. "Can I take them out?"

"Go ahead," she said. "Whatever makes me look more celestial."

He stood behind her and she felt a gentle tugging as he

pulled the dried leaves out one at a time. Closing her eyes, she felt the same warm rush that she used to get when Mama combed her hair after a bath. She didn't want to enjoy it. She shouldn't feel anything but disgust for a bandit. Yet she couldn't help it, because she knew this might be the last nice thing that happened to her.

When he finished, she followed him to the horses, which Ren had already bridled and saddled. Doi looked her over and spat on the ground.

"I thought I told you to clean her up," Doi said.

Ren kept his eyes fixed on Burden, lacing his fingers and boosting her into the saddle. "I guess I forgot the jewelry and the fancy robes," he said.

Kai sucked in her breath. It wasn't like Ren to say or do anything that would set Doi off.

"What was that?" Doi said with cold rage. Ren fixed his gaze on her foot in the stirrup. Doi shoved Ren in the shoulder, and Ren stumbled back, looking at the ground.

Goto rushed over and threw his arm around Doi. "The sooner we get there, the sooner we get paid," he said. "Once she has the bird cloak on, General Takagi won't notice anything else."

Doi stared at Ren for a long moment. When he grunted and turned to mount his horse, Kai finally exhaled.

Once they crossed the shallow river, they moved into a canter, passing through bright green rolling hills. Clouds of gnats hit her in the face, flying up her nose and catching in her hair. So much for cleaning her up. She tried to remember all the things Ren told her to do the day before. Keep her heels down. Move her hips with the rolling rhythm. It was harder to lose herself in riding today, and Ren didn't talk to her at all. He didn't say whether her reins were too loose, or point out if her calf had slipped too far back. She realized in the hard silence how lucky she'd been to grow up with her family, her warm, loud, funny family, and her twin most of all. She had never been lonely, not really. Kai thought she felt lonely when Kishi disappeared behind the ginkgo tree with the village chief's son. But that was nothing compared to how she felt now.

Every so often when they reached a narrow or uneven section of trail, they slowed to a walk, and in those moments she tried to come up with what she could say to General Takagi to convince him to not only buy her but then let her go. But no words came to her, only an image of a hairy red ogre with horns and fangs.

Once they crossed the second tine of the Three-Pronged River, the gnats disappeared. Instead bee clouds moving in perfect ovals swarmed trees with floppy purple flowers. Since she didn't want to make Burden nervous, Kai told herself that bees were like schools of fish. They traveled as one, and as long as the flowers distracted them, there was no danger of being stung. Still, when they crossed the last tine of the Three-Pronged River, Kai was relieved to leave the Perpetual Plain of Eternal Afflictions behind. The land became rockier and more spare in the Valley of the Windswept Pine. At least they seemed to be taking her in the right direction, toward Sky Mountain and not away. They climbed uphill past flat white rocks and pine trees that had been bent into hard angles. As they came around a turn, Kai saw a fortress in the distance, a wall surrounding a cluster of brown roofs. It looked like a hard, unforgiving place. Her chest tightened. Burden snorted and tossed her mane.

"Is that it?" Kai asked, forgetting that Ren wasn't speaking to her.

Ren nodded. "That's it."

Without thinking, she tugged on the reins and Burden stopped. Ren looked over his shoulder and stopped, too. She wanted to stay in this moment in the only safe space left to her, riding Burden, with Ren at her side.

"Have you met General Takagi?" she asked. "Is he worse than Doi?"

"I've only been in the stable area," he said. "He takes good care of his horses. They're the best I've ever seen. If you were a horse, you'd be all right."

"That's reassuring," she said. Bile rose in her throat and she covered her mouth to keep herself from vomiting on the horse. But it was too late. Ren jumped off Encumbrance and pulled her to the ground, holding back her hair as she doubled over and dry retched.

"What's going on?" Doi shouted, pausing at the next bend. "Get her back on that horse."

"She's fine," Ren called out. "We're coming."

Not wanting to get him in trouble with Doi, Kai straightened up. Her head still felt buzzy, as if the bee swarms had streamed in through her ears to her brain. Instead of leading her to Burden, Ren boosted her onto Encumbrance and jumped on behind her. As they wound up the wide switchbacked trail that led to the fortress, she sagged into his chest. She was a mess when she needed to be strong. She couldn't even pretend to be brave. Where the path leveled off at the top, plants that looked like bloody red mouths with thorny teeth bordered a wide moat. One snapped closed and trapped a butterfly. She thought she'd rather be eaten by a bloodthirsty plant than face General Takagi.

Goto and Doi stopped at a bridge that spanned the moat and led to a wood gate topped by a thatched awning. Goto called out to the guard. The clan crest, a silhouette of a pine tree, had been painted in dark green in the center of the gate.

"What do you want?" the guard said to Goto. "Unless you have useful information this time, General Takagi said not to let you back in."

"Oh, you'll want to let us in," said Goto in a slippery voice. "We have something valuable that he'll be interested in."

There was a long pause, and then the gate rolled open. They entered a dusty strip between the exterior and interior walls, with the stable to the right and what looked like barracks to the left. Presumably General Takagi's quarters were on the other side of the interior wall. Ren dismounted near a hitching post and placed a hand on Kai's back as she swung her leg over and dropped to the ground. Her knees buckled as she landed, and had he not been steadying her, she would have fallen over backward. Ren tucked the bundle containing the feathered cloak under his arm and greeted the old man who came to collect the horses with familiarity. He didn't ask Goto and Doi if he could come along. He just did, and Kai was grateful because his kindness was the only thing holding her together.

A man with gray-flecked hair waited for them at the interior gate. He wore wide brown trousers and a tunic patterned with the pine tree motif. Since the soldiers at the gate wore dark green, Kai thought he must be a servant. They followed him into an expansive rectangular courtyard. Trees peeked over the top of a smaller gate immediately to their right. Just past the garden gate, a mansion stretched the length of the courtyard. Elevated on a platform and built out of dark wood, the grand house had three sections: a main building in the middle and two smaller buildings on either side connected by covered breezeways like two pincers and a crab body. All three buildings had deep eaves and wraparound verandas.

To the left of the courtyard, soldiers on horseback practiced archery on a vast grass field. As the horses thundered across the turf, their riders turned to the side at the midway point to shoot at the target boards. Both the soldiers in their uniforms and the horses with an emblem of the pine tree on their saddle pads looked crisp and intimidating.

In the capital, the servants always led them through a side

entrance, not up the main stairs from the courtyard, which was strictly for ladies and gentlemen. The servant here did the same, taking them up to the veranda of one of the smaller buildings, then through a breezeway that connected to the main house. The interior was dim and cool. The wood floorboards gleamed with polish. In a reception room, another servant laid out floor mats that faced a folding screen depicting a bloody hellscape of demons attacking people. Goto and Doi kneeled on the two mats in front. Goto took the bundled feather cloak from Ren and set it next to his mat.

Ren led her to the mat behind Goto. She was trembling with fear and almost fell over as she kneeled. Once he settled on the mat next to her, he studied the demons on the screen. Her throat tightened and a dull pressure built behind her eyes. She wanted to curl up in a ball on the floor. She wanted to tell the Dragon King and Benzaiten that she gave up, that she was scared and tired of being scared and just wanted to go home. It took every last bit of strength not to dissolve into a puddle of tears.

The floorboards creaked and a tall, brawny man who would have dwarfed Papa strolled around the screen. The scent of pine and something musky filled the air, which meant that his dark green robe had been perfumed like those of the ladies and gentlemen in the capital. He held a book in his hand that he studied with the lofty air of a priest reading the sutras. The book confused her. Could this be General Takagi? Schooling was for monks and the children of the nobility. Warriors weren't known for being cultured. Looking up, he closed the book and handed it with theatrical flourish to his rabbity aide.

"Goto, what is it that you need this time?" General Takagi was about her father's age. Despite his powerful build, he didn't look like an ogre. He had tufted eyebrows like an owl and his left arm seemed longer than his right. That had to be an illusion. But no, he wasn't slouching or leaning to one side. When his curious gaze met hers, she stared at the edge of her mat until he looked away.

"We've brought you something very special, General," Goto said, rubbing his hands together. "A few days ago, we went hunting and saw a most unusual bird flying over Mirror Lake, twice the size of an eagle and more colorful than a mandarin duck. We shot it out of the sky. Then we discovered that this creature was not a bird at all, but a tennyo. Immediately we thought such a rare prize should belong to you."

"A tennyo," General Takagi said with an arrogant smile. "From the fairy tales that my daughters read."

"Yes, imagine our surprise," Goto said.

General Takagi held up his hands, each one big enough to crush a skull. "Where is this creature from the heavens?"

"She's right here," Goto said, turning and gesturing toward her. Kai thought she must have looked like a street urchin, with gnats in her hair, tiny scabs on her face and arms where the crows had pecked her, and a rip in her jacket sleeve ringed with dried blood.

General Takagi laughed heartily. "This girl is a tennyo?"

"Well, of course we took away her gown so she couldn't fly off," Goto said, untying the cord around the cloak and holding it up.

Frowning, General Takagi took it from him and examined both sides. They all fell silent as the feathers shimmered in the dim light, blues, yellows, reds, and greens popping against the whites, browns, and blacks. *An empress or a goddess should be wearing that cloak, not me*, Kai thought.

"I suppose you have a price in mind," General Takagi said.

"You have always been most generous," Goto said. "I leave the question of compensation to you. However, we have had inquiries. The chancellor thinks she'll make a wonderful gift for the emperor."

Now that she'd seen General Takagi and he seemed like a reasonable man, she was pinning her hopes on him. Setting her up as a gift for the emperor seemed foolish.

General Takagi coughed and cleared his throat, a glint of amusement in his eyes. "How much is the chancellor offering for her?"

Goto glanced at Doi, then blurted out: "Twice her weight in jewels."

"A celestial nymph clearly belongs at court," General Takagi said. "Who am I to take away a gift from His Royal Highness?"

Goto seemed at a loss for words. Kai was tempted to jump to her feet and negotiate her own price. She didn't know which was worse, Goto's greed or his stupidity.

"Who are you?" Doi said in a crafty tone. "You're the one who's going to stick it to those crybabies in the capital, the ones who wear their swords for show and swoon over their own poetry." He clasped his hands together and his voice shot up in a falsetto. "Like the leaves that fall from the autumn tree, so do my tears dampen these sleeves."

General Takagi let out a deep booming laugh. His shrewd eyes fell on Kai again. "Let's see her fly," he said.

He strode out of the reception room with her cloak over his arm. They trailed him down the main stairs to the court-yard. The archers immediately halted their practice and lined up at the edge of the field. Foot soldiers with swords hanging from their belts appeared out of nowhere and formed a circle around them. General Takagi motioned to her to join him. As she stepped forward, she felt the weight of their stares. Her eyes barely lined up with General Takagi's broad chest. She tried to swallow but her mouth had gone dry.

"There's no need to tie her up," he said pleasantly, as he removed the rope from around her wrists. He took the feathered cloak from his aide and draped it over her shoulders. "Give us a demonstration. But know that if you try to escape, my men will shoot you down."

Kai pushed her arms through the sleeves. When she didn't immediately feel a tug skyward, she worried that the tear in the sleeve might have ruined the cloak. But once she extended her arms, the rip seemed to have no effect. She levitated several feet off the ground while the soldiers murmured with amazement. Tipping forward, she flapped her arms in a rolling motion and flew in a lazy circle above their heads. The drawn arrows of the archers winked at her in the sunlight. Behind Goto and Doi, she spotted Ren with a look of wonder on his face. As she glided in circles, Ren started to drift backward, and it occurred to her that he might be trying to slip away. Wanting to buy him time, she swooped headfirst into the center and pulled out of the dive at the last second to a collective gasp. Then she flew in circles, tighter and tighter until she landed in front of General Takagi, who watched her with guarded admiration.

"Tell me, little bird," he said. "Are you truly from the heavens?"

Since Kai hadn't been able to picture this moment, she hadn't practiced her answer in her head. And she'd never been a good liar.

"This cloak is enchanted and allows me to fly," she said. "But I'm not a tennyo. My name is Kai and I'm just a normal girl. A commoner. A pearl diver from the Freshwater Sea."

Astonishment rippled through the soldiers. Between two men, she thought she spotted Ren's long gaunt face and wished he would keep going and get away from Goto and Doi. Goto lost his oily composure and stepped forward, his eyes bulging.

"She's a liar," he said. "This girl promised us treasure from the gods."

"When they shot me out of the sky, I promised them pearls if they let me go, pearls from the Freshwater Sea," Kai said. "That was not a lie. My parents would give them every-thing they had."

"This girl can't be trusted, General," Goto said. "We had every reason to believe she was a tennyo."

General Takagi silenced him with a look. "How does a pearl diver come into possession of a magic cloak?"

"It all started with the ghost whale, sir," she said. She told the whole story, only leaving out that Kishi was her twin, since most people believed that twins were unnatural. Goto kept huffing with disbelief. When General Takagi glowered at him, Doi nudged him in the ribs, trying to get him to stop. As she described the Dragon King scaring off the ghost whale, General Takagi's eyebrows shot up.

"I know it sounds strange," she said. "If you'd asked me a week ago if I still believed that the Dragon King lived in a castle in the Freshwater Sea, I'd have said it's a myth. But he's real. He's as big as your mansion, with gold scales and black fins."

"This is a preposterous story, General," Goto said, moving toward him.

She heard the metallic screech of soldiers unsheathing their swords. Goto froze.

General Takagi held up his hand. "Why should I believe you over him?" he asked her.

"If I was going to lie, I would have claimed that I was a tennyo so that you would buy me and take me away from these bandits," she said. "A tennyo has more to offer you than a commoner from the Freshwater Sea, even a commoner who happens to have an enchanted cloak."

General Takagi clasped his hands behind his back and stared off at some point in the vast green field. In the silence, all Kai could hear was her own heart beating. The soldiers seemed to be holding their breath.

"Kai, your loyalty to your sister warms my heart," he said. "You are a welcome guest in my home."

Guest, not prisoner. "Thank you, sir," she said, elated. She could still save Kishi. Tears welled in her eyes.

"But, General," Goto pleaded. "We were on our way to ambush pilgrims on the route to the capital. Once we found her, we had to abandon those plans. We hurried back here to bring her to you."

"You mean you changed your plans because you thought selling her to me would be more profitable," General Takagi said, lifting the cloak from her shoulders and folding it over his forearm. "Don't worry. I'll have this repaired."

Kai started to thank him, but Goto interrupted, pressing his hands together and forcing his lips into an oily smile.

"Exceedingly generous of you, sir, to take in the young lady," he said. "Your reputation as a wise and just leader is well deserved. If we could trouble you to compensate us for our time, we would be most appreciative."

General Takagi's left eye twitched. Kai felt like she was watching water in a pot on the brink of boiling over. She wondered why Doi wasn't pulling Goto away.

"What do you think your time is worth, Goto?" General Takagi asked. "A roll of our best silk?"

"You are too kind, General," Goto said.

"That is without a doubt the truest thing you've ever said," General Takagi said. Then he turned to his aide. "Show Kai to our guest quarters in the west wing. Have my wife send some of her attendants."

"Right this way," the aide said to her, nodding his head toward the wing at the far end of the courtyard.

As she followed the aide, she heard Goto say, "Perhaps your kitchen could throw in some food and drink as well. We're nearly out of rations. It turns out tennyos have quite an appetite."

"Why not?" General Takagi said, an underlying menace in his tone. "Let's add a pair of our finest horses, too."

The aide began to walk faster. "The hydrangea are in full bloom in the west garden right now," he said. "They're absolutely stunning."

Because the aide was speaking, she couldn't hear Goto's response. The aide was walking so quickly now that Kai almost had to jog to keep up.

As they reached the veranda steps, General Takagi thundered, "Goto, you are the thief who eats his neighbor's pig and then tries to sell him the bones."

Hearing a strangled scream, she turned around at the top of the stairs. But the soldiers ringing General Takagi blocked her view.

"Right this way," the aide said, trying to lead her inside.

The shutters separating the veranda from the interior

suddenly opened and a maid appeared inside the rectangle. The maid's gaze went past Kai to the courtyard, and she gasped. This time when Kai turned around, the aide said nothing, because he too was transfixed. General Takagi was climbing the steps to the main house, cleaning his bloody sword with a rag. A soldier pushed a wheelbarrow toward the gate, and what appeared to be a man's leg dangled over one side. The rest of the crowd had dispersed, leaving a lone servant shoveling sand over a large pool of blood.

8

"Inside, inside," the aide said, ushering her in through a sliding door. "Back to work," he said to the maid, who finished opening the bottom panels of the floor-to-ceiling shutters and immediately lowered a bamboo blind in their place. Then she moved to the next row of shutters. Kai stood rooted to a spot near the door and watched her blankly. It was still sinking in that the pool of blood and the dangling leg belonged to Goto and that Goto was dead. She decided that she didn't care that Goto had died. She only hoped that Ren had time to escape the compound.

The maid opened shutters along the veranda all the way around the west wing. Kai had seen this at mansions in the capital, shutters instead of walls. She felt like she should offer to help, being a commoner and all. But she didn't. She was afraid to touch anything.

Meanwhile the aide left, hurrying across the covered walkway that connected the west wing to the main house. With nothing to do, Kai decided to explore her new quarters, which were larger than her family's entire cottage. First she peeked inside the interior room, a dressing area that contained a low cabinet with drawers, a mirror, and a clothing rack. Behind a thick curtain she found the sleeping area, where a thin mat covered a low platform.

The outer rooms along the veranda had makeshift partitions created out of folding screens and portable curtains. In the area facing the courtyard, two legless chairs with single armrests angled toward each other as if in conversation. Around the next corner, a low desk inlaid with mother-of-pearl overlooked a bamboo grove. In the back of the west wing, a stack of floor cushions had been left near the bamboo blind. When she pulled back the blind, she saw a smaller courtyard bustling with servants. Near the main door, folding screens created a room with a view of an interior garden walled off by the west wing, the covered walkway, and the main house. An intricately carved go table with a square grid on top had been placed by the veranda, where the players could gaze at the purple-and-white hydrangea. The black and white stones that served as playing pieces engaged in battle on the grid, though Kai did not know enough about the game to discern which side was winning.

A nervous giggle escaped from her mouth. It seemed ludicrous that she, who emerged from the sea pruny-fingered and sun-browned each day, had an entire wing of a mansion to herself. During her family's trip to the capital, Kishi had joked that they could probably sneak into a room in a remote wing of a villa and stay there without anyone knowing. Her sister, who had been more swept up by the glamour of the noble houses, would relish the opportunity to stay in a fancy house like this. But Kai wished General Takagi had sent her to the servant quarters instead.

Suddenly Kai heard the door whoosh. When she stepped out from behind a folding screen to see who had come in, she found a woman as elegant as the ladies she'd glimpsed in the capital. Her glossy black hair, parted down the middle, almost reached her feet. She wore several layers of long, loose silk robes in pinks and pale greens. A large mole on her chin had been powdered over.

"Are you the general's wife?" Kai blurted out. Then she turned scarlet, realizing she probably should have bowed to show respect.

At first the lady looked puzzled. Then she burst out laughing. "Me? Oh, no. I'm Nene, one of her attendants."

A girl who looked a few years younger than Kai traipsed in carrying a branch with white flowers. With her round flushed cheeks and layered robes in shades of orange, she reminded Kai of a plump sweet potato. She set the branch in a large jade vase near the door.

"I'm Ruri, but everyone calls me Little Nene and my mother Mama Nene," the girl announced, her coppery eyes bright and knowing. "Soon I'll be as tall as my mother, and I don't know what they'll call me then. But I'll probably be in the capital with General Takagi's oldest daughter by the time that happens. It's good that you arrived today. If you'd come yesterday, we wouldn't have been here. We returned very late last night with the general's wife from a pilgrimage to the Grand Shrine. Have you taken a pilgrimage there?"

Kai shook her head, feeling out of breath just listening to her talk. *Nene* meant "tranquil," but there was nothing calm about her.

"We were supposed to get home three days ago," Little Nene said. "But the master of divination said that home lay in an unlucky direction, so we had to travel in a roundabout way to avoid the evil spirits. I find unlucky directions tiresome, don't you?"

"I wouldn't know," Kai said. "We don't have masters of divination in my village."

She watched with curiosity as Mama Nene adjusted the branch in the vase so that it leaned in the opposite direction. Then Mama Nene shifted the vase to the left. After stepping back to study the effect, she moved the branch ever so slightly to the right. She did this several more times. Kai wanted to tell her that it looked pretty no matter which way she positioned it in the vase, but she didn't want to offend Mama Nene.

"I heard you were kidnapped by bandits," Little Nene said as three women filed in carrying basins of water and a wood trunk. "That must have been exciting. Nothing exciting ever happens here."

The servants, like Mama Nene and Little Nene, were also dressed in beautiful silk robes. Kai only knew they were servants because they were the ones carrying things. Mama Nene followed them into the dressing room and began unpacking robes from the trunk, handing some to a servant to hold and draping others on the clothing rack. Little Nene wandered in and plucked a pink outer robe with a floral pattern from the servant's arms and held it up to herself.

"Are we in Boso Province, then?" Kai asked from the bedroom door. That was where the Grand Shrine was located.

"This is Mikawa Province," Little Nene said, dropping the robe carelessly on the floor. "General Takagi also controls Omi, Boso, and Jomo. Four so far. The chancellor calls our general the claws and teeth of the Heiwadai Empire."

Kai nodded. Mikawa Province was on the Saltwater Sea, to the south and east of her home province. At least the bandits had brought her in the right direction. "Maybe I imagined it," she said, "but I thought General Takagi's left arm was longer than his right."

Little Nene nodded. "Yes, his left arm is three inches longer, which gives him even more power with a bow. He can send a single arrow through two armored men."

"Ruri, please don't talk our guest's ears off," Mama Nene said, handing Kai a wide-sleeved white blouse and a purple trouser skirt. "Let's give her some privacy."

Mama Nene and Little Nene left while she changed. First she set the compass and the magic bowl on the cabinet. Then she slipped into the fresh undergarments, made of an exquisite silk that made her rough, dirty clothes seem even rougher and dirtier. When she finished dressing, Mama Nene asked her to her lie down with the nape of her neck resting on the edge of one of the stone basins. Kai felt her body go limp as Mama Nene's fingers massaged her scalp and washed her hair. Lying there with her eyes closed, she wondered if Ren was alone or if Doi had caught up to him. She wanted to believe that he was now galloping free through the windswept pines on Encumbrance.

Next she sat in front of the mirror while the Nenes combed out the tangles in her hair, yanking on her roots like the Crows of the Eternal Night as she winced and tried not to cry out. When they finished, she almost didn't recognize herself. Her hair usually looked windblown and wild from the ocean air. Now it lay flat and smooth and felt almost as soft as her undergarments. Once Kai's hair was done, Mama Nene selected five silk robes in gradations of pink and helped Kai into each one, adjusting the sleeves and the necklines so that a hint of each color could be seen.

"How do you decide the colors and the order of the robes?" Kai asked. She'd thought it was all silly, how the ladies in the capital stayed hidden behind curtains and screens and only allowed their hems to peek out. But Kishi had been fascinated by what the color choices meant, and how the combination of colors created a lady's reputation in society. Kai didn't like the idea of being judged by what she wore.

"Of course it depends on the season," Mama Nene said, helping her into a stiff robe with boxy sleeves. "Also we choose colors that suit the lady and that say something about her personality. Is she elegant and refined, or is she bold? As I get to know you, the colors will reflect that. This is perhaps too traditional."

For the final layer, Mama Nene chose the pink floral robe that Little Nene had discarded on the floor. Kai felt like an overdressed doll.

"She looks so much prettier, Mama," Little Nene said. "Like the story of the girl with the bowl stuck on her head who turns out to be beautiful."

"Yes, she looks very pretty," Mama Nene said with an indulgent smile.

"What's this?" Little Nene picked up the coral compass from the vanity. Panic shot through Kai. She'd meant to put the necklace back on before Mama Nene and Little Nene came in to wash her hair. How could she have been so careless with something that important?

"It was a gift," Kai said, reaching for it as Little Nene danced away.

Little Nene pivoted right and then left. "The pin is pointing at your chamber pot," she said with a giggle. "I think this is an example of an unlucky direction."

Kai thought Little Nene seemed young for her age, at least compared with the girls in her village. Back home, Kai would have found her annoying. But after spending the last few days with bandits, she didn't mind.

"The hydrangea in the garden is beautiful," Kai said, changing the subject and hoping that in doing so Little Nene would set the necklace down.

"Hydrangea is my fourth-favorite flower," she declared, dropping the necklace inside the magic bowl, which thankfully was so plain that it hadn't attracted her attention. "First is wisteria because the branches look like they're weeping purple tears. Second is the cherry blossom because it's such a happy, frilly flower. Third is the moonflower. When they open all at once at dusk, it's magical."

A smile tugged at Kai's lips as she slipped past Little Nene and quickly put the necklace on. Then she hid the bowl inside her sleeve until she could find a better hiding place. A powerful exhaustion seeped through her bones. All she wanted to do was lie down, close her eyes, and listen to Little Nene rank flowers. "You have strong opinions," Kai said.

Little Nene twirled a lock of her long dark hair around her finger with a cheeky smile. "It's important to have opinions about nature, poems, paintings, music, and characters in stories," she said. "Once General Takagi's oldest daughter is in the capital, these are the kinds of things we'll be expected to discuss."

"It sounds like you're ready," Kai said. She found General Takagi's ambition puzzling. Warlords were supposed to be ruffians who looked down on the gentlemen in the capital as weak. Yet he was willing to play their game of raising his family's status through marriage.

That evening Mama Nene set up a portable curtain, behind which Kai was supposed to eat her meal: thin slices of fish, pickled vegetables, nuts, and melon that came served on many dainty plates. When Kai asked why, Mama Nene said General Takagi took pride in running his house the same way gentlemen did in the capital, where family members had their meals privately.

"The act of eating is considered unpleasant to the eye," she said.

"But I'm a commoner," Kai said.

"Right now you are our guest," Mama Nene said.

Kai could see that there was no point in arguing and went to sit behind the curtain. For the first time since leaving the Freshwater Sea, she was ravenous, and the small servings only made her more hungry. She wished she'd brought the magic bowl behind the curtain instead of hiding it in the bedroom in a cedar box she'd found. She could have eaten ten bowls of rice.

After her meal, Little Nene challenged her to a game in which they balanced as many go stones as they could on one finger. Little Nene stacked eleven with ease, which Kai found astonishing since she could barely balance three. It felt so nice to be clean and to sit around playing games in a beautiful house that she almost dreaded having to leave the next day.

At bedtime, Little Nene lay down next to her, chattering about how dull she found her koto lessons and how the music teacher was always blowing her nose.

"She looks like she has a strawberry in the middle of her face," Little Nene said with a giggle.

"That's not her fault," Kai said. "You shouldn't make fun of her."

"But it's distracting," Little Nene said. "How am I supposed to play the koto when she has a nose like that? But the general's wife says there's not another decent koto teacher in the entire province. This wouldn't happen if we were in the capital."

Kai wondered what Little Nene would be saying about her once she left. Would Little Nene make fun of her ear that stuck out, or the calluses on her hands? Yet when she closed her eyes, she missed Little Nene's chatter, because it kept her from picturing the pool of blood in the courtyard, the sea serpents slithering around Kishi, the sickening stab of the arrow into her shoulder. To banish those thoughts, she tried to think about something good, something comforting. Ren jogging alongside her as she trotted on Burden. Ren pulling leaves from her hair next to the river. Her eyes popped open and she immediately pushed him from her mind. He had been kind, but that didn't make him a friend. She wasn't going to see him again.

In the morning, she woke up alone and disoriented. She sat up ramrod straight as her eyes adjusted to the dim room. No trees, no hard ground. It took several seconds for her to remember how she came to sleep in a bed, that she was safe inside General Takagi's compound, and that she had nine days to get to Sky Mountain.

Kai got out of bed and shuffled out to the sitting room, where the latticed wood shutters had been opened and the thin blinds had been lowered. Little Nene lolled on a cushion in the room that overlooked the courtyard. In the morning light, her skin was as pale and unblemished as a steamed dumpling. From outside Kai heard the ting-ting of sword-play. She pulled back the blind to see soldiers dueling in pairs in the courtyard.

"How many soldiers does the general have?" she asked.

"Here?" Little Nene looked up from her book and frowned. "Two hundred. But he has other compounds, too. They're preparing to attack Biwa Province."

Kai whirled around. "What? That's my province."

"It's a good thing you're here and not there, then," she said. "General Takagi says he needs to control the port in order to take the capital."

Kai gasped. "He's going to overthrow the emperor?"

"Oh yes," Little Nene said. "But first General Takagi needs to marry his oldest daughter off to a son or grandson of a retired emperor. That way when the general takes over as chancellor, he can put his daughter and son-in-law on the throne."

Kai sat down on the floor in a daze. Coups had been attempted before. That part wasn't surprising. She just couldn't believe that Little Nene was so casual about it.

"I'm going to be a lady-in-waiting to an empress," Little

Nene said with a dreamy smile.

Papa used to tell them never to talk politics outside of their house. He meant about the village chief, because gossip spread quickly in their hamlet. But it seemed like good advice now.

"What are you reading?" Kai asked.

"'The Legend of the Star Festival,'" she said, tilting the page. "This is my third-favorite story. 'The Tale of the Bamboo Cutter' is first, because having a princess small enough to fit inside a stalk of bamboo would be so cute. 'The Mirror of Matsuyama' is second, because it makes me laugh. The girl doesn't realize she's seeing her own reflection."

Little Nene read "The Legend of the Star Festival" out loud. It was about two constellations in the sky, the weaver and the cow herder, who fell deeply in love and neglected their duties. The weaver stopped weaving and the cows wandered off. As a punishment, the emperor of the heavens separated the lovers and decided they could only meet once a year, on the seventh day of the seventh month. The illustration showed the weaver and the cow herder with their arms outstretched, a river of stars between them. Kai had Little Nene read it out loud twice so that she could commit the story to memory and share it with Kishi one day when this was all over. Of all the tales that Hamako had told them, Kishi liked the love stories the best.

"It's so romantic," Little Nene said with a sigh. "Do you have a suitor?"

Kai smiled, not because it was far-fetched for a girl her age to be married off but because it seemed far-fetched for her. "No way."

"General Takagi's oldest daughter just came of age and she has three suitors," Little Nene said, with the same tone of reprimand that the village matchmaker had for Kai and Kishi's mother. After the last pearl season, the matchmaker stopped Mama in the village and said she could probably find a family willing to overlook their pearl diving background for Kishi. Mama had laughed and told her not to bother.

"Things are different in my family," Kai said. "The women dive for pearls and the men take care of the boat. As long as we have someone who can row, we don't need husbands."

Her mind wandered to Ren, to his dark messy hair falling over his sullen eyes. She wondered if he knew how to fish.

"You look weird," Little Nene said, crinkling her brow. "Is something wrong?"

"Nothing's wrong," she said. "Everything's fine."

What was she saying? Everything was wrong. Kishi was dead. Yet here she was lounging around the west wing and getting caught up in fairy tales. Kai jumped to her feet. It was time to tell General Takagi that she was ready to leave.

She'd gone out the door and had just started to cross the breezeway to the main house when Little Nene grabbed her sleeve.

Panic roiled her face. "Kai, where are you going?"

"To see the general," she said.

"You can't do that," Little Nene said. "Ladies are supposed to stay in their quarters."

"I'm not a lady," Kai said. "I'm a pearl diver."

"While you're here, we're to treat you like a lady," Little Nene said. "The general said so. If you leave the west wing, you'll get Mama in trouble."

"But you can come and go as you please," Kai pointed out.

"I'm an attendant," Little Nene said. "But the general's wife and their oldest daughter stay in their quarters in the north wing." She gestured toward a roof that extended behind the main house.

"We're not in the capital," Kai said. "He's a warlord, not a gentleman. There's no need for any of this."

"He's in charge," Little Nene said softly.

A male servant passing along the veranda of the main house paused to give them a curious stare. Little Nene tugged on Kai's sleeve and looked at her with imploring eyes. Kai grudgingly retreated to the west wing, a knot of dread forming in her stomach. After what had happened to Goto yesterday, she didn't want General Takagi to blame Mama Nene for her behavior.

The hours stretched and yawned. There was nothing to do in the west wing besides play with the go stones and watch the soldiers do their drills. To pass the time, Little Nene offered to bring more books from the library. Kai asked her to look for any stories involving foxes. She might as well do some research as long as she was stuck here. About an hour later, Little Nene returned wielding a scroll like a magic wand. Two maids trailed her, each carrying an armful of books. Little Nene instructed them to set the books on the floor, in order from her most favorite story to her least.

"Let's start with the best story," she said, with an authority that made Kai marvel. "Number one is about the white nine-tailed fox, the most powerful kind of fox, who shape-shifted into a beautiful woman and bewitched the emperor—yes, the emperor himself was fooled! Not long after she became empress, her true identity was revealed, and the emperor sent an army to kill her. She escaped by sending her spirit inside a rock. The ending is a bit disappointing. But I suppose it would be terrible to spend the rest of your eternal life inside a rock."

Little Nene summarized all nine stories. None of them gave Kai any ideas about how to steal the pearl.

"What's that?" Kai asked, pointing at the scroll in her hand.

"Oh, I almost forgot." Little Nene took the scroll to the writing desk, where she weighted one end with an ink stone and unrolled it. The illustrated scroll showed the inside of a cave where a group of orange foxes held glowing white orbs on the tips of their tails. Two white nine-tailed foxes in the center faced each other, their white balls in front of them. They stood on their hind legs with their front paws in the air by their ears. One wore a crown on its head. The orbs had to be pearls, Kai thought. The kinetic swirl of the brushstrokes suggested something momentous was happening.

"What is this?" she asked.

"I don't know," Little Nene said with a shrug. "I found it in a dusty old box."

Kai stared long and hard at the illustration, willing it to give up its secrets. But the scroll refused to comply. After rolling it up, she took it into the bedroom and placed it in the small cedar chest next to the bed where she kept her magic bowl. As she emerged from the bedchamber, Mama Nene arrived, looking flustered.

"Why isn't her hair done?" she said to Little Nene. "The general is coming to visit soon."

Mama Nene ushered Kai back into the dressing room. Kai watched in the mirror as Mama Nene combed her hair and parted it down the middle like hers. Unlike Mama Nene, whose hair almost reached her feet, Kai's only hit her waist and didn't look nearly as elegant. Once again Mama Nene layered her in robes, this time in pale yellows, light greens, and dark greens. On top of the stiff boxy layer, Mama Nene chose a golden-yellow robe with a leaf pattern. Kai thought she looked like a giant puffer fish.

"Mama, what about her eyebrows?" Little Nene asked.

"No time to pluck them," Mama Nene said. "I'll just powder her face. If he takes a peek at her, he might not notice. Can you set up the curtain, please?"

"Is this necessary?" Kai protested as Mama Nene attacked her face with a powder brush. But Mama Nene didn't answer.

"Come," she said, beckoning Kai to follow her to the spot near the veranda where Little Nene had set up a portable curtain. Kai kneeled on a floor mat and watched with dismay as Mama Nene arranged her hems so that they peeked out on the other side of the curtain, as if she were a lady in a noble house.

"Why do I have to sit behind a curtain?" Kai asked. "General Takagi has already seen me. He knows what I look like."

"We follow proper etiquette here," Mama Nene said. "When the bandits brought you, that couldn't be helped."

She handed Kai a fan with pink flowers painted on it. Then she and Little Nene disappeared behind a folding screen to her right. Kai could hear their robes rustling as they sat down. The two of them going behind another barrier to eavesdrop made her feel both trapped and exposed, like a firefly in a jar. She suddenly missed Kishi fiercely. Once, five or six summers ago, the circus came to their village and the performers had pulled them up to the stage. Kai remembered instinctively knowing that Kishi was worried about saying something dumb that would cause the audience to laugh. She'd taken Kishi's hand in hers and felt her sister relax. That's what she needed right now—for Kishi to hold her hand.

Kai smelled General Takagi's robes, the spicy pine, before she saw him through the crack in the curtain. She opened and closed the fan nervously. There was a shuffling as he kneeled on the other side of the curtain. Through the crack in the drapes, Kai saw him in slivers. Dark green robe, beard patch, one flared nostril. She heard more rustling as a second figure kneeled next to General Takagi. Probably the aide.

"So, little bird, how are you finding the west wing?" he said in a hearty voice. "I hope my Nenes are taking good care of you."

"It's more than a commoner like me deserves," she said. "You're very kind."

"Your parents must be very worried," General Takagi said. "If you tell me where they live, I will send a messenger to let them know you're safe."

Kai felt a stab of guilt that she hadn't thought to ask him to send a message earlier. Yet she hesitated. After seeing the fear in Little Nene's eyes at the prospect that her mother could get in trouble, she wasn't sure if she wanted General Takagi to know where her family lived. Kai decided to buy some time. "Thank you. I'll ask Little Nene to write the letter for me."

"Excellent idea," he said. "When it's ready, have Little Nene bring your letter to my aide. Now that that's settled, I'd like to introduce you to my son, Yugiri."

So the other person wasn't the aide. Kai leaned over, trying to get a glimpse of the son through the gap in the curtain. His build was small and twiggy compared with his father's, and he kept his face turned away from her.

"Nice to meet you, Yugiri," she said.

When Yugiri mumbled in return, General Takagi prodded

him with his fan. "Speak up, Yugiri," he said.

"Welcome," he said in a loud whisper.

An exasperated sigh came from General Takagi. "You'll have to excuse Yugiri. He has not yet learned how to make a strong impression."

"Can I go now, Father?" Yugiri asked, his voice sullen and his eyes still cast away from them. Probably Yugiri found her circumstances, a commoner pretending to be a lady, as ridiculous as she did. She couldn't blame him for not wanting to speak to her.

"To do what?" General Takagi said. "When is the last time you rode a horse or practiced archery? From what your tutors say, you don't apply yourself to your studies, either. Kai, I apologize for my son's lack of manners."

Kai winced. Her mother would never criticize her publicly like that. But she knew how it felt to fall short of expectations whenever Mama said things that started with, "Kai, look at what a nice job your sister did."

"General, now that I'm rested, I'm ready to go to Sky Mountain," Kai said, jumping in before he got too annoyed with his son and left. "The sooner I get the pearl, the sooner I get my sister back."

"What a quick recovery," he said. "You're strong, like a warrior. Do you hear that, Yugiri? She was hit by an arrow and kidnapped by bandits. Yet after one night of rest, she is determined to continue her journey. Most impressive. Now tell me, why does Benzaiten want the pearl? How will she use the foxes to her advantage?"

Kai glanced over at the folding screen, as if the Nenes could help her find the answer that General Takagi wanted to hear. "I don't really know. She said the land gods are too powerful."

Through the crack, she saw his hand rub his chin. "There is a story I once read to my daughters," he said. "A young woman had been possessed by a fox. She was playing with a white ball, tossing it in the air and catching it. A young warrior snatched it away to get her attention. She begged him to return the ball, but he refused. Finally she admitted that she was a fox. 'You don't know how to use the ball. But if you give it back to me, I'll always protect you.' He thought that was a good deal. One night, he was lost in the woods where thieves and bandits lurked. He asked the fox to come protect him, and she appeared and led him to safety. So even for a mortal, the fox can be a powerful ally."

That story hadn't been among the nine that Little Nene had read to her. The ball had to be the fox's pearl. The general's interest made Kai uneasy.

"The risk of fox possession is high on a mission like this," General Takagi said. "Did Benzaiten tell you how to take the pearl from Dakini?"

"No," Kai said. "She didn't give me any helpful advice."

"I believe I can help you," he said. "I'll send some of my men to Sky Mountain to scout the situation. Then we'll come up with a plan."

Kai knew she should be thankful for help from a grown-up, from a man who knew how to fight battles. But she couldn't get past this uneasy feeling. "You've already done so much for me," she said. "I don't want to impose any further."

"I insist," he said. "I'll send a scouting party this afternoon."

"I don't want anyone else to be hurt or killed by a fox on my behalf," she said.

"Nonsense," he said. "It is far safer this way. Information is the key to any battle. Haste is a hero's downfall. Sky Mountain is only a day's ride from here. They'll be back in plenty of time. While we wait for their report, enjoy yourself. Ask for anything you need. We have a library full of books. We can arrange for the music tutor or the art tutor."

I can't leave unless he lets me, Kai thought. Hamako would have warned her not to argue. *Ants are drawn to sweet things*, she'd say. "As long as I'm here," Kai said, "I'd like to learn archery."

There was an extended silence. Kai opened and closed the fan and prayed that she hadn't offended him. Then came his booming laugh. "I have always said that women and girls should learn to defend themselves. But my wife has never allowed it. I will see what I can do."

"Thank you, General," she said, feeling the same flutter of excitement that she had when Ren taught her how to ride.

"Perhaps you can inspire my son to brush up on his skills,"

General Takagi said, the floorboards creaking as he rose to his feet.

After he and Yugiri left, Kai listened to the horses thundering across the turf and the thud of arrows, a sound she now found as beautiful as surf crashing against the shore.

9

As the sun went down, Kai sat at the go table, staring at the hydrangea in the garden but not seeing the flowers. She was lost in a daydream, imagining herself flying in the cloak and aiming an arrow at Doi while he blubbered and begged for his life. *Laugh*, she would say, shooting two arrows in quick succession that would pin him by his jacket sleeves to a tree. *You're supposed to laugh.*

A maid coming through to light candles and lamps jolted her back to the present. Little Nene plopped down on the other side of the go board from Kai, resting her dimpled chin in her hands. "Want to play a game?" she asked.

"That depends," Kai said. "Do I have any chance of winning?"

Little Nene gave her a coy smile. "Since you're interested in foxes, we should play fox fist," she said. She raised her hands to her head and pointed her index fingers at the ceiling. "The fox bewitches the village chief." Then she set both hands palms down on her knees. "The village chief outranks the hunter." Finally she raised her hands as if shooting a bow and arrow. "The hunter kills the fox. The game ends when one of us wins three times in a row."

"Oh, my sister and I used to play that," Kai said. "Only we did frog, slug, and snake."

She and Kishi had gone through a phase where they played frog-slug-snake to decide everything, from who had to fetch the firewood to who got to eat the largest rice cake. The problem was, neither of them could win because they read each other so well. They'd match each other twenty, thirty, forty times in a row, their games only ending when Mama ordered them both to get the firewood or Papa threatened to eat the rice cake himself.

"We count to three," Little Nene said, demonstrating by clapping on one, crossing her forearms on two, and clapping again on three. "And then choose."

Clap, cross, clap. Kai threw up her hands to make the fox and so did Little Nene. "No score," Little Nene said.

Clap, cross, clap. Kai made the fox again, bewitching Little Nene's chief. "One to nothing," she said.

Clap cross, clap. This time Kai pulled back the hunter's bow, shooting Little Nene's fox. "Two to nothing," Little Nene said.

Even though this was only a practice round, Kai thought all those endless games with her sister might give her an advantage.

Clap, cross, clap. Kai went back to the fox, but Little Nene took the hunter's stance. "Zero to one," she said.

Kai interrupted. "Shouldn't we be tied at one?"

Little Nene shook her head. "You either get three in a row or you start over," she said.

Clap, cross, clap. Her village chief bested Kai's hunter. "Zero to two," she said.

Clap, cross, clap. Kai threw up her fox ears again, only to be shot by Little Nene's hunter. Game to Little Nene.

"This time, we bet," she said. "The adults play with sake. But since we can't do that, the loser has to do something for the winner. If you lose, you have to tell my mother that you want shaved ice and you have to give your dessert to me."

Now she knew why Little Nene was so eager to play this game. "All right," Kai said. But she struggled to come up with something that she wanted from Little Nene. "If you lose, you have to go into the garden and pick some hydrangea."

Little Nene gasped. "The gardener will be furious. He'll know that the flowers are missing."

"Just one."

She twisted her lips and tilted her head as she pondered. "Fine."

Little Nene won again, so Kai asked Mama Nene for the shaved ice, which Little Nene ate slowly, savoring every bite, the way Kishi did on the rare occasion when they had sweets.

In the morning when Kai woke up, a single purple

hydrangea in a glass jar waited next to her pillow. Her heart swelled at the sight of the flower.

It was a strange feeling, knowing she could lie in bed all day if she wanted. There were always chores at home, even if the weather didn't allow for diving. But the thought that she had only eight days to get to Sky Mountain and that she was here until General Takagi said it was time to go made it impossible for her to enjoy lounging around. She got up and went to sit at the go table. A drumbeat marked the time, 9:00 a.m., the Hour of the Snake. She heard servants calling out to each other in the back while a soldier barked orders out front. Bored without Little Nene, Kai stacked go stones into towers that alternated between black and white. A boy's voice that she didn't recognize came from the back of the west wing.

"Miss Kai! Miss Kai!"

Curious, she hurried toward the voice and pulled back the bamboo blind. A chubby page boy stood on the veranda with a cloth bundle tucked under his arm. He appeared to be about Little Nene's age.

"Why didn't you come to the door?" she asked.

"I've been sent on a secret mission," he said, puffing out his chest. "The general would like you to put these on and come with me. Make sure your hair is hidden by the jacket."

He offered her the bundle, the same light brown page-boy uniform and cap that he wore. She stared at the outfit in her hands. "Why?" she asked warily. "Where are we going?"

"To the archery range," he said. "It's just beyond the barracks."

Her lesson. A smile broke out across her face. Taking the uniform into the dressing room, she cast off her robes and put on the boxy long-sleeved tunic, the trousers, and the round cap. She studied the effect in the mirror. Kai thought with the cap she looked boyish, kind of. Mostly she looked like someone with something to hide.

She followed the page boy down the stairs to the servant courtyard, where the sun struggled to break through the steely sky and the air smelled like boiled rice. The kitchen was directly across from the west wing. Bungalows, probably for the servants, lined the other two sides. A cook sat outside the kitchen, shelling beans and scolding a chicken.

"We're taking the back way," the page boy whispered, even though there was no one close enough to overhear him. "It's a longer walk, but those were General Takagi's instructions."

He kept up a stream of chatter that Kai didn't hear because she was too busy looking around. They walked past the bamboo that walled off the west wing's interior garden and along the back side of the main house. The blinds were open, revealing a corner room with a massive wood writing desk and swords hanging on the wall behind it. General Takagi's aide leaned against a pillar, reading over a paper scroll. Turning to the left, they walked alongside another breezeway that connected the main house to the north wing—where Little Nene said the general's family lived. Kai realized the mansion wasn't shaped like a crab but like a lobster, with the north wing forming the lobster's tail. The smell of incense mingled with the lavender growing in a garden on the other side of the path. In a room with the blinds half lowered, she recognized the two servants who had brought the washbasins to the west wing. One was kneeling and sewing. The other was draping a green robe with a bird-wing pattern over a wood frame with a smoking incense burner beneath. Kai had never seen a robe being perfumed before.

"One of your panels is upside down," the servant perfuming the robes said.

The one sewing held up the fabric and sighed. "If we weren't so rushed, this wouldn't happen," she grumbled as she pulled out stitches. "Why does the wedding have to happen so soon?"

General Takagi must have chosen among the suitors for his oldest daughter. After meeting Yugiri, Kai was curious to see what the general's three daughters were like. But the rest of the blinds had been lowered all the way. At the end of the north wing, they passed by a kickball court divided into four squares. On the other side of the family quarters, a lavish garden took up the entire northeast corner.

Kai had seen gardens in the capital, but this was her first time walking through one. Every living thing seemed to be the best version of itself, from the bright green moss on the rocks to the bell-shaped rhododendrons shading the path. They walked along a stone walkway past a gardener clipping a pine tree. After each snip, he stopped to gauge the effect, just as Mama Nene had done with the branch in the vase. Next they came to a pond that was so still that it created an exact mirror reflection of the rocks, flowers, and trees on the opposite side. The garden was flawless. Too perfect. Kai decided she liked nature better.

Halfway around the pond where a mossy stone lantern stood sentry, the path forked and the page boy took the one that veered east, going beneath a vine-covered arbor. On the other side of the arbor, a high wood gate had been left propped open. Workers unloaded crates from a cart and carried them into a storehouse on the left. To the right was the stable. The page boy turned to the right. Was Burden still here? She wanted to stop and look. But the old stable hand was grooming a horse in the aisle and she didn't want to call attention to herself and get the page boy in trouble. She wondered which direction Ren had gone and how he would live, if he would just ride around the country, living off the land. She didn't think he would go back to being a bandit. Papa liked to say there were only two kinds of people, those who fixed things and those who tore things down. Ren was a person who wanted to fix things but had been forced to tear things down. Kai had told him the name of her village, and even though it was silly, she imagined him coming to find her, trotting into their yard on Encumbrance.

Past the stable, they crossed through the area between the main compound gate and the interior gate. Kai counted three rows of barracks. Soldiers loitered outside in groups, but not a single one looked at her. In the page-boy uniform, she was invisible to them, beneath their notice. Even in her own commoner clothes, she was certain they would have stared at her. General Takagi had been smart to dress her as a page boy. The archery range had been set up on the other side of the barracks. General Takagi and another soldier were already there. Every time the general shot an arrow, it struck the target with such force that the entire board rocked back and forth. His bow was taller than he was.

"It takes the strength of three soldiers to use that bow," the page boy whispered.

Kai found General Takagi so intimidating that she wouldn't be surprised to learn that other warlords surrendered before a single arrow had been shot. He tucked the bow under his arm as they approached.

"Good morning, Kai," he said. "I apologize for the disguise. It was easier this way. If my wife found out that I was teaching you, she would be furious. She believes my eccentricities, as she calls them, will hurt our oldest daughter's marriage prospects. What she doesn't understand is that we'll always be outsiders to the noble houses in the capital. They'll always look down on us. The only way to gain their respect is on the battlefield."

A chill ran through her at the prospect of war. All villages had to provide a certain amount of rice and other goods to the capital every year. The military clan that controlled her province came through to collect the provisions. She didn't see General Takagi caring how many commoners died in the crossfire so that they could give their rice to him instead.

General Takagi frowned and looked past them. "Where is Yugiri?" he asked the page boy.

"He said you don't need him, sir, since you have a tennyo to protect you," the page boy said. "I told him that Kai was just pretending to be a tennyo to fool the bandits. But he told me to go away and started blowing his flute right in my ear, so I left."

"All right, I'll deal with him later," General Takagi grumbled, then turned to Kai. "This is Commander Sato. He will be instructing you."

Kai wondered if Commander Sato might resent having to teach a girl. But as she turned to bow to him, she saw fear in his eyes. He probably didn't know that she had no special powers without the feather cloak. When he handed her a bow, she realized she had a dilemma. A right-handed person would hold the bow's grip in their left hand. But Kai was a lefty. Her father was, too, and he used to tell stories about how his parents forced him to use chopsticks with his right hand, and how he was not to let anyone else know that he favored his left hand. That was why he liked to row, because as a boy he could use both hands and not have to think about it. Her parents had never tried to make her right-handed, dismissing the superstitions around left-handedness as old-fashioned. But since they didn't interact with other families much, other villagers weren't likely to find out.

Kai decided she wasn't going to hide anything. She gripped the handle with her right hand and pulled the string back with her left index finger. When she released the arrow, it fishtailed toward the target, catching the edge. Commander Sato's eyes flitted from her hands to General Takagi, but he said nothing.

"Very good," General Takagi called out. "You have a natural ability. Results are what matter."

Once she became comfortable with the mechanics, Commander Sato told her to think of the bow as an extension of herself and to move fluidly from one step to the next. The page boy, who had stayed to practice, shot at a target that was about twice as far as hers, and Kai was determined to catch up to him. Each time she shot, her aim improved. The arrow stopped glancing off the board. Every time she hit the center, Commander Sato moved the target farther back. Just like when she learned to ride Burden, she found herself deeply absorbed in the lesson.

Commander Sato ended their session with a contest between Kai and the page boy. They each shot ten arrows. The contest came down to the last shot. To win, Kai needed a bull's-eye. She loaded the arrow and pulled back the string. The target's black center loomed large. She unhooked her finger and the arrow flew with authority, striking the center with a hollow thunk.

"Game to Kai," Commander Sato said as the dejected page boy groaned.

"Yes," she said under her breath, wishing Ren could have seen it. The thought shocked her. Why would she want him to know and not Kishi? *Because Ren would care and Kishi wouldn't understand why I wanted to be good at this*, she thought. And that was fine. They didn't have to be everything to each other all the time as long as they could be together again. Kai thanked Commander Sato for the lesson. Over the commander's shoulder, she noticed General Takagi watching her through narrowed eyes and wondered if she would have been better off losing. She wasn't sure the general was somebody she wanted to be noticed by.

When she returned to the west wing, Mama Nene and Little Nene were still out. She stashed the page-boy uniform in a cabinet near the go table. Even if Mama Nene knew about the archery lesson, Kai didn't want the uniform sent off with a servant for cleaning. She liked the feeling of invisibility and wanted to keep it handy just in case. As she closed the cabinet, Little Nene hurried through the door carrying a small bamboo cage.

"Come look," Little Nene called out. "I caught a bell cricket in the garden."

She set the cage in the middle of the go table. Kai kneeled to look at the cricket, which she had heard many times but never seen. She examined the flat black bug with long white antennae. Suddenly the cricket puffed out its heart-shaped wings and made a melancholy trill.

"The bell cricket is my third-favorite insect, after the

ladybug and the dragonfly," Little Nene said. Her top layer was a cheery red today, with a circular pattern that made her look like a plump ladybug.

"Why isn't the butterfly in your top three?" Kai asked.

"Everybody puts the butterfly first," she said. "It's too predictable."

Propping her chin in her hand, Little Nene poked at the bell cricket with the handle of an ink brush until the poor bug jumped and landed on its back. Kai felt sorry for it.

Before they went to bed, they played fox fist again. Little Nene had her eye on a gold comb with rubies that had come in the trunk filled with robes. Though the hair ornaments that General Takagi had sent weren't Kai's to give away, who was she to say no?

"If I win, you have to free the bell cricket," Kai said.

"That's silly," Little Nene said. "Play for something real."

"That's what I want," Kai insisted.

Clap, cross, clap. Kai shot her hands up to make the fox and so did Little Nene.

Clap, cross, clap. They both took the hunter stance.

They matched each other seven times in a row. Kai went up one when her village chief trumped Little Nene's hunter. But she lost that edge when Little Nene's fox bewitched her chief. They matched two more times. The tempo increased. Little Nene scrunched up her face with concentration and reeled off three in a row for the win. They played three more times and Kai lost them all.

"I don't get it," Kai said with frustration. "It's a game of luck. Why do I keep losing?"

With a knowing smile, Little Nene picked up and examined each item that she had won, two hair ornaments and two painted fans. "Because it's not a game of luck," she said.

"What do you mean?" Kai said. "It's not like you can read my mind."

"No," she agreed. "But most players have patterns. Or they give away their next move."

Kai was stumped. "What am I doing that makes my next move obvious?" she asked.

"If I tell you, I won't have an advantage anymore," Little Nene pointed out.

"Come on," Kai said. "I'm here for a few more days. The worst that can happen in the meantime is you have to let the poor bell cricket go."

"All right," she said grudgingly. "Your go-to move is the fox, and all but once the fox was your opening move. Also, when you're about to make the hunter, your hips shift to the side."

Kai was amazed by how observant she was. For the rest of the night, she practiced drawing back her imaginary bowstring without moving her hips. Through a gap in the top shutter, the half-moon looked like a broken rice cracker. The notes of a koto floated in, played with deep feeling by an accomplished musician. The music trembled with sadness in the dim, sparsely furnished room.

"Who is that?" Kai asked.

"The general's wife," Little Nene said, lying on her stomach on the floor and poking at the bell cricket with the ink brush handle again.

"Does she have a name?" Kai asked.

Little Nene looked up from the tiny cage and frowned. "Not that I remember," she said.

That night when Kai lay down to go to sleep, the notes lodged in the spaces between her ribs, like a side stitch from surfacing too fast. It used to make her mad when people in the village called Papa "the pearl diver's husband." Now she was proud that Mama hadn't lost her name and that Papa didn't care what other people said about him. Kai didn't want to ever be known as someone's wife, no matter how rich or powerful that man might be.

The next day was mostly the same. In the morning, a servant brought a note telling Mama Nene and Little Nene to report to the main house. Not long after they left, the page boy appeared at the back veranda to take her to the archery range, where she continued to improve in both distance and accuracy. Then she spent the afternoon with Little Nene trying to dodge the servants who came to exchange the old bamboo blinds for fresh ones. Mama Nene asked which ones she liked best, the blinds edged with light green silk or the ones edged with light blue.

"I'm leaving soon," Kai said. "The color doesn't matter to me."

A ripple of something that she couldn't read crossed Mama Nene's face. "Perhaps you'll come back and see us again," she said. "Let's go with the blue."

That evening Kai played fox fist with Little Nene. She still lost. But this time she noticed that Little Nene tucked her chin into her chest when she was about to play the village chief. With this new knowledge, she was excited to play Little Nene again. Kai wanted to beat her once before she left.

The next day Kai surpassed the page boy in shooting distance, and when they competed at the end of the lesson, eight of her ten arrows hit the center. General Takagi nodded at Commander Sato but left without speaking to her. She was disappointed because she wanted to ask him about Sky Mountain. There were six days until the full moon. Where was the scouting party? She couldn't shake the nagging fear that he was going to leave her here and go get the pearl for himself. But why train her in archery if he didn't plan to bring her along?

The following morning, Commander Sato set up two platforms on either side of the shooting range with an almost-invisible slanting rope between them. From the higher platform, he hooked clay birds that traveled down the rope, creating a moving target. It took most of the lesson for her to figure out the timing. But by the end, she was hitting every single bird.

"She'll be the one leading you into battle one day, young man," Commander Sato said to the page boy.

When Kai returned to the west wing, she kept hearing his words in her mind, and she couldn't stop smiling. Pulling back the blinds in the front room, Kai watched some soldiers out in the field sprinkle two long lines of white sand on the grass and plant banners with the pine tree symbol at each end. Behind her, the door slid open. Little Nene rushed in with excitement on her face.

"They're having an archery contest today," she said. "I love contest days."

The entire household was expected to watch. More chests arrived with more robes and hair ornaments. Mama Nene ushered Kai into the dressing room and combed her hair with cloudy rice water to make it shine. This time Kai didn't escape the eyebrow tweezers. She yelped every time Mama Nene yanked out an eyebrow hair.

"Can't you just use the powder to cover them up?" she complained.

"If another attendant comes to the west wing on an errand, you might be seen," Mama Nene explained. "The other ladies are curious, and not always kind."

"I'm nobody," she said. "They don't need to judge me."

"As your attendant, they're judging me, too," Mama Nene said.

Kai stopped complaining then. Mama Nene had been so nice when she could have been upset about waiting on a commoner. Once she finished plucking, Mama Nene applied powder to Kai's whole face, painted her lips red, and added two small circles in black paint where her eyebrows had been. Kai felt like a hideous porcelain doll. She wondered if the general's wife and the oldest daughter looked like this, too.

When Kai finally emerged from the dressing room weighed down by a dozen robes, the portable curtains had been set up by the veranda so that they could watch the contest without the soldiers being able to see them. Along the veranda of the main house, a rainbow of silk hems snaked beneath the edges of the curtains belonging to the general's wife, his three daughters, and their attendants. Mama Nene arranged Kai's hems, a mix of summery greens and blues, so that they peeked out, too. When she turned her head, Kai tried to pull hers back inside. But Mama Nene immediately noticed and slid them out again.

On the grass field, three tall black screens had been set up facing the main house, each with a ringed target affixed. The soldiers lined up in straight crisp rows in the courtyard, leaving a wide swath open in the center. Deep drumbeats signaled the start of the contest. A drummer and two flag bearers marched through the courtyard gate. General Takagi followed on a magnificent white horse with dark green ribbons braided into its mane and tail. Behind him ten archers, divided into two columns, filed in on horseback. The procession marched along the entire perimeter of the courtyard, passing directly in front of the west wing and then the main house. They filed up the center, coming to a halt. General

Takagi proceeded out to the field and turned around to face the troops.

"Today we celebrate the way of the horse and the bow," he announced. "Our finest warriors will compete for the title of champion. But perfection is not about striking the target. Perfection is the rider and the horse becoming one, and the target is their reflection. When we achieve this harmony, our aim is always true."

The ten contestants on horseback lined up near the west wing by the banner. Meanwhile General Takagi settled in a tall bamboo chair at the other end of the track and held up a red fan. When he lowered the fan, the first archer galloped down the field, turning sideways in the saddle and shooting three quick arrows at the targets as he flew by. Though Kai had seen them practicing, she was still awed by their skill and athleticism, and that they could hit not one but three targets while moving at such high speed.

"The horse that just went is Blaze," Little Nene said. "He's my favorite. The golden one is Summer. She's my second favorite. Third is Star. Then Wizard."

As she chattered away, Kai imagined charging down the field on Burden and shooting at the targets. It probably took years of archery and horseback riding practice, and she had only a few more days. Maybe she could ask to ride Burden to Sky Mountain. Maybe General Takagi would let her keep Burden afterward, too.

For the next round, the large ringed targets came down

and in their place hung clay pots that burst into confetti clouds each time an arrow struck. It was a small detail, yet she oohed and aahed each time one was hit. The rider on Blaze was the only one to shatter all three pots. As the confetti swirled and glittered in the sun, she and Little Nene clapped.

General Takagi announced the two finalists, the rider on Blaze and the rider on Wizard. A group of servants rushed out to remove the target boards. Once the field was clear, two soldiers carrying a cage entered the field through a gate at the far southeast corner by the barracks and the archery range. Inside the cage cowered a fox with three bushy tails. Kai gasped. A shocked murmur ran through the crowd. General Takagi held up the red fan and silenced them.

"Last night my scouting party captured this three-tailed fox near Sky Mountain," he said. "For the final round of our contest, the archer who kills the fox will be the winner."

The two soldiers let the cage door fall open and then they sprinted toward the courtyard, no doubt afraid that the fox would try to possess them. But the fox didn't go after them. Instead it left the cage in a crouch. The riders on Blaze and Wizard had been waiting on the west side of the green. They raced their horses across the field, arrows flying. The fox darted toward the east wall. Kai found herself rooting for the fox to escape. One arrow pierced the fox through its spine and it collapsed. The soldiers cheered. Then one of its tails seemed to dissolve into thin air. Kai blinked to make sure she wasn't seeing things. The fox jumped to its feet and the arrow fell to the grass.

"Did you see that?" Little Nene exclaimed.

The fox took off toward the east wall again. This time Wizard's rider hit the fox in the neck. Again, it collapsed, one more tail dissolved, and the arrow fell to the ground. The fox, down to a single tail, got up and ran. As the horses closed in, the fox wheeled around and darted between them, racing toward the west wall. Blaze's rider turned in a tight circle, galloping ahead of Wizard. Both archers shot at the fox. Kai wasn't sure whose arrow hit, but this time the poor animal stayed down. She remembered the Dragon King saying that with one tail the fox became mortal again, and that seemed to be true.

"Blaze won!" Little Nene exclaimed.

Kai started to say, "Hooray for Blaze," but was distracted by a servant leading General Takagi's white horse toward the bamboo chair. Lanky, mussed hair, a gait so quiet that it almost disappeared. Ren. How was that possible? She strained to catch another glimpse amid the troops who had swarmed the field to congratulate the winner. Once General Takagi mounted his horse, the servant turned around and stared straight at her through the curtain. At least that's how it felt. She quickly hid a giddy smile behind her sleeve. Ren was here.

10

Kai had to fight the impulse to run out to the courtyard. How had Ren gotten a job as a servant? Did he work in the stable? Did General Takagi know who he was? Then a terrifying thought popped into her head: What if Doi was still in the compound, too? Once the contest ended, she went to the back room and peeked around the blinds at the servant courtyard, hoping to catch sight of Ren. She slid her hand beneath her robes to check the arrow wound below her shoulder, which she'd forgotten about since arriving at the compound. The skin felt rough and bumpy but didn't hurt. She smiled as a cook waved a large wooden spoon and shouted at the chickens to go lay more eggs, and cringed as a servant carrying a tray dropped food on the ground and, after looking around to make sure nobody was watching, returned it to the bowl. She hoped that dish wasn't meant for her. Probably the servants had strong opinions about the commoner being treated like a lady.

"Kai, come quickly," Mama Nene called out. "The general and Yugiri are here to see you."

Kai returned to the front room. Through the crack in the drapes, she saw General Takagi's disembodied ear like the inner whorl of a conch shell. Yugiri again sat off to the side with his eyes downcast.

"Good afternoon," General Takagi said. "What did you think of our contest?"

"How in the world did your men catch the fox?" she asked.

"It tried to trick one of my men by shape-shifting into a beautiful woman," General Takagi said. "He played along and the other soldiers were able to grab it. After the contest, we checked the dead fox for its pearl but could not find it. So we've learned that we will not be able to take all of Dakini's nine lives in order to get her pearl. We will have to apply other methods."

Other methods. Threats and torture. Kai couldn't believe that he was calling this "their" plan when it was only his plan.

"What about the feather cloak?" Kai asked, to change the subject. "How are the repairs coming along? Will it be ready by the time we leave?"

"I have my best seamstress working on it," he said. "We will set out for Sky Mountain at dawn on the day of the full moon."

Four more days. Kai was about to ask if maybe they

shouldn't leave sooner when she felt her hems grow taut.

"Look, Yugiri, this is a bold combination," General Takagi said, his voice playful. "How does the poem go? 'My mountain door of pine has opened briefly / to see a radiant flower not seen before.'"

Even though he dropped her hems, she felt flustered. She didn't understand why he was reciting poetry.

"I will go check on the status of the cloak and leave you two young people to get better acquainted," General Takagi said.

Did that mean Yugiri was coming with them to Sky Mountain? Why would they need to get to know each other? When his father's footsteps faded, Yugiri cleared his throat.

"I will sit here awhile, long enough to satisfy my father," he said. "But you don't need to stay."

"I don't understand," she said.

"He's watching from the main house," Yugiri said. "He can see me but he can't see you. So you don't need to keep me company."

"Why does he want you to speak with me?" she asked.

"Because we are all stones on the go board for him to move around as he pleases," Yugiri said.

"Tell me what he's planning," Kai said, pushing the drape aside.

Yugiri kept his head bowed. Deep lines creased his forehead. "There is never one plan," he said. "There are plans upon plans upon plans."

When he left, he went the long way around, behind

the west wing to the servant courtyard. Even his footfalls sounded sad and resigned.

Rain fell. The two guards posted at the stairs to the main house stood like statues and stared across the courtyard into the empty field. Little Nene rubbed an ink stick on the ink stone at the desk and practiced calligraphy in smooth, elegant brushstrokes while Mama Nene straightened up the dressing room. Bored and restless, Kai went to the back to practice fox fist moves. She couldn't take her mind off Ren. She wanted to tell him everything that had happened so far. She had to find a way to sneak out of the west wing and find him. When the sky darkened, Little Nene tried to teach her how to play go, but the game required too much concentration. Kai swept the stones to the side with her hand, startling Little Nene.

"Let's play fox fist," Kai said. "If I win, I want you to take me to the stable to see the horses. Tonight."

She didn't care anymore if Little Nene found out that Ren was one of the bandits. Making Little Nene into a coconspirator increased the odds that Kai could leave the west wing and get to the stable.

"What?" Little Nene's eyes and mouth widened with horror. "We can't do that."

"Mama Nene's in the north wing," Kai said. "She'll never know."

"We'll get soaked and we can't hide a pile of wet clothes," Little Nene countered.

Kai pulled a big-sister move. "You're scared."

She stuck out her lower lip. "I am not. It's not worth getting in trouble over."

"You are," Kai said, folding her arms across her chest. "You're a big chicken."

"We'd both get in trouble, you know," Little Nene said.

"The general likes people who are brave," Kai said. "Not cowards."

Little Nene's mouth quivered. Kai felt a twinge of guilt for manipulating her like this.

"Fine," Little Nene said. "But if I win, I get your special necklace."

Kai couldn't risk losing the compass. She didn't understand why Little Nene liked it so much when she already had so many beautiful things to wear. "I can't bet that," she said.

"Then we're not playing," Little Nene said.

Kai bit her lip. She had to see Ren. After figuring out some of Little Nene's tells, Kai felt confident this time she could beat her. "All right. Let's go."

They went back and forth, with neither of them able to go up by more than one point. Kai had been right about Little Nene tucking her chin when she brought her palms to her thighs for the village chief move. Little Nene seemed to struggle now that Kai had stopped shifting her hips when she went to the hunter. They fell into a hypnotic groove, matching each other seven, eight, nine, times in a row. Then, with a slight frown, Little Nene's eyes darted over Kai's shoulder.

Kai glanced to see who was there, which broke her concentration.

Clap, cross, clap. Little Nene's fox bewitched Kai's chief.

Clap, cross, clap. Little Nene's hunter shot Kai's fox.

Clap, cross, clap. Little Nene's hunter shot Kai's fox again.

Little Nene held out her hand for the necklace. Kai looked over her shoulder to confirm that no one had come into the west wing.

"You tricked me," she said.

"You fell for it," Little Nene said with an imperious smile.

"Best two out of three," Kai said.

She shook her head. "We'll play again tomorrow."

Kai simmered with rage. She never should have bet the necklace. But a deal was a deal. She handed over the compass. Little Nene put the chain around her neck and danced around, pointing the needle this way and that. Meanwhile Kai plastered a smile across her face and pretended not to care. But losing the compass shook her up. She couldn't sit around and wait anymore.

At bedtime, once Little Nene's breathing settled into a steady rhythm, Kai rolled up three robes and placed them beneath the covers. If Little Nene woke up or Mama Nene checked the bedroom, at a glance it would appear that she was asleep in bed. The bedroom was pitch-dark. In the dressing room, she jostled the robe stand and nearly knocked it over. When she reached the doorway, she poked her head out to make sure she was alone. All was quiet. Hurrying to the cabinet near the go table, she threw on the page-boy tunic and cap over her bedclothes.

She slipped out the back to the servant courtyard, going down the short staircase and dodging the rain puddles on the path to the north wing. The shutters had not been closed yet, and in the lamplight Kai saw a delicate nose, a peaked white face in profile, looking out from behind the blinds. Somehow she knew that this was the general's wife.

"You humiliate your family with this marriage," the woman said. "We had a chance to form a powerful alliance and instead you throw it all away."

"Don't be a fool," General Takagi said. "They were only using us to make a better match. We don't need them. This marriage is our secret weapon. You'll see."

Kai wondered if Little Nene knew who General Takagi planned to marry his oldest daughter off to. Maybe she wasn't going to the capital after all. Rounding the corner, she skulked past the ball court. A white kickball glistened on the stairs leading up to the veranda. She was about to step onto the path leading to the garden when she heard men's voices. For several heartbeats, she crouched down and listened. The voices appeared to be coming from the veranda overlooking the garden. Slowly she raised her head. In the lamplight, she saw three uniformed men lounging on the veranda and knocking back cups of sake. A door slid open and General Takagi stepped out.

"Let's see if you're as good at kemari as you are with the bow and arrow," he said.

The other men stood up and they all walked toward her. She backtracked to the stairs and crawled beneath them. Cold water soaked through her trousers at the knees. Footsteps clomped overhead, then she heard the thwack of a ball being kicked. She groaned inside. She was stuck here until they finished their game.

Peering out from beneath the stairs, she watched the men kick the ball high in the air without letting it hit the ground. When General Takagi lunged and caught the ball with his foot in the corner, the return caught the soldier diagonal from him by surprise. He tripped over his own feet and fell heavily. The others laughed at him.

"What's the matter? Did you see a fox?" one of the soldiers said.

"You were running like a scared pig when you opened that cage today," grumbled the soldier who fell.

"Why are we messing with foxes at all, chief?"

"Benzaiten wants Dakini's pearl," General Takagi said as he let the ball roll down his chest and leg to rest in the crook of his foot before launching it in the air. "We will get it for her. And I will promise her that if she helps me overthrow the chancellor, then I will make her our country's one and only god."

He might as well have kicked the ball straight into her chest. Was General Takagi going to allow her to get Kishi back as part of his plan? Just then the ball sailed toward the building. Kai pulled her head back. It bounced off the veranda and landed next to the stairs. General Takagi's boots came into view. Maybe because he'd been drinking, he bobbled the ball, sending it under the stairs. Kai knocked it back, but not quite hard enough. Cursing under his breath, General Takagi crouched and his arm reached inside, his hand almost brushing her knee as he swiped at the ball. Finally he corralled the ball and stood up. Kai exhaled with relief.

The game started again. As Kai debated whether she should wait or make a run for the garden, light footsteps creaked overhead. "I'm sorry to interrupt you, sir," the page boy said.

"Yes, what is it?" General Takagi said tersely.

"The lady of the house would like a word."

General Takagi grunted and excused himself. The soldiers said good night. Once their voices faded, Kai crawled out from beneath the stairs and jogged through the garden, running past the pond and beneath the vine-covered arbor to the gate. But when she tugged on the handle, the gate didn't budge. She tried to turn the latch by inserting a twig into the iron keyhole. Then she stood on the gate's lower rail, grabbed the top of the slats, and tried to pull herself up. Without any momentum to carry her over, her arms shook, her feet scrabbled, and she had to let go.

Wiping her sweaty palms on her tunic, Kai backed up and took a running start. She launched herself into the air, then grasped the top of the gate with her hands and hooked her right ankle over the slats. As she pulled herself up, the rough edge of the wood ripped her trouser skirt and scraped the back of her leg. But she managed to swing her left leg over and hopped down to the ground.

The barn had deep eaves and wood-lattice siding. Slipping inside, she waited for her eyes to adjust to the dark. She was facing the stalls, which ran along one side with only a horizontal bamboo pole hemming the horses in. They rustled in the hay and whinnied to each other. Across the aisle an interior door rumbled and a lantern glowed. Kai froze. She'd forgotten about the old man. When a tall, lean figure stepped out, a smile broke across her face. Holding up a lantern, Ren frowned as he looked up and down the aisle.

The light didn't quite reach her. So when he turned to go back inside, she called his name. He whipped around and flinched.

"You scared me," he said. "Kai, what are you doing here?" His thick brows knit together with concern.

"I didn't know you were here until you brought the general his horse at the archery contest," she said. "I wanted to see you, but I had to wait for my attendant's daughter to fall asleep."

"How'd you get a uniform?" he asked.

"The general arranged for me to have archery lessons," she said. "But he doesn't want anyone to know that he's teaching a girl."

"Your time here hasn't been a complete waste, then," he said. "You want to see Burden?"

Kai followed him down the row. Burden was lying on her side in the hay. When Ren made a kissing sound at her, she stood up. Ears pricked forward, Burden nickered and nuzzled Kai's chest. Kai laughed with amazement and threw her arms around Burden's neck, feeling a rush of pure joy. *She remembers me*, Kai thought. That's when she knew why the bandits had not managed to stamp the kindness out of Ren. He had the horses.

"She misses you," Ren said, one corner of his mouth twisting into a half smile.

"I miss her, too," Kai said, patting Burden's neck and looking into her wide trusting eyes.

"I have some tea if you want some," he said.

"Tea sounds good," she said, feeling shy all of a sudden.

He slid open the door to a storage room. Lead lines and bridles hung from pegs on the wall. Buckets of hard-bristled brushes filled the shelves. In the corner, a pile of horse blankets formed a makeshift bed. He took one of the blankets and set it on the floor for her. She kneeled and watched him search through a jumble of dishes stacked on a crate. He picked up a cup and filled it with tea from a small pitcher. "It's cold," he said apologetically, sitting across from her and handing her the cup.

After only a few days, he seemed transformed. The clean uniform, and probably regular meals, made him seem less gaunt. His face looked more relaxed. He still wore a bandanna around his forehead, but his dark hair no longer looked wild and matted. It was shorter and tidier.

His gaze went to the muddy wet ovals on her knees. She was a mess, and he couldn't even see the rip in her trouser skirt since she was kneeling. "I had to hide under the veranda stairs to avoid the general, and then I climbed over the gate to get in here," she said.

"So you're not a celestial being after all," he said.

"Nope, just an ordinary girl," she said. Their eyes locked. Her face went hot and she looked down at the chipped edge of her cup.

"So tell me what happened," she said to cover up her embarrassment. "How did you wind up here?"

Wonder filled his eyes. "The stable manager, Jiro, saved me," he said. "I could tell that General Takagi liked you and that things weren't going the way Goto planned. The thought flashed through my head that this was it. This was the time to get away from them. So I left while everyone was focused on you. I figured I'd get on Encumbrance and ride as far and as fast as I could. Jiro was at the inner gate watching with a group of soldiers and as I passed through he said, 'The general's not in a forgiving mood today. Your friend is going to die.' And I said, 'He's no friend of mine.' Then he started walking alongside me and said, 'If you're looking for a new line of work, I could use a hand. You might want to start now.' I said, 'Now is good.' A minute later, Doi sprinted up to the hitching post, jumped on his horse, and managed to get out through the delivery gate. A group of soldiers went after him. When they came back, I asked one what happened. He said Doi took a couple arrows and fell over the side of the mountain."

"I can't say I'm sorry," Kai said.

"Yeah, me neither," he said.

Kai sipped her tea. Knowing that she would never see Doi again was a relief. "Do you like working here?" she asked.

A dazed smile spread across his face. "I have a roof over my head. They feed me. All I have to do is take care of the horses. It's the best thing that ever happened to me."

"Good," she said. "You deserve it."

"Rumor has it you're living like a princess in the west wing," he said.

She nodded. "It's a very beautiful prison."

She told him everything that had happened since Goto was killed. How she wasn't allowed to leave the west wing because otherwise something bad might happen to Mama Nene. How they dressed her up and treated her like a lady. How General Takagi wanted to use the pearl to get Benzaiten's support.

As she spoke, the question that had been nagging at her bubbled to the surface. "Why is he keeping me here? He doesn't need me to get the pearl. He can do that himself. Or at least he thinks he can."

"Maybe he's hoping that living like a princess will make you want to stay," he said.

Kai nearly choked on her tea. "Why would he want me to stay?"

He bit the inside of his cheek, as if trying not to smile. "You mean besides the obvious reason?"

"There's an obvious reason?" she asked.

"Maybe he wants his own onna-bugeisha," Ren said.

An onna-bugeisha was a woman warrior like the legendary Empress Jingu, who centuries ago borrowed the Dragon King's tide jewels and sailed into battle to defeat Silla on the Freshwater Sea. She laughed at the notion. "I'm a pearl diver. I don't know how to fight."

Ren studied her with pensive eyes. "You're capable and you're strong and you're brave. He could train you—he *is* training you. A flying onna-bugeisha would be a pretty awesome sight on the battlefield."

She shivered even though she wasn't cold. "He's not letting me go, is he?" she said.

"No, I don't think so," he said.

Kai sat there, stunned. A dull exhaustion washed over her. She wished she could stay here with Ren and go to sleep on the horse blankets and not have to go anywhere or do anything. The drumbeat marked the Hour of the Ox. It was 1:00 a.m.

"I need to find a way out of here," she said. "Could I hide in a delivery cart?"

"The guards check every cart that leaves," Ren said.

"Is there a place where I could get over the wall?" Kai asked. "Maybe with a ladder? The gardener must keep a ladder somewhere."

Ren shook his head. "Even if you managed to find one, that's a bone-breaking drop on the other side. The moat's not that deep."

"So you're saying it's impossible," she snapped. "I should just accept my fate."

He rolled his eyes and gave her a look that said she should know better. "What I think is that you're better off getting your cloak back and flying over."

She threw up her hands. "He gave it to a seamstress. It could be anywhere."

He leaned over and poured more cold tea into her cup. "I bet it's still sitting in his office," he said.

"So I'll just waltz in past the guards and the servants and look for my cloak," she said. That seemed about as wise as, well, going into the belly of a sea monster.

He smirked. "Lucky for you, I know a few things about breaking and entering."

An ache rose in the back of her throat. "I can't ask you to do that," she said. "I would feel terrible if you got caught helping me."

"Old habits die hard," he said with a shrug. "I'll poke around tomorrow, see what I can learn. Meet me at the pond by the stone lantern after dark. Bring whatever you need with you. Once you have the cloak, you should go."

"Thanks, Ren," she said. Even though she worried that he was taking too big a risk, she couldn't say no. Not with her sister's life at stake. She stood up to leave and slid the door open.

"Kai," he said.

When she turned around, he was standing behind her. He smelled like hay and liniment and campfires, and she had the fleeting thought that he was close enough to kiss her, which made her feel weird and fluttery inside. Instead he reached for something on the wall next to her ear.

"You don't have to climb the gate," he said. "I have a key."

11

On her way back to the west wing, Kai only had to hide in the shadows once when a servant passed by. Creeping up the back stairs, she tiptoed inside the west wing and stashed the page-boy uniform in the cabinet. Then she carefully slipped into bed without waking Little Nene. Closing her eyes, she saw Ren's face, grave but with a hint of a smile in his eyes and on his lips. The thought of kissing made her squirm and roll on her side. Why had she thought that? Because he had complimented her? Maybe. Once, when Mama had chastised her for being stubborn and impulsive, Aunt Hamako pulled her aside later and said, *Stubborn means strong. Impulsive means brave.* But she hadn't truly believed her aunt until Ren used the same words.

She pressed the back of her hand against her lips. Was that what a kiss would feel like? She wished she could talk to

Kishi. But then she had a disturbing thought. What if Kishi had kissed the village chief's son and hadn't told her? She pictured the moment she saw them under the ginkgo tree, Kishi giggling in his arms. But had Kai walked up before or after? Would Kishi have kept something that big from her, simply because Kai didn't like the chief's son? If Benzaiten brought Kishi back, Kai swore to never say another word against him or any other boy her sister liked.

In the morning, Kai woke up to find Little Nene gone. As she sat up and stretched, she wondered what Ren was doing right now. Brushing horses? Cleaning out the stalls? Maybe she'd see him on the way to her archery lesson. Hearing the door slide open, she got up to see if Little Nene was back. As she crossed the dressing room, Kai heard Little Nene speaking in a loud whisper.

"It's not fair, Mama," Little Nene said. "The general's wife said I won't get to go to the capital if I help you today. She'll send Shosho in my place. Her calligraphy isn't nearly as good as mine and she has no opinions about anything."

Kai peeked out the dressing room door and saw Mama Nene from behind, her glossy black hair forming a cape over her floral robe. Though Little Nene was facing toward the bedroom, she'd turned her head in order to avoid her mother's gaze.

"Don't be silly," Mama Nene said. "Who do you think makes these decisions? The general does. I need you here. I can't do all of these preparations by myself."

"But Mama." Little Nene snuffled and burst into tears.

Mama Nene sighed. "Fine. Pack up the books you borrowed and then you can go."

Kai's heart began to pound. Preparations for what? Mama Nene and Little Nene moved to the front room. Kai went to sit by the go table where she could keep an eye on the door. A few minutes later, Little Nene came back holding a wood chest filled with the fox stories. Her face looked splotchy and puffy from crying.

"What's wrong?" Kai asked.

"Nothing," she said, pausing by the door. "When the general's wife is in a bad mood, she takes it out on everybody."

"I heard you say his wife might not let you go to the capital," she said.

Little Nene shrugged. "She thinks I'm horrid. But I'm the one who knows the most about poetry and art and music. She has to let me go."

"You're the farthest thing from horrid," Kai said, indignant.

Little Nene flushed and looked away. "It's only because she thinks Mama is more loyal to the general than to her. She thinks we're his spies." Little Nene kept her eyes trained on the courtyard, blinking away tears. "Guards should always be good-looking, don't you think?" she said with forced cheer. "I mean, they're the ones we have to look at, and the daytime guards have such serious faces. I much prefer the nighttime guards. The most handsome one is on the night shift because the servants complain that he's gassy. You can't have a smelly guard during the day in case there are important visitors. But we can't smell him from here, so I still rank him number one."

Had Kai not been so anxious about the mysterious preparations, she would have teased Little Nene for being boy crazy. From the breezeway, footsteps and voices approached. Little Nene opened the door to an army of servants carrying large wood chests. Then she left without saying goodbye. Meanwhile Mama Nene rushed over to give instructions. Out of the chests came vases, wall hangings, floor mats, and drapes. A polished wood lute that looked too beautiful to touch appeared in the corner near the go table. Afraid that a servant might toss out her belongings, Kai hurried to the bedroom and snatched up the small cedar box where she stored the magic bowl and the fox scroll. Mama Nene came into the dressing room and began hanging robes on the rack. When she held up a green one with a bird-wing pattern, Kai realized she'd seen it before, being perfumed by the servant when she walked past the north wing for her archery lesson.

"What's happening?" Kai asked with alarm.

"We're sprucing up the west wing," Mama Nene said with the same false cheer that Little Nene had used moments ago.

Kai moved to the other side of the rack, forcing Mama Nene to meet her eyes. "Why? Mama Nene, please. I need to know what's happening."

Mama Nene forced a smile. "You're very lucky," she said. "The general wants to make you part of the family. You and Yugiri are to be married right away, as there are exactly three nights before you leave on your expedition."

Kai felt like she'd been knocked down in the surf by a ferocious wave. "But I don't want to be Yugiri's wife," she said. "The general can't decide for me."

"You're no longer a little girl," Mama Nene said. "This is the real world, not a fairy tale. Rarely do we have a choice."

"But I'm a pearl diver," she said, tears welling and blurring her vision. "That's not how it works in my family."

"And you are far from home right now, aren't you?" she said gently.

To marry, the groom visited the bride on three consecutive nights. He was supposed to sneak in late at night and sneak out at dawn as if they were having a secret romance. Only it was all pretend, because the bride's parents knew and would leave out wine and rice cakes. Kai walked to the go table and looked out at the hydrangea, covering her mouth with her hands in a futile attempt to silence the screaming in her head. She wasn't ready to marry anyone. And she definitely did not want to marry Yugiri.

Agitated, she paced the length of the west wing, then went to the blinds and looked out at the courtyard, at the pair of not-so-handsome guards at the base of the stairs. She could go confront General Takagi. But would that be wise? Hamako would have told her to stay quiet and stick to the plan. Go meet Ren tonight and escape. If she made General Takagi angry, he might send a guard to the west wing to watch over her, or he might tell Mama Nene to stay close. Then she wouldn't be able to sneak out. No, she needed to be patient and slip out the back tonight before Yugiri arrived, but with enough time to search for her cloak in General Takagi's office. Kai felt like she was back in the jaws of the bakekujira with the current pulling against her.

Because Mama Nene was busy overseeing the exact placement of every new item, she assigned two servants to help Kai get dressed.

"You can tell she's had too much sun," one grumbled. "There isn't enough powder in the Heiwadai Empire to cover up her brown face. And look at these calluses on her hands."

The other one yanked a comb through her tangles. "Her hair is as dry as a broom," she declared.

"I didn't ask for this," Kai snapped. "I'd rather be put to work and stay in the servant quarters."

"Dumb as an ox, too," the first one said. "A rich man wants to give her a life of leisure and she complains."

Kai shut up then, because these women were going to criticize anything that she said. Thankfully she was used to the villagers making comments about "those pearl divers" and "those twins." She did what her mother taught her— sat up straight and held her head high. After what felt like hours, the servants finished her makeup and hair. Mama Nene handed them robes from the rack to dress her in, saving the bird-patterned robe for last. The sweet jasmine perfume made her nose itch.

For the rest of the afternoon, Kai kept hoping the page boy would show up to take her to her archery lesson, though she knew how unlikely that was, given that she was all dressed up. A servant brought her meal tray behind a portable curtain where she picked at the persimmon cakes, nuts, orange slices, grilled fish, and pickled radishes in doll-sized china dishes. She was too nervous to eat. At dusk, a group of maids arrived with jars of fireflies that they released amid the hydrangea in the interior garden. Then they kneeled on the veranda to enjoy the light show. Mama Nene moved the go table and placed a portable curtain there, along with a sake carafe and bowls of tangerines and nuts on the visitor's side. Then she walked through the west wing lighting candles. Kai's mouth was dry. It was hard to swallow.

"Is Little Nene coming back tonight?" Kai asked Mama Nene, who kneeled on the floor near the door and arranged flowers in a vase by lamplight.

"No, she's with the general's daughters this evening," said Mama Nene, her full concentration on the flowers.

Kai felt her heart sink. How was she going to get to Sky Mountain without the compass? She never should have bet the necklace. It had been arrogant and stupid. "But we always play fox fist," Kai said.

"Not tonight," she said. "This is no ordinary night."

"What time will the general bring Yugiri?" Kai asked, trying to make her voice sound calm. Trying not to show how scared she was.

"Not for a few more hours," Mama Nene said.

"Aren't there supposed to be rice cakes?" she asked dully.

Mama Nene held a flower stem in midair and frowned.

"I'm sure there will be rice cakes," she said. "That's not until the third night."

The maids either got bored of watching the fireflies or had more work to do, because they filed out the back to the servant courtyard. Through a gap in the blinds, the almost-full moon hovered over the compound gates.

"I'm tired," Kai said. "I'm going to lie down for a bit."

"I'll wake you when he gets here," Mama Nene said.

Kai walked into the dressing room, her stomach jittery from the deception she was about to pull. She shed her robes down to the first layer, then rolled up four and stuffed them under the bedcover. Then she took her indigo jacket from the drawer where Mama Nene had stored her old clothes and placed the magic bowl, the fox scroll, and a pair of scissors inside the pockets. After extinguishing the lamp, she ducked down next to the dressing room door in the dark and spied on Mama Nene, waiting for her to walk toward the front out of the line of sight or step out onto the veranda. Kai waited and waited, until her calves ached from crouching. Suddenly there was a light rap on the door. Her heart banged in her chest, fearing General Takagi and Yugiri had arrived. Instead a woman called out a hello, and Mama Nene stepped outside. Kai exhaled and tiptoed closer to eavesdrop.

"His wife has every right to be angry," the visitor said. "The general has lost his mind, marrying Yugiri off to a peasant. Does he think because he dresses her up in fancy clothes that we'll forget who she is? Not only is he giving up an alliance with the northern general, but he's jeopardizing his daughters' chances to marry into a good family in the capital. It's embarrassing. He's completely bewitched. She must be a fox."

"She's not a fox," Mama Nene said. "I've helped her dress. She has no tail. The poor girl only wants to go find her sister. This was not her idea."

Kai didn't wait to hear any more. She rushed to the cabinet, grabbed the page-boy uniform, stepped into her sandals, and slipped out the back. The summer air was warm and soupy, and she felt like she was walking against a stiff current. Hiding behind a servant bungalow, she changed into the uniform and put her jacket on over the tunic. Then she hacked at her hair with the scissors, kicking dirt and pebbles over the fallen locks. Now she really could pass for a boy. She pulled the cap low over her forehead. As she passed the north wing, she heard General Takagi and his wife arguing. Stopping at the stairs where she had hidden last night, she shoved her clothes and the scissors beneath the steps. Kai couldn't quite make out what they were saying, but she hoped they would be fighting for a long time.

Under the cover of darkness, she ran. It felt good to dash through the garden's winding paths. She ran away from General Takagi and his plans, away from Mama Nene's warning that she was no longer a little girl. She ran so hard that when she came to the pond, she almost slammed into Ren. In his dark clothes, she could barely distinguish him from the shadows.

"Whoa," he said, grabbing her by the shoulders. "Kai? Is that you?" His eyes went to her shorn locks.

She nodded and took a ragged breath. "You were right."

His hands dropped from her shoulders and his brow furrowed. "About what? What's happening?"

"The general." She struggled to get the words out. It was too upsetting. "His son. The general is making us get married."

She took in another ragged breath. Surprise, shock, and something she couldn't read—anger, but not quite—rippled across his face.

"Good thing we're getting you out of here, then," he said.

Kai nodded. Now that she was out of the west wing and with Ren, she felt calmer. He started walking along the path toward the east wing and she fell into step with him, trying to copy his quiet gait.

"There's nobody staying in the east wing, as far as I can tell, so we're not likely to run into any servants," he said. "We'll go up to the veranda there and cross the breezeway into the main house."

"They don't lock it at night?" she asked.

"They do," he said. "But it's not very secure. They're more concerned about keeping outsiders out of the compound than they are about people moving inside the compound."

They passed elegant rocks that looked like miniature mountains and pruned trees forced into unnatural positions. The moon loomed large beyond the compound wall. Kai was suddenly stricken with doubt. Even if they found the cloak and she flew away, General Takagi would probably still show up at Sky Mountain to take the pearl. She had too much against her, too much to overcome. Benzaiten and the Dragon King were probably laughing over tea right now. Ren paused at the edge of the garden, staring up at the dark, silent east wing.

"I got a look around inside this afternoon," he said. "One of the horses went lame so I went to ask the general's assistant how he wanted the horse treated. They both have their offices on the back side of the main building."

"That's good, right?" she said. "It's far away from the guards."

"Yeah, and it means I can keep an eye on the breezeway to his private quarters while you look for the cloak," he said.

"Let's do it, then," she said, pushing the doubts from her mind. She was nervous, but the good kind, the kind that made her sharp.

"Stay low and follow me," he said.

They crept up the stairs to the veranda, keeping their heads level with the rail. When they reached the door to the breezeway, Ren reached into his pocket and pulled out a thin strip of wood, about the length of a chopstick. He slid it between the door and the frame and popped open the latch. They slipped through the door and ducked down again as they crossed the breezeway. She could just make out the profile of one of the guards in front of the house, staring straight ahead into the courtyard. She wondered if he was the good-looking one. Ren cracked open the door to the main house and put his eye up to it. Satisfied that no one was inside, he slid the panel just wide enough for them to slip through.

The shutters had all been closed, and only tiny specks of moonlight seeped through. As her eyes adjusted, she made out rows of books along the walls. A story scroll had been left abandoned next to a floor cushion, the paper looping in larger and larger circles like a ghost snail. Around the next divider, they entered a space with maps hanging on the walls, and what looked like a low wide drum in the middle of the room. Kai paused to look at the drum, which had a large seahorse painted on the taut fabric. Examining the painting more closely, she noticed that each part of the seahorse had been made a different color. When she saw two castles, a big one on its belly and a smaller one on its back, she realized she was not looking at a seahorse but at a map of the Heiwadai Empire, with each province painted a different color. The big castle closer to the Saltwater Sea had to be General Takagi's compound and the little castle closer to the Freshwater Sea had to be the capital. Papa would laugh for days at General Takagi's arrogance, if she ever had the chance to tell him.

Ren suddenly grabbed her by the arm and pulled her deeper into the map room, behind a cabinet next to the divider. He put his eye up to a crack in the divider and she did the same. On the other side, General Takagi's aide hunched over a desk in a small cramped space partitioned off by folding screens and a portable curtain. Long minutes passed as the assistant penned his letter, his face bent over his paper so that he could see in the weak light. Sweat trickled behind her knees.

In the distance, a drum marked the Hour of the Rat, and the sound seemed to break the aide's train of thought. He shuffled papers around the desk. Then he picked up the lamp again and came toward them. They shifted away from the cracks so that he couldn't see them spying on him. Kai looked at Ren as he bit the inside of his cheek and shook his head ruefully. A drawer banged shut. They crouched behind the cabinet as the aide passed through the map room with a lantern. When his footsteps grew distant, they slinked past his office to General Takagi's on the other side. A large clean desk inlaid with mother-of-pearl commanded the center of the room. Cabinets and shelves lined the walls.

"Start in here," Ren whispered. He moved to the corner and cracked open the shutter so that he could see the breezeway connecting the main building to the north wing.

General Takagi's office was tidy, the opposite of his aide's. Kai started with the cabinets along the wall, which looked like the most likely place to hang a cloak. In the first one, she found several wide-sleeved jackets hanging on rods. The next contained medals and other awards. The third was locked. She checked the desk for a key, feeling the items in a small lacquered tray. She didn't come across a key, but her fingers brushed across something rough and familiar. She picked up the round object and moved next to Ren, where she could see better. She gasped. General Takagi had her coral compass.

"What's that?" Ren asked, glancing at her hand.

"The compass that the Dragon King gave me," Kai said, outraged. "My attendant's daughter must have given it to him. I can't believe she did that."

"The compass isn't going to get you over the wall," he reminded her.

She put the chain around her neck. Had Little Nene planned this all along? She clearly had no intention of ever playing fox fist again if she'd given the necklace to General Takagi. She was only a child. Still, Kai felt sick. This place was like the sea, changing colors on the surface depending on the time of day and the weather, but never revealing what lay below.

Ren tapped her arm. "Someone's coming from the north wing."

She hurried back to the desk and dumped out the contents of a lacquered box, finding two keys, one smaller than the other.

"If the general comes into the building, we'll go around to the reception side," he said in a loud whisper.

Kai turned to the locked cabinet. Her hand shook as she tried to insert the first key.

"There are two of them," Ren said. "They're coming down the veranda."

Ren closed the shutter. She looked over her shoulder as

the light from a lantern flickered against the shutter panels. It was a strange feeling, knowing the general's intent and how joyless her life would be if she had to be Yugiri's wife. She tried the second key in the lock and heard a click. The cabinet opened and she jumped back as three demon faces leered at her. Kai reached out and touched one. It was steel, an armor mask to scare the enemy on the battlefield, as if General Takagi needed a mask for that. Below them hung a row of daggers, tips down.

"How's it going in there?" Ren didn't tell her to hurry, but his tone had an edge.

"I'm still looking," Kai said.

"They're in the west breezeway."

Maybe Mama Nene would chat with them and that would buy a few more minutes. Kai slid open a compartment door at the bottom of the cabinet and rifled through the stacks of fabric, flags or banners based on the thick rough feel. When she slid the panel the other way, she found a large silk bag. As she pulled out the bag and loosened the drawstring, there was a sharp whistle outside.

"Kai, he knows," Ren said.

The whistle repeated twice more, from the guards in front of the house and then the guards at the interior gate. She plunged her hand inside the bag. Feathers.

"I found it," she said, jumping to her feet.

They ran back the way they'd come, through the map room and the library. Instead of taking the breezeway to the east wing, Ren turned up the veranda toward the north wing, then climbed over the rail and dropped to the ground. Kai clambered after him. As they dashed into the garden, she heard soldiers shouting in the courtyard. It wouldn't be long before they fanned out to search the grounds. They ran around the pond, past the stone lantern, and beneath the vine-covered arbor toward the gardener's gate.

Ren stopped. "This is as good a place as any. You'll want to fly north, over the back wall," he said.

She kneeled and opened the drawstring. "Thank you," she said. "I'll never forget this."

"You don't need to thank me," he said. "I shot you in the arm, remember?"

Kai wished she had time for a real goodbye, but she didn't. Reaching inside the bag, she grabbed the cloak but felt no resistance. Opening the mouth of the bag wider, she saw only loose feathers.

"No, no, no, no," she wailed, pawing around inside the bag and pulling out a handful. "The cloak is ruined. He destroyed it."

Ren brought a hand to his forehead. "You're sure it's not just the ones on top?"

Lanterns glowed on the breezeway between the east wing and the main house. They'd be in the garden soon.

"It's been picked apart," she said, her voice jumping an octave.

"We can't stay here," he said. "Let's get to the stable."

Kai shoved the feathers back into the bag and pulled the drawstring closed. As she stood up, a white feather at the top fluttered out and sailed over her shoulder. Hearing a rustle, she turned and saw a snowy egret with a long arched neck standing by the arbor. The egret had appeared out of nowhere, but she didn't have time to think about it. Ren ushered her through the garden gate, and as soon as she stepped through, he locked it behind them. They darted inside the barn, where the horses snorted restlessly and one kicked the wall of its stall with a bang. They seemed to know something unusual was going on. Kai thought Ren would tell her to go hide in the hay. Instead he went into Encumbrance's stall and put her bridle on.

"What are you doing?" she asked.

"Getting you out of here," he said, hurrying into the next stall.

She didn't know how he expected to get past the guards. But there was no point in asking, since she didn't have a better plan. He pulled Burden into the aisle. Kai held the silk bag against her chest and used the drawstrings as straps over her shoulders. Maybe there would be a way to salvage the cloak later. Ren boosted her onto Burden and then tethered Encumbrance and Burden together. From somewhere in the garden, she could hear a soldier barking orders. They were getting closer.

Ren handed her the reins and fixed her in his steady gaze. "I'm going to talk to the guard at the delivery gate," he said. "When I come back, we're going to move fast, so be ready."

Through the barn door, she watched Ren jog toward the guard. Encumbrance danced in place. Kai patted Burden on her neck.

"What's going on in there?" the guard called out to Ren.

"The new girl is missing," Ren said. "The search party's tacking up. They want the gate open now."

"That's against protocol. I need the code."

"The wind is in the pine."

"Not from you. The squad leader needs to give me the code."

"Come on. I can't go back and tell him that."

The garden gate rattled. The men's voices grew louder. Kai bit her lip, willing the guard with her mind to let them out.

"All right, all right."

The guard started to push the gate open. Kai couldn't believe it. Ren dashed back and leaped onto Encumbrance. The horses sprang forward. As they bolted out of the barn, she saw movement to her right. General Takagi and some soldiers were running toward the barn.

"Stop," General Takagi shouted. "That's an order."

Ren kicked Encumbrance and they hurtled forward.

"Nobody leaves!" General Takagi roared. "Stop them."

The guard looked from them to General Takagi and started to push the gate closed. The horses were at a full gallop now, so they were either going to get out or they were going to crash. The gap narrowed. The guard planted himself in the opening, then realized Ren wasn't going to stop and leaped out of the way. Burden and Encumbrance squeezed through, squashing Kai's leg between them. Then they were flying down the hill, around a series of hairpin turns. Her body jerked side to side and she thought for sure she was going to tumble off the edge. She kept her eyes straight ahead, trained where she wanted the horse to go as Ren had taught her. Just as they straightened out of a turn, an arrow whizzed past Ren's head. Kai looked over her shoulder and saw General Takagi and five soldiers riding bareback several switchbacks above them.

At the bottom of the hill, the path flattened out. Arrows zinged by, streaking past her knee, grazing her ankle. They seemed to be aiming low, at the horses. They wanted to take down the horses but keep her and Ren alive, she realized. The path veered between two rocky hills, the curve protecting them from the arrows for a moment. But once they were on a straightaway the soldiers would start shooting again, and Kai doubted they would miss. Poor Burden was lathered in sweat and her breathing was labored. The lead line between Burden and Encumbrance grew taut as she struggled to keep pace.

Kai suddenly remembered the white feather floating over her shoulder and the appearance of the egret. She remembered the fierceness of the Crows of the Eternal Night. Plunging her hand into the bag, she grabbed a fistful of feathers and let them go. The second the wind caught them, the feathers sprouted into birds. Black birds, blue birds, yellow birds, red birds, in all different sizes. They squawked and flew toward the soldiers. Kai poured more feathers out in a steady stream. Eagle, hawk, blue jay, robin. She heard shouts and screams behind them. Grasping Burden's mane with one hand, she shook more and more feathers out of the bag.

Ren glanced over his shoulder at the river of birds and brought the horses to a halt. When Kai turned her head, she was amazed to see that the birds had not only flown at General Takagi and his men, but they continued to attack. The frightened horses bucked off their riders and ran in wild circles. Meanwhile the birds swarmed the soldiers, forcing them to the ground. Kai checked inside the bag and found a lone brown feather caught in a deep corner. Placing it in the palm of her hand, she blew on it. As the feather caught air, it morphed into a cute murderous finch that darted at General Takagi, who stumbled around waving his arms to bat it away.

"See, I told you he didn't bother to get the cloak fixed," Ren said.

"That's all right," Kai said. "I didn't really like flying anyway."

With the soldiers' shrieks and the birds' squawks still ringing in their ears, they turned their horses around and galloped into the night.

12

With only the light from the moon and the stars, Ren led them through the Valley of the Wind-swept Pine. The question that nagged at Kai was where he was leading them.

"The compass from the Dragon King will take us to Sky Mountain," she said, holding up the coral pendant.

"Not now," he said, his jaw clenched.

"Shouldn't we stay on course?" she said.

"I know what I'm doing," he said. He had that flinty, closed-off look that he used to have around Goto and Doi. His ability to read the land, to know which two trees to go between and where to cross a creek, was not that different from her spying a mussel on the seafloor. So even though his tone stung, she said nothing more. Every time she looked at him in the moonlight, her heart twisted. He should have been at the compound, asleep on his bed of horse blankets. He was only here because of her.

Every so often, Kai glanced over her shoulder. If anyone could survive a violent bird attack, it would be General Takagi. She fretted about the birds and what would happen to them, if they would go back and join the Crows of the Eternal Night, or if whatever spell that had created the cloak had been broken and they would each go their separate ways. She hoped they stayed together.

As dawn seared the sky, Ren stopped the horses near a cluster of stout pines with low-hanging branches.

"Why are we stopping here?" she asked, sliding to the ground and nearly toppling over because her leg muscles were so stiff. "Shouldn't we find a cave or something?"

"Only if you like bears," Ren said as he pulled the reins over Encumbrance's head and slipped the bridle off. He hung the bridle on a branch and then turned to Burden.

Kai took the magic bowl out of her jacket pocket. "What did the horses eat at the general's compound?" she asked.

"Oats," he said, removing Burden's bridle. "Why?"

She held the bowl with both hands. "O Great Source of Bounty, please give me oats," she said. A puff of steam rose from the center, growing wider until it covered the entire surface. When the cloud dissipated, the bowl was filled with oats. She still felt a sense of wonder every time. Burden turned around and shoved her velvety muzzle into the bowl. Kai ruffled her mane with her free hand. They were free and they were together again.

Ren did a double take. "How did you do that?" he asked.

"The Dragon King gave it to me," she said. "You can ask for anything you want to eat." Encumbrance nuzzled her shoulder, wanting a turn.

"Great," he said with a smirk. "The whole time we were with Goto and Doi and I was sharing my food with you, you were feasting on—I don't even know—whatever delicacies an empress eats."

Kai thought he was being sarcastic, but she wasn't sure. "The eyelashes of an electric eel on a bed of lotus leaves? Shaved ice topped with phoenix tears?"

He crossed his arms and sucked in the side of his cheek. "Eels have eyelashes?"

"In rainbow colors," she said. "Actually, this is the first time I've used the bowl since I met you. I've been afraid to get caught using it. Are you hungry?"

He yawned and pushed together a bed of pine needles beneath a tree with his foot. "That's all right," he said. "Just get the horses. I'm too tired to eat."

Ren flopped down on his stomach on the bed he'd made, resting his head on his hands. Burden wandered away and scratched the side of her head against a pine branch. Kai asked the bowl for more oats and fed Encumbrance. While she ate, Kai rubbed the white star between the horse's eyes. "You're not worried they're going to run off?" she asked Ren.

"They could," he said, his eyes closed. "But now that they

know you have oats, they won't."

When Encumbrance finished eating, she moved to stand nose to tail with Burden. Kai crawled beneath the same pine tree as Ren and leaned against the trunk with her arms wrapped around her knees, her left foot near the crown of his head. She didn't know how he could sleep. She still felt jumpy. "So you're saying they only care about where their next meal is coming from."

"That's how people are, too," he said drowsily. "Animals are more honest about it."

Tears that she didn't know she'd been holding back suddenly spilled out, because if what he said was true, they couldn't trust each other. And wasn't it true that she was only concerned about herself? It was her need to win that put Kishi in the path of the ghost whale. Then she made it worse by running off without telling their parents. Now her escape could put Mama Nene's life at risk. And Ren's. She had ruined everything for him. Kai sniffed and wiped her tears with the back of her hand. Ren propped himself up on his elbows, his dark messy hair flopping over his forehead.

"What's wrong?" he said, alert again.

"It's my fault that you're here," Kai said, the tears falling faster than she could wipe them. "It's my fault that you left the horses."

He sat up, stray pine needles dropping from his chest. "We have horses," he said, nodding in their direction.

"I mean your job," she said. "You had a place to stay. It was perfect for you."

"You didn't make me do anything," he said, sitting next to her, his elbow brushing hers as he rested his forearms on his knees. "Eventually the general would have told me to do something to the horses that I didn't agree with and that would have been it for me."

"You're not just saying that to make me feel better, are you?" She rested her head against the trunk and looked at the glittery stars through the black web of pine needles.

"If you think I would do that, then you don't know me at all," he said.

He bumped her shoulder with his and she smiled at the stars. She had known him for less than two weeks, yet it was true. She did know him.

"We should get some sleep," he said.

She nodded and made a pillow out of pine needles. Falling into a fitful sleep, she dreamed Little Nene ran around a meadow catching the birds from the cloak with a net. Then she lined them up in order from her most favorite to her least. Little Nene ranked the egret number one, followed by the cute murderous finch.

When the heat of the sun filtering through the pine woke Kai a few hours later, the horses were still there.

"O Source of Great Bounty," Ren began.

"O Great Source of Bounty," she said. They were sitting on a sun-warmed rock near the pine tree where they'd slept.

Ren cupped the magic bowl in his hands.

"O Great Source of Bounty—" He stopped and broke into laughter. "I can't do it. It sounds ridiculous." He handed the bowl back.

"It does," she agreed. "What do you want?"

He raised both hands up. "I don't know. You pick. I can't think of anything."

"None of the rich people you robbed ever had provisions that made you think, 'If I could eat this every day, I would'? What kind of bandit are you?" she said.

"Not a very good one," he said. "I remember when I lived at the inn we had winter melon soup once."

"Winter melon soup it is, then," she said. "O Great Source of Bounty, please give me winter melon soup." The bowl frothed over, and when the steam cleared, it was filled to the rim with a light green soup.

He shook his head with disbelief. "Amazing. You should ask the Dragon King to let you keep that."

They shared the soup and some oranges and laughed at the horses rolling on their backs in the dirt and kicking up their legs. They seemed as happy as she was to have escaped the compound. But she had no business being happy, not without Kishi.

She felt Ren's eyes on her. "Are you all right?" he said.

She twiddled the ragged ends of her chopped hair between her thumb and index finger.

"Every now and then I realize I haven't been thinking about my sister and I feel bad," she said.

Encumbrance came over to snuffle the orange rinds that they'd dropped at the base of the rock. Ren slid down to stop her from eating one. "So what's she like?" he asked.

It took Kai a few seconds to answer. This was the first time that she'd ever been asked to describe Kishi. The villagers didn't need to ask. They already had their opinions.

"She's the fastest swimmer in the family," Kai said. "She loves the color purple and collecting sand dollars and performing the Dance of the Blue Waves at the summer festival. She's also the good twin—the responsible one, the sweet one, the one everyone likes."

Ren swiped the dust off Encumbrance's back with his bare hands. "That may be true, but I'm guessing she wouldn't have taken out a warlord with a bag of feathers," he said. "Maybe she's lucky to have a bad twin."

"I don't know about that," Kai said. "She would have been in the boat when the ghost whale came if I hadn't egged her on."

A dusty cloud rose as he ran his hands along Encumbrance's side. "I hate to tell you this," he said. "If there's ever an award for the baddest of the bad twins, you've got no shot. It's going to be me."

She knew he was trying to cheer her up. But the most she could give him was a melancholy smile. If she were Ren, she'd always be on the lookout for her twin. It would be constant, like breathing.

Since Kai always felt better when she was moving, she jumped down from the rock and copied what he was doing, using her palms to sweep the dust from Burden's broad back and her sides. Then he showed her how to put the bridle on, working the metal bit past Burden's long bony teeth. While he finished getting Encumbrance ready, Kai led Burden to the rock, stepping up high enough that she could get on without Ren's help.

Once she settled on Burden, she held up the pendant. "O Wandering One," she said, "show me the way to Sky Mountain."

The needle spun in a silver blur. When it stopped, it pointed at eleven o'clock. Kai turned Burden around, kicking with her left heel and pulling out her left rein, until the needle pointed straight ahead.

Ren mounted Encumbrance. "I want to make a stop," he said. "There's a bow maker not far from here. We have to expect General Takagi will be at Sky Mountain and I don't want to be unarmed."

Kai nodded grimly. "Yeah, that thought occurred to me, too. I never should have told him the truth."

"You did the right thing," he said. "If you'd stuck with the tennyo story, he would have thought you were one of us and that the whole thing was a con, to get someone on the inside."

Whenever the path was wide enough, she and Ren rode side by side. Every so often his ankle brushed her calf and she liked this easy feeling between them. In her old life, she would have rushed to tell Kishi that she liked a boy. Already sensing big news, Kishi would have been fluttering her hands with pent-up excitement. This was life now without her sister.

They emerged from the forest and started up a mountain trail. The sun burned her neck where she used to have hair. She could tell by looking at her shadow how uneven her hair was. Ren had to really like her for who she was on the inside. To pass the time as they rode, she told him all the fox tales she knew.

He guffawed when she finally ran out. "Where did you hear all of these stories?" he asked.

"Some Little Nene told me," she said. "The rest are from my aunt. She loved fairy tales. Once she was out swimming and surfaced near a fishing boat. The men thought she was a honengame, a turtle mermaid. She told them that if they weren't nice to their wives, a tsunami would wipe out their villages."

A smile hovered on his lips. "So that's who you get it from," he said.

"Are you calling me a liar?" she said, only pretending to be indignant, since she had in fact passed herself off as a tennyo. If she made it through this journey, maybe one day she'd be the aunt telling the unbelievable tales. Everyone said she was just like Hamako, and Kishi was just like their mother.

"Your word, not mine," he said.

His eyes laughed at her. But when he looked ahead and squinted into the distance, his grin faded and his face paled. Kai scanned the area where the trail leveled off, fearing an ambush. But all she saw was a strange tree, two trees, actually, one on either side of the path, fused together by a single branch. "What is it?"

Ren stopped to examine the conjoined branch that spanned just above their heads and ran his fingers over the rough bark. A haunted look entered his eyes.

"Nothing," he said. "I know where we are, that's all."

He moved ahead. But Kai couldn't shake the feeling that this place had deep significance for him. "What happened here?" she asked.

He didn't answer right away. The horses plodded along in silence toward the summit.

"I had a growth spurt two summers ago and I couldn't ride with Goto or Doi anymore. I needed my own horse," he said, patting Encumbrance on the neck.

A chill went through her as she realized what that meant. The bandits got their horses from the noblemen who they robbed and killed. "Who did they belong to before?"

He shrugged. "Some government lackey and his son."

"Are they—" Her voice caught. She couldn't say the word.

"Dead? Yeah," he said. "The kid was about the same age I was at the time."

"And did you . . ." He let her flounder for several long seconds. She didn't know why she was struggling to say what she knew to be true. She knew that he had hurt people, probably more times than she could fathom.

"Kill him? What do you think, Kai," he said with painful coldness. "He was bawling like a baby. Doi liked to toy with them, you know. I did him a favor."

Kai pictured the page boy, soft and innocent, blubbering until snot bubbled from his nose and fell on his sleeve. Ren wouldn't have been able to stand it, the suffering. But he would have pretended to Doi that he couldn't stomach the sight of weakness. It must have been exhausting, to always look for the least evil choice available and then act like you'd done the vilest thing that you could.

Kai had stopped looking over her shoulder for General Takagi. But that night Ren said since he wasn't tired, he would keep watch while she slept, which meant he was still worried. She made him promise to wake her when he got sleepy. But by the time he shook her arm, it was dawn.

The sun was nearly overhead when they reached a valley where dozens of cottages dotted either side of a wide road. They passed fruit orchards and grain fields, and commoners going about their work. Four young men loaded up a cart with barrels. A grandmother and a young girl sat side by side on their veranda and wove bamboo strips into baskets, the grandmother showing her where to place her fingers. A blacksmith clanged his hammer against red-hot metal. Ren came to a halt in front of a cottage with a neat vegetable garden.

"The bow maker's name is Nomura," he said. "He and his wife are good people."

He dismounted. As she jumped down from Burden, a woman about Mama's age with kind eyes and a gap between her two front teeth greeted them.

"Hello, welcome," she said. "My husband will be back soon. He says he likes to test his own merchandise. But if you ask me, he just likes to shoot things. If you're in a hurry, I can help. After twenty-seven years of marriage, I know all there is to know about bows."

Kai hid a smile behind her jacket sleeve. Mrs. Nomura reminded her of the shopkeepers in her village.

"Mrs. Nomura," Ren said. "I don't know if you remember me. It's been a few years."

Her face lit up. "Ren. Of course! I'd recognize that wild mop of hair anywhere. Take the horses around the back and come inside."

Kai followed him across the yard to the field, where they left Encumbrance and Burden. Inside the cool, dim cottage, Mrs. Nomura kneeled at the hearth slicing peaches and then set out a bowl of walnuts. They kneeled on the mats that she'd laid out around the edge. Ren introduced her, and though Kai could also be a boy's name, Mrs. Nomura still gave her a long curious look. Kai picked up a peach slice and stared at the charred wood in the hearth.

"What happened to those men, the bandits?" Mrs. Nomura asked.

Ren had taken a handful of walnuts and was popping them into his mouth one by one. "Goto and Doi are dead," he said.

"Good riddance," she said with a snort. "Does this mean you're out of the bandit business?"

"All done with that," Ren said, though it occurred to Kai

that they were bandits of a sort, going after a prized possession and then bartering it.

"We stopped by because I need a new bow," he said. "We can pay you with rice." He glanced over at Kai for confirmation and she nodded.

"Yes, of course," Mrs. Nomura said. "You can take a look in the workshop now if you want. Where are you headed?"

General Takagi already knew their destination, so Kai didn't see any harm in telling the truth. "We're on our way to Sky Mountain," she said. "Have you heard of it?"

"Sky Mountain," Mrs. Nomura said with trepidation. "Oh yes, everybody knows about Sky Mountain. It's not far, less than a day on foot. But nobody goes there by choice."

"I've been sent to find something," Kai said. "Something important."

A door rattled in the back and a deep voice called out hello. A burly man with a sunburn on his bald spot burst into the room. "Sorry to keep you waiting," he said. "I hurried back as soon as I saw the horses."

Mrs. Nomura clapped her hands together. "Look, dear, it's Ren."

Mr. Nomura lit up. "Ren, my boy. How wonderful."

"He's free of those bandits at last," Mrs. Nomura said. "They're traveling to Sky Mountain."

Mr. Nomura's furry eyebrows shot up. "Most people steer clear of Sky Mountain. Foxes, you know."

"That's the thing. We don't know," Ren said. "How do we

avoid fox possession? The scariest bandit out there is this guy named Twitch. He's fox-possessed. Talks to himself. Totally unpredictable. We crossed paths with him once. One minute he was telling Goto a joke and the next he had his hands around Goto's throat."

Mrs. Nomura wagged her finger at her husband, who leaned his brawny shoulder against the doorway. "You know who they should talk to is the priest," she said. "He's at Cypress Pillar, up on the next ridge. He used to go all over the province conducting exorcisms. Foxes are his specialty."

"Old Basho spent a lot of time at Sky Mountain," Mr. Nomura said. "He became an expert in exorcism after being possessed by a fox himself."

During her family's trip to the capital, Kai had seen a priest and his medium, a girl not much older than her, arrive to conduct an exorcism at the home of a nobleman. Amid the smell of poppy incense and the priest's fierce chanting, the servants gossiped about who had possessed their master. One speculated that he'd been possessed by a fox while traveling back from the provinces. Another thought he had been possessed by the ghost of a friend whom he had wronged. Kai had wondered ever since what happened to the medium if the exorcist removed a fox. A ghost had no personal grudge against the medium and therefore no reason to inhabit her. But what about the fox? Would it leave the medium or did the medium have to be exorcised, too? Maybe Old Basho could tell her.

"Do you think he'd talk to us?" Ren asked.

"Sure, sure," Mr. Nomura said. "He loves visitors. Come pick out a bow first. Business first, Basho and the foxes later."

Mr. Nomura led them to his workshop in the back of the house, where dozens of bows lined one wall. Along another wall, dried bamboo poles tilted at precarious angles in buckets. In the middle of the floor, a whittled length of bamboo had been bent into the shape of a flat-topped mountain using short wood strips of varying lengths that protruded like fish bones. Mr. Nomura picked out a bow with a red handgrip.

"This one I call the Dragon Slayer," he said. Then he lifted one with a purple handgrip. "This one is the Dormouse Slayer." He winked and said in a loud whisper, "The only difference is the price. Don't tell anyone."

Ren reached for the bow with the purple grip. "It's harder to hit a dormouse," he said.

Mr. Nomura gave a loud, honking laugh. "You're a smart young man. Come on. I have targets set up in the field."

The workshop had a sliding door to the yard, where Mrs. Nomura was clipping orange flowers, some type of lily. Kai was about to follow Ren and Mr. Nomura through the gate into the field when Mrs. Nomura called her over and turned over a washbasin for her to sit on. "Let's fix your hair," she said.

"It looks that bad?" Kai said, sitting down.

"It could look better," she said.

Kai felt Mrs. Nomura tug her hair and then the metal

blades squeaked. "I think also, when you meet strangers, talk as little as possible. That will be safer for you."

"I will," Kai promised. Out in the meadow, Mr. Nomura and Ren carried target boards. The grain fields in the distance formed a gold band behind them.

"Ren was always a sweet boy," Mrs. Nomura said. "Quiet and hardworking. Those bandits left him here a few times while they went off and did whatever bandits do. We offered to adopt him since we don't have any children of our own. But they wouldn't let him go."

Ren would have liked growing up here. Mr. Nomura would have taught him his trade. Mrs. Nomura would have doted on him. Kai was sad for all three of them for what might have been.

When Mrs. Nomura finished, she handed Kai a tarnished round hand mirror. It was disorienting how something as simple as a haircut changed her face. Mrs. Nomura had evened out her hair so that in front it came to her ears. In the back it was longer, about chin length. Kai didn't quite see Kishi in the mirror. Everyone said that they looked like their mother, but with her hair short, Kai saw a young version of Papa. Her cheeks and nose seemed more prominent, her jaw more square.

Kai handed the mirror back to Mrs. Nomura and thanked her. When she went through the gate into the field, Burden and Encumbrance lifted their heads and nickered their approval. As she walked toward Ren and Mr. Nomura, Ren peppered a target board with arrows. Neither one of them commented on her hair as she approached. Mr. Nomura held out the Dragon Slayer.

"Ren is not good enough for this bow," he said with a wink. "I think you should give it a try."

Ren collected the arrows from his target board and moved the one next to it closer. When he reached the distance she'd been shooting at the compound, Kai told him to stop.

Ren raised one eyebrow. "You sure?"

She took an arrow from the quiver that rested against the fence. "Watch and see."

Ren shrugged and went to stand next to Mr. Nomura. The bow was lighter and more stable than the one that she'd used at the compound, and she liked how the grip fit in her hand. She nocked the arrow, pulled the bowstring to her ear, and let the arrow fly, hitting the board but not the target. She shot three more, getting successively closer to the center.

"Very nice," Mr. Nomura said. "The bow always finds its rightful owner."

The bow did feel natural, though she'd have to change the name. She had no intention of hurting dragons, especially after all the Dragon King had done for her.

"Not bad," Ren said, looking befuddled.

"What, you didn't think a girl could shoot?" Kai said.

"I would never doubt you," he said.

They practiced until dusk and then settled up for the bows. Since she didn't want the Nomuras to see the magic bowl, she whispered to it in the garden and filled a basket with rice to pay them. The secrecy was probably unnecessary. They were so kind, she was sure they'd be amazed and it would never occur to them to try to take it. For dinner, Mrs. Nomura cooked the rice that they paid for the bows with, roasted a pheasant, and picked fresh vegetables from their garden. It was a simple meal, but it reminded Kai of home. The carrots were sweet, the radishes crunchy with a hint of heat, and the greens had the right amount of bitterness. The pheasant was crisp on the outside and juicy within. The flavors, the glowing hearth, Mr. Nomura's joyful honking laugh—it all made her feel warm inside. That dinner was better than anything she could have asked the magic bowl for. She missed her family so much that she could hardly speak.

The next morning, Kai woke up in the workshop to the thud of arrows hitting the boards. Through the window, she saw Ren and Mr. Nomura practicing. She went to join them. After they finished, Mrs. Nomura fed them porridge and peaches. Then Mr. Nomura used an arrow tip to draw directions to Cypress Ridge in the dirt outside. With their new bows slung over their shoulders, they set out to find the priest. As they climbed toward the ridge, sunbeams slanted through the maple and cypress trees. Ren was quiet, a moody kind of quiet, and Kai wondered if he was thinking about what his life would have been like if the Nomuras had adopted him. Of course he might not have been thinking about the Nomuras at all. He might have been thinking about the boy he killed, and Kai wondered, too, if it was possible to truly know someone if you didn't understand their silences.

As they neared the top of the ridge, she smelled salt water an instant before she saw the stunning aqua blue in the distance. An "ohh" escaped her lips at the sight of the coastline hugging the sea. She'd been to the Saltwater Sea only once, to visit their father's cousin who was like a brother to him. She and Kishi had played in the break zone, and she vividly remembered getting slapped hard by a wave in the chest, taking in a mouthful of salty water, and having her airways explode as if she'd gorged on horseradish. Seeing the ocean made every part of her body crave its cool slickness. She'd never gone this long without going into the water. Sensing her attention was elsewhere, Burden came to a halt, and Kai had to kick her into a trot to catch up to Ren.

They continued along the spine toward the summit. Soon the path narrowed and the drop-off on either side was dizzying. The green valley where the Nomuras lived spread to their right while the sea called out from the left. Puffs of steam trickled from the mountain slope as if baby dragons napped beneath the surface, and every so often she caught the stench of rotten eggs, which meant those had to be hot springs below. The path ran out in front of a stout raggedy tree trunk charred at the top from a lightning strike—the Cypress Pillar.

They tied the horses to the shards of the trunk as best they could and continued on foot up a trail. Where the path circled back to the seaside, the drop-off was sharp. Ren treaded with soft assurance, becoming one with the cliff. Kai concentrated on walking where he walked and not looking down. When Ren stopped short, she nearly bumped into him.

"What the—" he said under his breath.

Kai followed his gaze up. A wood platform braced with stilts had been built into a recess in the cliff. Hanging upside down from the platform was an old man, bald, with a full white beard. His sun-bleached trousers sagged to his knees, displaying a pair of knobby ankles. Kai rubbed her eyes, but the upside-down man was still there.

"Excuse me," Ren called out. "Are you Basho?"

The man turned his head to look at them. His forehead was bright red from the blood rushing to his scalp. Bending at the waist, he grabbed the rope that tethered him to the platform and hauled himself up.

"People have called me many things, and Basho is one of them," he said. "You'll have to use the ropes to come up."

Three thick, knotted ropes had been anchored to the cliff face at intervals. Ren climbed up the first one, reached out with one hand to the next, and then stepped on the bottom knot of the second rope, moving steadily and without fear. The drop was steep. *This is no scarier than going inside the bakekujira*, Kai told herself. And at least the air was fresher. Grasping the rope in her hands, she set her feet on the bottom knot. The rope swayed but seemed sturdy. She climbed to the top and grabbed the second rope with her hand. As she stepped over, her left foot knocked against the cliff, releasing a shower of pebbles. Of all the dangerous things she had done since leaving home, this was somehow the scariest. She had too much time to think. That was the problem. Why couldn't the priest just live in a cave like the other mountain hermits? At the top of the third rope, she had to step across a gap to get to the platform. Kai eyed the distance, which was just far enough to make her pause.

"Look at me," Ren said, extending his hand. "Don't look down."

The cool confidence in his eyes, his certainty that she could do this, helped her trust herself. Holding her breath, she stepped across the gap and grabbed his hand. Once she was safely across, she moved to the middle of the platform. Meanwhile, Basho did a frenzied dance from one foot to the other in his straw sandals, like the fairy-tale teakettle that had the legs and head of a badger.

"Pins and needles," he said. Kai laughed. There was something very endearing about him.

Basho kneeled, and Kai sat down next to Ren with her back against a latticed wood divider that created a compartment inside. The priest probably slept in there. She wondered how he went to the bathroom, then answered her own question—his toilet was most likely the edge of the platform to some part of the cliff below.

"Why were you hanging upside down?" she asked.

"To catch my thoughts," Basho said, tapping his forehead. "Or to make them fall out. I can't remember which. What brings you to see Old Basho?"

"The Nomuras told us that you're an expert on foxes," Ren said.

"Oh, yes, the bow maker," he said. "I'm much more of an expert than I'd like to be. A fox possessed me for three years before it got bored and left. It was a strange, terrifying experience. I was fully conscious, yet I could hear the fox in my head all the time arguing with me. I would get up in the morning and think, *I'd like to hike to the waterfall today.* And the fox would think back, *No, you foolish old man. We will go into town and steal tofu and show people what a fool you are.* I was in a constant battle for control with the fox. It would force me to leap and twirl instead of walk. If I met a villager, I would try to explain that I had been possessed by a fox. My own words would slur as if I had been drinking. Once I could fight the fox no more, it would make me sing nursery rhymes at the top of my lungs, or throw my rosary beads at people, or do cartwheels down the street. Once I went inside a villager's home and took tofu out of a bowl from a small child. To this day, I can't stand the sight of tofu." He fluttered his lips like a horse. "Compared to fox possession, hanging upside down is not so bad."

Kai shuddered. It had been strange enough having the Dragon King in her thoughts, and he hadn't been trying to control her. "But you got it to leave," she said.

Old Basho beamed. "Oh, I did not. I simply got lucky. In the old stories, foxes are always possessing young beautiful women who trick silly men. The truth is, foxes will possess anyone—men and women, old and young. Every month on the night of the full moon, the fox would make me go to Sky Mountain where all the foxes gather. Once as we danced in the moonlight, a fox decided to leave its host, an old washerwoman. She lay on the ground sobbing and saying, 'Ten years. Ten years I've lost to this fox.' That's how it happened to me. After three years, the fox suddenly decided to leave."

She looked at Ren, who seemed mesmerized by Basho. "Mr. Nomura said you can exorcise them," he said. "How does that work?"

Basho cocked his head to one side and scratched his temple. "It's no easy task," he said. "For a time, I tried to help those I met at Sky Mountain. I had a disciple with me. We would capture the possessed person and tie them up. What most priests do, with the incense and the chanting, puts on a great show, but it's not terribly effective on foxes. First we would try to reason with the fox. Then we would try to bribe them with tofu. If that didn't work, we would threaten to drag them beneath a waterfall. The cold rushing water is often unpleasant to the fox."

"In stories, sometimes the possessed person is burned with fire and other terrible things to make the fox leave," she said. "Did you ever do things like that?"

"No, that would injure and possibly kill the person who's

possessed," Basho said. "The fox has taken over our bodies, but we still feel everything."

"Can a fox be killed? On its own, outside of a host body, I mean," Ren said.

She knew the answer from the Dragon King and from watching General Takagi's archers in the contest. But she was curious to hear if Basho would say the same thing.

"Yes, but that is not easy, either," Basho said. "As I'm sure you know, the fox grows an extra tail for every century that it lives until it becomes a white nine-tailed fox. What you might not know is that every tail provides the fox with an extra life. In order for the white nine-tailed fox to truly die, you would have to kill it nine times."

Ren glanced down at his quiver. He only had twelve arrows.

"I'm happy to keep talking," Basho said. "However, I would like to know why you're so interested."

"Benzaiten sent me to take Dakini's magic pearl in exchange for my sister's soul," Kai said.

As she explained the whole saga, sorrow entered the old man's eyes. "My dear boy. That's a fool's errand."

Her fingers reached for her hair that was no longer there. "I have to try," she said.

"It would be better for you to accept your sister's passing," he said. "In a way, that is the braver choice."

His words pierced straight through her heart. This was her twin, the person she loved more deeply than she would ever love anyone. She shouldn't have been surprised. He was a priest, and all they talked about was giving up desires and shedding earthly concerns.

"I can't do that," she said. "That's what it means to be a twin. We aren't whole without the other."

He studied her and something seemed to relent inside him. "What else can I tell you?"

"Where does Dakini keep the pearl?" she asked. "Is it always with her or does she store it somewhere?"

"Those pearls contain their fox magic," he said. "There's only one situation I know of when she would be required to take out the pearl. That's if she's challenged to a hunt. On the night of the full moon, any white nine-tailed fox can challenge the reigning Dakini to be their leader."

Kai was stunned. "Wait, Dakini is not one being?"

"No, Dakini is the title of the head fox," he said. "I only witnessed the hunt once. At midnight, there's a call for challengers. Then they battle to see who will be the pack's leader."

The more she learned from Basho, the more discouraged she felt. Would she be allowed to challenge Dakini? How could she fight a fox? "Do they fight to the death?" Kai asked. This did not bode well. She couldn't kill a fox with her bare hands, and it seemed doubtful that she'd be allowed to use her bow.

"No, the foxes are more humane than, say, a warlord," Basho said. "Death in the hunt is an illusion. However, only the most powerful, confident, and ambitious nine-tailed fox dares to challenge the queen. The loser not only becomes a mortal fox, but she is left with only a stump for a tail. Her humiliating defeat will mark her for the rest of her life."

Kai suddenly remembered the illustrated scroll. She pulled the paper out of her pocket and smoothed out the drawing on the floor. "Is that what this is?"

Ren and the priest both leaned forward, and Basho laughed with delight. "This is marvelous. I wonder who could have painted this? As it's shown here, both Dakini and the challenger place their pearls between them in the center of the ring. The music strikes up. Through fox enchantment, it will appear that Dakini and her challenger are hunting each other in a field. The winner keeps both pearls."

"We could steal the pearl while they're playing," Ren said.

Basho shook his head. "Go into the ring with two nine-tailed foxes? That's suicide. To walk out of Sky Mountain alive, you'll have to beat Dakini at the game. That strips her of her power. I can't predict what the foxes will do then. They're accustomed to having a leader. I don't know whether a human can control them with the pearl or not."

They all went quiet. The sea ebbed and flowed in the distance. "How do I convince Dakini to let me play?" she asked.

"I'm afraid I can't be of any help there," he said with a sad smile. "But I can give you one thing that might be helpful." He stood up and opened the door to his tiny cell. When he reemerged, he shook out the contents of a small bag, four pea-sized balls, into his palm. "It's an herbal remedy that I took when I conducted exorcisms. You won't see the illusion that the foxes can create. You'll only see what's real. It wears off in about an hour."

Basho dropped the pills back in the pouch. Kai thanked him and put the pouch in her pocket.

"Where will we find them?" Ren asked. "How far up the mountain are they?"

"Oh, they're not up the mountain," Basho said. "Their burrow is under the mountain."

Kai shot Ren a confused look. Of course she knew foxes lived in burrows. But like Ren, she'd also envisioned Dakini and her foxes gathering at the summit.

"So we're looking for a hole in the ground," Ren said. "That could take forever."

"The entrance is on the northeast side of the mountain," Basho said. "I would tell you more. But it's quite striking. I wouldn't want to ruin the moment. Trust me when I say it's impossible to miss."

As a token of thanks, Kai left the fox scroll with him. She was glum as they rode back to the Nomuras. She'd always known that stealing the pearl would be a near impossible task. But somehow as long as that was in the distant future she hadn't dwelled on it. She figured she'd find a way. Now that time was here. Basho had laid out what to expect and Kai was scared. She didn't want to be torn to pieces by foxes, or possessed by them, or see either of those things happen to Ren. The Dragon King wasn't going to swoop in and save her this time. Wrapped up in despairing thoughts, she hadn't noticed that Ren had turned down the ocean side of the ridge instead of the valley.

"I thought we were going back to the Nomuras," she called out.

"We will," he said.

"Where are we going?"

"Take a wild guess."

He was taking her to the sea. Tears welled in her eyes and a grin spread across her face. When the horses stepped on the sand, they nickered with excitement. Ren brought Encumbrance to a halt. He dropped his bow and quiver on the sand, and took off his jacket and shoes. Kai did the same. Then they rode the horses into the surf. Burden and Encumbrance whinnied as a breaking wave sprayed their faces. The next one drenched her as it hit Burden in the chest. Then they were past the break zone in deeper water. Kai could feel Burden running beneath her without impact.

"They're swimming," she shouted to Ren.

He grinned. "They can swim."

As her legs floated up behind her, Kai gripped Burden's mane. It was magical, feeling the power of the horse beneath her yet smoothly gliding along the surface. A set of waves rolled through, lifting them up and down, each one bigger than the last. Pelicans circled nearby and dove headfirst for fish. The late afternoon sun dappled gold across the ocean's mottled blue. When Burden tired and turned toward shore, Kai let go and floated out. Ren waved as Encumbrance carried him back to the beach. She treaded water for a moment, then took a deep breath and dove down, deep down, through golden vines of seaweed, past dour red fish and silly puffers. She slithered through seagrass and spotted a turtle. When she felt a slow burn around the edges of her lungs, she arced toward the surface with a little flutter kick. Bobbing in the current, she watched Burden and Encumbrance roll on the sand and kick up their legs. Ren crouched on the beach to examine a shell. Riding a wave back to shore, Kai emerged from the sea cleansed and exhilarated and grateful. She might not be able to read Ren's silences, but he could read hers, and he knew that on what might be her last night on earth, she would want to go to the sea.

13

That night she couldn't sleep. She lay awake in the dark workshop on a straw mat next to Ren's and stared up at the pitched ceiling. Her hair was tangled from the sea breeze, her skin was chalky with salt, and her clothes smelled like brine. In the moonlight, the bows formed a wavy pattern against the wall. Tomorrow she would fight a nine-tailed fox. But when she tried to picture herself winning, she had no idea what that looked like.

"I wish I still had my bird cloak," Kai said. "I wouldn't even have to challenge Dakini to a hunt. I could just grab her by her nine tails and fly her to Benzaiten."

"Too bad you didn't save that last feather," Ren said. "That was one mean sparrow. It could probably take Dakini and all of her foxes out."

Kai laughed and rolled on her side to face him. The horses had taught him how to be gentle and kind and funny, carving out a safe secret space for him that Goto and Doi couldn't touch. She wished Kishi could meet him. She wished that she didn't have to be grieving and fighting for her sister and having these deep yet fluttery feelings for him at the same time.

"Kai, I need you to promise me something," he said. "If a fox gets to me tomorrow, if it jumps inside me, you need to take the shot."

She closed her eyes. If only she had closed them a moment sooner, she could have pretended to be asleep and then she wouldn't have had to answer. The magnitude of what he was asking took her breath away. She'd never killed anything except for mussels and the occasional mosquito or fly. She thought she could shoot an animal or a man if her sister or her parents were being attacked. But she could not shoot Ren, not even in a mercy killing.

"I don't think I can," she said.

"When Basho talked about the washerwoman who lost ten years—I can't live like that," he said. "I've already spent too much of my life doing things I didn't want to do. Promise me you'll take the shot."

Her throat tightened and she couldn't swallow. She didn't want to lie. "I promise," she said. "But I won't have to because I'm going to win that magic pearl fair and square. And then you'll have to escort me to the Freshwater Sea, since I'll be carrying this valuable jewel, and who knows how bandits think better than an ex-bandit? And then we'll have tea with

Benzaiten and the Dragon King, and take my sister home. And if you want to watch us dive, you'll have to take an oath to never share our secrets with our rivals, the saltwater pearl divers."

She made up the last part. If she ever met a saltwater pearl diver, Kai would consider her a sister. The corner of his mouth cricked upward in a smile.

"I'm sure your parents would be thrilled if you brought a bandit home," he said.

"Former bandit," she said.

"They might not see it that way," he said.

"They'll see it the way I see it," she said. It was a terrible thing to admit, that she was so caught up in what was happening to her and so absorbed in what she had to do that her own parents had become an afterthought. "If I don't make it out and you do, will you tell them?"

"I will," he said.

But there was a catch in his voice. Either he was lying, too, or he didn't think there was a scenario in which they survived.

Ren woke Kai up early the next morning to do one last round of target practice in the field, so early that she could see the shadowy outline of the rabbit who lived on the full moon. Of course now that Kai knew what she might have to do with that training, she wasn't as enthusiastic about practicing archery. Ren was quiet and businesslike as he set up the targets. Standing at the line, he aimed and shot off each arrow with such intensity that octopi and jellyfish could have rained from the sky and he wouldn't have noticed. He had very straight posture for someone who managed to make himself invisible.

Mr. Nomura drew directions for Ren with an arrow tip in the dirt and then he and Mrs. Nomura saw them off, hiding their concern beneath stoic smiles. As they left the valley, Kai yearned for a final glimpse of the ocean between the trees. But all she could see was land and sky.

"How do bandits decide who to rob?" she asked once the trail was wide enough that she could ride alongside him. "Do you roam around until you see someone who looks rich?"

"We staked out certain routes that court officials took," he said.

"What about pilgrimage routes?" Women often took pilgrimages, noblewomen and their daughters. Kai wanted him to tell her something that would make her hate him, something that would make her want to put an arrow through his heart.

"Sometimes," he said.

"What happened to them, to the mothers and daughters? Did you kill them, too?"

His eyes flicked over at her. His jaw tightened. She could tell that he was sifting through the past, and the longer that took, the more afraid she became.

"I didn't," he said. "But I didn't stop anything from happening, either."

She didn't press any further because the question of guilt suddenly didn't seem so clear-cut. There were degrees and it was hard to know where the line was. Did the fact that Ren had been powerless to stop Goto and Doi clear him of any responsibility? If Goto and Doi had killed Mama and Kishi while he stood by, she'd be angry with him for not trying to help.

She had to think about the boy he had killed, about that boy's mother and his sisters and the grief they had to carry around because of Ren. That would be the only way she could do it.

Late in the afternoon, they came to a dead, decaying forest where purple fruit about the size of a fist grew from brittle leafless trees. Beyond the forest rose a lone mountain. Nothing about it screamed "Sky Mountain." It seemed average as mountains went, green about halfway up, bare around the summit. It wasn't particularly tall or shaped in a memorable way. But the compass seemed to be taking them straight to it. Kai didn't understand why supernatural foxes would choose such an ordinary place for their abode, unless the name was meant as a trick. Ren halted Encumbrance and scanned the trees.

"Benzaiten said we would pass through Laughingstock Forest," Kai said. "Do you think this is it? It doesn't seem like a happy place."

"Whatever it's called, I think we have to go through it," he said. "Watch the roots. Horses have delicate legs."

She studied the skeins of gnarled roots that broke through the ground. "Horses seem so big and strong," she said.

"Yeah, but if they break a leg, that's it," Ren said. "The kindest thing you can do is put them down."

But it was not the roots that they had to watch out for, at least not at first. As soon as Encumbrance took one step into the tree line, a wild eerie giggling broke out. She spooked and reared up, dumping Ren off her back. Then she turned around and bolted past Burden, who pranced and bucked, knocking Kai forward on her withers. Encumbrance stopped, her tail swishing and her nostrils flared. Kai dismounted, led Burden over to Encumbrance, and grabbed her reins.

"Ren, are you all right?" she called out over the strange laughter that had to come from some kind of bird or animal. But she didn't see a thing. Maybe tree spirits were to blame.

Ren was already on his feet, dusting himself off and looking up at the branches. "I'm fine," he said. "I think it's coming from the fruit."

Kai stared into the branches of the closest tree and focused on the fruit, which looked like a short stout eggplant, and saw what Ren was seeing, two puckered eyes and a hollow for a mouth. Encumbrance reared and tried to run again, dragging her a few steps. Ren jogged out and the laughter stopped.

"That's creepy," she said. "What do we do?"

"I don't know," Ren said. "We can't take the horses through

there, at least not Encumbrance. But we might burn a lot of time trying to find a way around."

They both turned to look at the horses. Encumbrance tossed her mane while Burden waited patiently by her side. Kai knew that they would have to leave the horses at Sky Mountain to go into the burrow and that they might not return. Ren would have to unbridle them and set them free. She didn't want them to be free. Not yet.

"I'll go ahead and you stay here with them," Kai said.

"I'm not letting you go alone," he said.

"But—" she said.

"Kai, no," he said.

She was racked with indecision. They were her family now, Ren and the horses. She wanted to keep them with her as long as possible. Taking an arrow from her quiver, she shot at a piece of low-hanging fruit. It squealed and made an ugly baby face, then dropped to the ground and shriveled up.

"Great, so all we have to do is knock down every single piece of fruit from every single tree," Ren said. "We'll be doing that until the next full moon."

Something about seeing the ugly baby face jogged her memory. Hamako had told Kai and Kishi a story about a tree on a mythical island where only women lived. Since they had no husbands, a magic tree grew their babies and they would cry at anyone who passed. But if the babies cried too loudly, they fell off the tree and died. Maybe these trees were related to that tree.

"There might be another way," she said. "Hold their reins so they don't run. If the fruit doesn't fall, I'll be right back."

Kai stepped into the forest and the giggles erupted all around her. "How do you make an octopus laugh?" she said in a loud voice. "With ten tickles." The laughter grew louder. "Where does a warlord keep his armies? Inside his sleevies." They began to cackle and squeezed their eyes shut from laughing so hard. Kai used to groan at Hamako's jokes, but hearing the fruit laugh made it hard to keep a straight face. "What's the best way to carve wood? Whittle by whittle."

The branches shook as the fruit screamed with laughter. Then all of a sudden, they went silent and fell to the ground. Kai picked her way around the splattered, shriveled droppings and went to the next section of trees.

"Want to hear a joke about paper?" she said. "It's tearable."

The sun was low in the sky by the time Kai cleared the trees and they reached the other side. The compass pointed straight at the mountain. Ren caught up to her with Burden and Encumbrance in tow.

He shook his head. "I can't believe how many bad jokes you know," he said.

"My aunt would be very proud," she said. "I learned them all from her."

They mounted the horses and headed along a path that hugged the mountain base. Around the next curve, Kai saw two fox statues on stone pedestals standing sentry on either side of the trail. One held a ball in its mouth. The other held a ball with the tip of its tail. Pearls.

"Is this it?" she asked.

Ren scanned the area. "There's no burrow here. It must be farther down the path," he said, dismounting and crouching down. Kai tried to see what he was seeing, but she couldn't pick out anything in the hard-packed dirt.

"These track marks are fresh," Ren said. "Take the horses off the path. I'm going ahead on foot."

She knew with a queasy certainty that General Takagi was already here. She slid off Burden and Ren tossed her Encumbrance's reins. Though she didn't like the idea of stepping back into the eerie laughter of the forest, she was more fearful of what lay ahead. She told some more jokes to the trees to knock down the fruit, then took the horses far enough from the path that they'd be hidden. While she waited for Ren, she fed them, asking the bowl for oats and then apples as a special treat. As she held out the apple slices in her palm, she kept looking in the direction Ren went. He'd been gone awhile. The sun was setting and a honey-drenched moon hung over the ancient trees. At what point did it become the right decision to go look for him? She was about to leave the horses when he appeared out of nowhere at her elbow.

"The general's here with thirty men," he said. "I thought I saw the gardener, too. I guess he dealt with the fruit. The birds got the general pretty good. He has a bandage over his right eye. Let's hope that affects his aim."

Kai thought General Takagi could have two broken arms and it wouldn't affect his aim. Any disadvantage would just make him more determined. "Where are they?" she asked.

"There's a clearing up ahead where the burrow is," he said. "Someone carved foxes into the mountain face all around the entrance like the statues on the path. That's what Basho meant. The general and his men are camped in the trees across from the entrance."

"He's either waiting for his own men to take the pearl from Dakini, or he's waiting for us," she said. She wasn't sure which was better for them.

"Well, there are as many horses as there are men, so I don't think anyone's inside the burrow," Ren said. "Lucky for us, the general seems to have a healthy fear of foxes. As he should. He's probably planning to shoot us on the way out. He'll let us do the dirty work of getting the pearl for him."

If she managed to beat Dakini in the hunt only to have General Takagi take the pearl away, she'd rather not get the pearl at all. *Swim one stroke at a time*, she reminded herself. There was no point in worrying about General Takagi when she had to deal with the foxes first. Was it cruel that she was letting Ren help? She should make him go, have him take the horses and head back to the Nomuras. She bumped his shoulder with hers.

"Listen, I have to do this for my sister," Kai said. "But you don't need to be part of this."

He gave her a mysterious half smile. "Yeah, sorry, you're not getting rid of me," he said.

"Ren, I mean it," she said. "You've done enough, more than I can ever possibly thank you for. You should go."

"And miss you going up against a fox? No way."

She wanted to yell at him to leave and she wanted to throw her arms around him and tell him to stay. But she did neither of those things because Burden wandered over and nuzzled her in a search for more apples, and instead, Kai and Ren laughed at her. Then Ren went to Encumbrance, murmured something to her, and gave her a firm pat. Kai hugged Burden one last time and tried not to cry. Their bridles were looped around a tree branch, devoid of purpose like Hamako's tool belt.

Ren cocked his head toward the path to say it was time. If he was nervous, he didn't show it. She picked up her bow and followed him. They kept to the edge of the path, passing the fox statues. Trained to track and prowl, Ren glided along with cool confidence. As they neared the clearing, she heard the low murmur of men's voices. Since General Takagi and his men were probably expecting Kai and Ren to come clomping down the path on horseback like a couple of rubes, they didn't seem to think they needed to be quiet. It occurred to her that Ren was her secret weapon. General Takagi was underestimating him.

Basho had been right. The burrow entrance was impossible to miss. Larger-than-life foxes had been carved into the mountain face all around the low cave opening, twelve in all. Some had fierce eyes and teeth. Others had mischievous smiles. A few carried a pearl in their mouths like the statue on the path. If the clearing were a sundial, the burrow entrance would be at twelve o'clock, General Takagi would be at six o'clock, and the spot where the path met the clearing would be at four o'clock. Using the bushes as cover, they crept along the edge until they reached two o'clock. That's where the bushes petered out. Ren placed his hand on her shoulder and pointed to a boulder to the right of the entrance.

"We're going to run and take cover there," he whispered.

She tightened her grip on her bow and nodded. The rock was just big enough for the two of them to hide behind. "I'm ready," she said.

"Go," Ren said, and she sprinted toward the rock as fast as she could, with Ren at her heels. They'd covered half the distance when General Takagi shouted, "Stop or we'll shoot!"

Kai was still four or five steps away from the boulder. Even though she assumed General Takagi wanted her in one piece to go take the pearl, her heart banged in her chest. Ren, passing her, grabbed her arm to pull her along the last few steps. They crouched behind the boulder. Once Kai caught her breath, she peeked around the side and saw the soldiers in silhouette, standing with their bows drawn and their arrows glinting in the moonlight. General Takagi stepped in front of his men.

"Kai, if that's you, I'm here in the spirit of cooperation," he said. "Please come out. My men will stand down."

He raised his hand and his soldiers lowered their bows.

"Talk to him and I'll tell you when to go," Ren whispered. "As long as you're in conversation, their bows will stay down."

She nodded. "Why should I trust you?" she called out.

"I realize now my mistake in not sharing with you the partnership that I envisioned," General Takagi said. "Working together, we can flush out Dakini and take the pearl. I will give you safe passage to the Freshwater Sea. All I ask in return is for you to bring me with you before Benzaiten. I will offer to fight in her name, to unite the provinces and bring down the chancellor and his puppet, the emperor. No longer will villages like yours be subject to a corrupt government. You can fight alongside me if you wish, or go home with your sister. The choice will be yours."

She didn't believe him. She didn't trust him. After all that she'd been through, she couldn't help taunting him. "You know you can't outhunt a pearl hunter," she said. "That's why you're out here and not in there."

Ren tapped her shoulder. "Go," he whispered.

She dashed to the burrow opening, which was wider than it was tall. Ducking her head to get through the entrance, she slipped on the dirt and slid down. At the bottom, she jumped to her feet to get out of the way as Ren came tumbling through. Arrows thwacked against the mountain, sending gravel cascading through the opening.

"I guess the partnership deal is off," Kai said.

"Well, at least you know where you stand," Ren said, dusting off his clothes.

The tunnel was roomy for a fox. Kai could walk upright and Ren only had to stoop a little. A series of torches along the burrow walls lit the trail, which twisted and turned in a steady descent into the mountain. She heard the faint sound of music—a shrill flute, atonal strings, a drum. Smaller tunnels branched off, but they kept following the music. Soon excited chatter floated above the notes.

At the end of the tunnel, they came to an expansive chamber. Slipping inside and hiding in the shadows, Kai looked up. And up and up. The chamber seemed to have no ceiling, only rocky sides that narrowed into a dark blue that deepened into black. In the section of the chamber closest to Kai and Ren, three fox musicians stood on their hind legs on a low stage, performing on flute, strings, and drum. They were dressed in stunning silk robes in pastel colors with long trains like the ladies in the capital would wear. In front of the stage, hundreds of foxes and people danced wildly to the music. Kai kept rubbing and blinking her eyes. Sometimes the dancers looked like people, and sometimes they looked like foxes dressed as people.

In the center of the cavern rose a circular stage, and she thought that might be where the hunt would take place. The ring was silver with rubies and emeralds embedded along the edge. Past that, a grand marble staircase led to a series of branching gold platforms studded with pearls. On the highest platform, a regal being whose form seemed to hover between human and fox lounged on a dais.

Kai nudged Ren. "That must be Dakini," she said.

Dakini had a shock of white hair that stood up on end,

held in place by a glittering tiara. Her face was young and fox-like, with golden eyes, pointy ears, and a long chin. Strands of pearls encased her forearms and ankles. Her sheath dress appeared to be made from pearls. A group of handsome men with sharp cheekbones and tapering chins lounged at her feet. Kai couldn't take her eyes off them. They were the most beautiful people she'd ever seen in her life. Just then a fox dressed like a monk passed in front of her, breaking her line of sight and the spell. She and Ren had traveled halfway across the dance floor toward the dais without realizing it.

"Do you think they can tell that we're not possessed by foxes?" she said, glancing around nervously at the raucous dancers.

"I don't know," Ren said. "We should take those pills that Basho gave you so we can see what's real and what's an illusion."

They made their way through the crowd toward the edge of the cavern where groups of foxes played dice games. They paused to watch a warrior, an old woman in plain commoner's clothes, and two red foxes throw gold pieces and gems into a pot. Then they took turns rolling three dice. When the warrior rolled all sixes, he jumped up, did a jig, and tossed his winnings in the air. The foxes anted up again and the old woman threw the dice. The first one landed with four dots facing up. The second one bounced and also came up as a four. The third die sailed toward Kai and Ren, landing in front of Kai's feet and spinning on a corner. The old woman ran over as the die rattled around and settled on five. Blocking the other players' view with her body, she turned the die to four and started cheering.

"Cheater," hissed a fox with three tails. When the old woman went to grab the pot, the fox tried to wrest it away from her. They went careening in circles onto the dance floor, the jewels flying everywhere.

"That was brazen," Kai said. "I hope Dakini doesn't cheat in the hunt."

Near the circular stage, there was a commotion that seemed to center around a servant woman carrying a tray. Two gentlemen in black hats ran away from a white nine-tailed fox. When the fox growled at them, they each dropped a tofu pocket on the floor and scurried away. The nine-tailed fox gulped down the tofu pockets. It really was true. Foxes loved tofu.

Finding an alcove, Kai and Ren slipped inside where they could watch without being seen. Kai took out the pouch that contained Basho's anti-enchantment pills. Ren winced as he swallowed one. Kai popped the herbal ball in her mouth and gagged. It tasted foul, like charcoal. She'd barely choked the pill down when her tongue began to tingle. The prickly feeling traveled to her scalp, and then a red-hot sensation went down her arms and legs.

"Are you itchy?" she asked Ren. "I'm itching all over."

"I want to tear off my skin right now," Ren said, tugging at his hair with both hands.

Kai had a powerful urge to rub her body against the rough cavern wall. After a few minutes, the itchiness subsided and the room began to wobble and shimmer. She took a chance and looked up at the dais at Dakini. Her pearl gown and tiara dissolved. Her slender human form morphed into plush white fur. Nine bushy tails fanned out behind her. The handsome young men transformed into a fawning cluster of red foxes.

Kai's eyes traveled to the platform, which was not gold at all, but shabby wood. The pearls turned out to be coal. The ring in the center was also wood with plain rocks embedded in the side. Gazing at the crowd, Kai discovered that about half the human revelers had changed back to fox form. They were the shape-shifters. That meant the rest were people who had been possessed. As Basho had said, they came from all walks of life, male and female, young and old, rich noblemen and poor commoners. She wasn't sure if it was the effect of the pill, but the music seemed to slow down. Tapping Ren's arm, she pointed at the dice game. The players had not been betting with gold and gems, but with acorns and leaves. The dice were river rocks.

"Reality is actually stranger than the enchantment," she said.

"Yeah, I'm not taking the second pill," Ren said. "Now it all seems too real. It's too distinct. Like I can see every nook in this rock." He tapped a stone on the ground with his foot.

"Let's get a closer look at the ring," she suggested.

They dodged and weaved through the dancers. The whirling foxes kept almost knocking her over with their tails while the possessed humans threw out their arms and legs. Another fight broke out around a servant who came through with food. Amid the ruckus, she caught a glimpse of the tray, which didn't have tofu pockets but dandelion fuzz wrapped in bamboo leaves. Kai and Ren sidled up to the ring. Stairs led from the floor to the platform, which was at eye level and completely empty. Ren turned in a slow circle, scanning the cavern.

"What are you looking for?" she asked.

"Trying to figure out the best spot to cover you from," he said.

All of a sudden, her page-boy cap came off her head. She turned around to find the old woman who had cheated at the dice game putting her hat on. The woman's face lit up with delight.

"That's mine," Kai said. "Give it back."

The old woman shook her head. When Kai took a step toward her, she turned and ran. Kai started to chase after the thief, then realized how pointless that was. She didn't need the cap. When she turned around, Ren had disappeared. Kai felt a spike of panic. She'd only walked away for a second. He couldn't have gone far. Thinking she saw a dark flounce of hair in the direction of the band, she started making her way across the dance floor. The closer she got to the stage, the more crowded and frenzied it got. The air was sweltering and feral. As she pushed her way up to the stage, a six-tailed fox growled. A fusty scholar with overlapping teeth wagged his finger. The flute shrilled. Kai didn't see Ren anywhere.

She skirted the entire perimeter of the dance floor with her heart lodged in her throat. It took every bit of her self-control not to shout his name. He had to be here somewhere. But if they both kept walking, they might never find each other. Kai decided to go back and wait by the ring. As she sidled through the dancers, she was bumped from behind and stumbled forward, her shoulder banging into someone who grabbed her arm and kept her from falling. When she looked up and started to apologize, Ren was frowning at her.

"There you are," she said, flooded with relief. "I've been looking everywhere for you."

He continued to stare at her without recognition.

Kai touched his arm. "Ren, are you all right?"

Had a fox sensed that Ren wasn't one of them and possessed him? Her eyes locked with his, searching for a sign of familiarity. But then she realized that the fabric beneath her fingers was rough and that he was wearing a dingy brown hunting cloak that she didn't recognize. Was she seeing things? She glanced up at Dakini's platform, which was still wood and coal. Something must have happened to Ren. Or the pill was wearing off. This couldn't be Ren's twin. It had to be an illusion. But Ren had had that vivid dream about a fox attack. Even though they'd spent their lives apart, maybe Ren and his twin did have a connection. Maybe Ren had seen the moment before his brother's possession.

"You need to come with me," she said. But he was moving

away from her. She lunged forward and tried to grab his arm. At the same moment, a white nine-tailed fox walking upright with a menacing air glided through, parting the dancers. Kai stepped out of the way. By the time the nine-tailed fox moved on, she had lost Ren's twin.

Kai looked around frantically. A sudden cramping in her gut made her double over. The back of her teeth began to ache. When the cramping passed and she raised her head, everything in the chamber flickered. Dakini's platform and the ring wavered between dull and sparkly. One moment the foxes around her had only their fur, and the next they had on human clothes. Then the flickering stopped and Dakini was a human goddess again, with flowing white hair and a dress made of pearls.

"We have one last song for you," the musician playing the flute announced. That's when Kai saw him, Ren, in his dark blue tunic with his bow peeking over his shoulder, standing at the back of the stage and searching the crowd. Kai thought she might pass out from shock. Ren was fine. So the other Ren was either an illusion or his fox-possessed twin. They'd come here to rescue her twin, but what if they could rescue his, too? If they could capture him and take him to Basho, maybe Basho could exorcise the fox.

She weaved through the dancers and rushed to the side of the stage. "Ren," she called out.

He didn't look at her. "He's here," he said, his voice flat and tense.

"I know," she said. "I saw him, too."

Kai glanced over at the band. The drummer was eyeing Ren with suspicion. She reached up and tugged at his sleeve. "But Ren, you need to get down from there," she said. "You're calling a lot of attention to yourself."

He brought a hand up to his forehead and swayed a little like he might be dizzy. A startled look entered his eyes. "Yeah," he said, stepping down. "Yeah. You're right. Sorry."

Kai pulled him away from the stage and into the shadows. Ren bent over, bracing his hands against his thighs and staring dully at the ground. The pill was wearing off for him, too.

"I couldn't believe it," she said when he straightened up. "What happened when you saw him? How did he react?"

He looked over her shoulder, gazing fiercely at the crowd, his jaw working. "I don't want to talk about it," he said.

"We can help him," Kai said. "We can take him to Basho." What she didn't say, because she knew it was too much, was that then he and his brother could come with her to get Kishi and they could all go home to her village together.

He pulled his hands away and crossed his arms. "It was fox magic. It had to be."

"But I saw him, too," Kai said.

"Drop it, Kai," he said, his voice hard and cold. "That's not why we're here."

She stood with her hands hovering in midair, feeling awkward and alone. She didn't understand how the same person who'd taken her to the sea yesterday could shut her out like she was nothing today. The song stopped abruptly. When the drummer banged on a gong, a hush fell over the room. Floating paper lanterns appeared over the ring. A fox in a monk's robe stood in the center.

"All hail the great and powerful Dakini, Queen of the Foxes," the fox monk said. "Undefeated in twenty-eight full-moon challenges."

The foxes barked their approval as Dakini stood on her dais and transformed from a human back into a fox. Fanning out her nine tails, she strutted down the marble staircase. As she entered the ring, she gnashed her teeth.

"Do any Nine Tails wish to challenge Dakini to the hunt?" the fox monk asked.

Kai took a tentative step forward. But another white fox, maybe the one she'd seen earlier, had already bounded into the ring.

"I, Tamamo, challenge the queen to a hunt," she said in a husky voice, while the foxes in the cavern whooped and cheered.

Kai hadn't counted on another fox raising a challenge. She shot Ren a panicked look.

"This is good," he said. "You'll know what you need to do."

"What if they only allow one challenge a night?" she asked.

"Then you call her a coward and make it so she can't back down," he said.

Kai didn't like his tone, like he was telling her something obvious. He was angry. She understood that. He'd been separated from his other half because of a stupid superstition and didn't even know his brother's name. But why did he have to take it out on her now, of all times?

Dakini gave the challenger a withering look. "I didn't think you had it in you, Tamamo," she said slyly. "I look forward to taking your tails away."

The cavern suddenly brightened as every fox held up a glowing pearl on its tail, hundreds of luminescent orbs from the dance floor all the way up to the top platform. The fox monk held a tray and went to Tamamo, who opened her jaws to reveal a glowing pearl about the size of an orange, larger than the ones held by the regular foxes. The fox monk took her pearl and then went to Dakini, who opened her mouth. Her pearl was even larger than Tamamo's. The fox monk took it and set them both on the tray between them in the ring.

"Once you take your positions," the fox monk said, "the music will start. I'll call out when the hunt begins. You'll choose your stance on every third drumbeat. If you're late or change your move after the third beat, you lose a life. If you have one kill or two kills but lose on your next turn, your score resets to zero. You must have three kills in a row to win the game."

The fox monk retreated to the edge of the ring and kneeled behind a giant abacus with six beads, three white and three black. On the performance stage, the drummer held a paddle drum in one paw and a drumstick in the other. Tamamo and Dakini stood up on their hind legs. As the flute and the strings embarked on a bouncy tune, the cavern shimmered and blurred. The ring turned bright green, and then the color spread like moss across the entire floor and sprouted into a grass field. The ceiling turned into a cloudless blue sky. The illusion was so real, Kai thought she could feel the blades tickling her ankles. The drummer hit the paddle with the drumstick in time to the music and the fox spectators joined in, clapping along to the beat.

Clap, clap, clap. Clap, clap, clap.

"Go," the fox monk announced.

Clap, clap, clap. Dakini and Tamamo both transformed into hunters wearing cloaks, bows drawn.

Clap, clap, clap. Dakini and Tamamo turned into village chiefs wielding their scrolls like weapons.

Clap, clap, clap. Dakini's hunter shot Tamamo, who raised her paws and remained in fox form. She staggered backward and fell in a heap.

"One for Dakini," the fox monk said, sliding a white bead to the right on the abacus.

The foxes cheered. Recognition struck Kai hard like the hunter's arrow, and she gripped Ren's arm. "They're playing fox fist. I played this game with Little Nene."

"No way," he said. "So you have a shot at this."

"I said I played it, not that I was any good," she said. "We need to watch for tells. Something that gives away their next move."

Tamamo morphed into the village chief and pulled even

with Dakini, knocking her hunter down. The monk moved the white bead back to the center and slid a black bead to the side. On the next turn, Dakini stayed in fox form and a cloud of glittery stars engulfed Tamamo's village chief, who collapsed to the ground. They went back and forth for a while, neither fox able to get more than one kill in a row.

"Tamamo keeps her paws by her shoulders when she makes the fox," Kai noted.

Ren bent his head toward her. "Watch Dakini's paws when she makes the village chief," he said. "See how she swoops out her paws as if she's going to make fox ears, but then she brings them down to her thighs and does the village chief? She's tricked Tamamo with that move four times now. When she makes the fox sign, her paws stay more centered. It's subtle."

Kai wasn't sure which fox to root for. Dakini had survived twenty-eight challenges, so she'd be tough to beat. But if Tamamo won, would she be allowed to challenge the brand-new Dakini tonight?

Clap, clap, clap. Dakini did her fox-to-village-chief move again and Tamamo's paws floundered with indecision, losing her a life. A ripple of excitement ran through the crowd, which seemed to sense a shift.

"One for Dakini," announced the fox monk, sliding a white bead to the right.

Clap, clap, clap. Expecting Dakini to play the village chief again, Tamamo stayed in fox form. Dakini morphed into a hunter and shot her with an arrow.

"Two for Dakini," the fox monk said, his voice rising as he slid a second white bead over.

Clap, clap, clap. Dakini the fox showered stars on Tamamo's village chief. Tamamo fell to the ground.

"Dakini wins," the fox monk shouted, and the cavern erupted in cheers. The foxes threw anything they could get their paws on into the air—flowers, leaves, and pebbles. The field wavered and blurred and then shattered. In a snap, they were back in the cavern. Tamamo was no longer a celestial white fox but a mortal red fox, looking miserable and wretched with only a stumpy tail. She skulked off the platform and a group of foxes attacked her, chasing her away. Dakini fanned out her nine tails and strutted to the center, where she swallowed her pearl and then Tamamo's pearl. A glow traveled from her jaws to the tip of her tail. Then she brandished her new pearl, which had grown to the size of a grapefruit, at the base of her nine tails as she took a victory lap around the ring.

Now that the time had come, Kai felt alert and clear. She leaned her bow and quiver against the wall and wiped her palms on her indigo jacket.

"Wish me luck," she said.

As she started to walk away, Ren grabbed her sleeve and pulled her toward him.

"Good luck," he said.

His face remained stoic. But some deep emotion in his

eyes rippled right through her. This could be it, the last time they would ever see each other. She threw her arms around his neck. He was still for a moment, his arms at his sides. Then he wrapped her in an embrace that lifted her up on her toes. She breathed in the smell of horses, of a friendship that had come and gone too fast. When she let go, she turned around and walked away without another glance, because she suddenly grasped why he couldn't talk about his twin. If she let herself feel the feelings he stirred up in her, she was not going to be able to do what she needed to do.

As Kai jogged up to the ring, a shocked murmur ran through the foxes. "Who is that inside the possessed human?" "Don't they have to show themselves to challenge Dakini?" Puzzled that the crowd was no longer cheering, Dakini stopped preening. When she saw Kai climbing the steps to the ring, her dark lips curled under, revealing her sharp teeth. Up close, Dakini was massive, bigger than a wolf.

"Dakini, my name is Kai and I'm a pearl diver from the Freshwater Sea," she said. "I'm challenging you to a hunt."

Astonishment rippled through the crowd. Dakini's eyes narrowed.

"You're human," she said in a growly voice. "You can't challenge me."

"I've been sent by Benzaiten," Kai said.

This seemed to pique her interest. "Did she give you her jewel to wager?" she asked.

"Well, no," Kai said.

"Then I don't accept your challenge." Her white fur blurred and dissolved as she transformed back into a goddess with golden eyes and a shock of white hair shaped like a fox-tail. Then she turned around and waltzed up the stairs to her dais, her pearl sheath dress clacking and shimmering.

"If I lose, you can kill me or possess me," Kai said.

Dakini's laughter came out as a bark. She looked over her shoulder. "I can order any one of these foxes to slash your throat or inhabit your body right now," she said.

The only tactic Kai had left was what Ren had said to do: shame her into it. "I think you're afraid," Kai said. "It wouldn't look good to lose to a human."

"Sea girl, now you're boring me," Dakini said with a languid wave.

Kai thought back to the tray with dandelion fuzz and bamboo leaves. There was one thing that foxes loved that they could only get from humans. She pulled the magic bowl out of her pocket. "If you accept my challenge, I'll wager the Dragon King's magic bowl, which will provide you with tofu, as much as you want, forever."

The foxes barked their approval. Dakini turned around on the top step, intrigued. "Show me," she said.

Kai held the bowl in both hands in front of her. "O Great Source of Bounty," she said. "Please give me rice-stuffed tofu pockets." The plume rose. A cloud bubbled out from the center and extended to the rim. When the steam vanished, six deep-fried tofu pouches appeared inside. She tossed them into the crowd and the foxes fought over the morsels.

Dakini snapped back into fox form. "Unlimited tofu," she said, loping to the platform. "I would be happy to take this wondrous bowl away from you. I accept your challenge."

"But Dakini," the fox monk said, "she's human. There's no precedent for this."

"We'll make one, then," Dakini said.

"But if she wins?" the fox monk asked.

Rage filled Dakini's eyes and she gnashed her teeth. "You think that I, the Great Dakini, could lose to a human?" She feinted at the monk, who ran out of the ring and disappeared into the crowd. Another fox clad in a warrior's uniform came up to the ring to serve as the scorekeeper.

The fox warrior came up to Kai with the tray and she set the magic bowl on it. When Dakini opened her powerful jaws to reveal her pearl, Kai was momentarily dazzled by its opalescent sheen. Her mind went blank. All she wanted to do was bask in its glow. When the fox warrior stepped between them, blocking her view, she snapped out of the trance. The pearl's aura was powerful. The fox warrior set the tray between them and reviewed the rules again, which sounded like gibberish to her ears.

Dakini reared up on her hind legs, showing her fierce claws and pointy teeth. The bouncy music started up. Grass grew under Kai's feet and a flawless blue sky appeared overhead, the colors so bright that they hurt her eyes. It was different being at the center of the illusion than watching it from the margins. She couldn't see anyone except Dakini, not even the warrior keeping track of the score. The flute and the strings seemed to feed off each other, picking up in tempo. Then the drummer joined in. *Boom-boom-boom.* The foxes clapped to the beat.

"Go," she heard the scorekeeper say.

Clap, clap, clap. Kai didn't feel ready but she had to choose a stance. She shot her hands up into fox ears and got lucky that Dakini went with fox, too.

Clap, clap, clap. She threw up her hands and did fox again. The moment she registered the hunter in front of her, an arrow banged into her chest. Even though the arrow wasn't real, the force still knocked her to the ground.

"One for Dakini," the scorekeeper announced. Barking filled the cavern, drowning out the music.

Dakini and Tamamo had made the game look effortless. But the impact of the arrow left Kai wheezing. In a daze, she was slow getting back to her feet. Two claps had already gone by and the drummer was about to hit the third beat. She tried to take the hunter's stance, but the village chief smacked her across the face and she tumbled to the ground.

"Two for Dakini."

She could not lose in three. She could not. Scrambling to her feet, she kept her eyes on Dakini's paws this time. She was seeing double but it didn't matter. Dakini's paws arced upward. She was planning a final blow with her signature move. Kai hit her with the fox and a meteor shower pelted the village chief. They were tied at zero again. She was back in it.

The time between beats seemed to slow down. Kai fell into a rhythm, mirroring Dakini so many times that she lost count. It was like playing with Kishi, anticipating her every move. The foxes had grown quiet. Kai kept searching for another tell. Then she saw it: Dakini's right hind paw angled out a split second before she made the hunter's stance. The next time Kai saw her back paw shift, she set her palms on her thighs. Kai's village chief smacked Dakini's hunter across the face with the scroll.

"One for the human."

Dakini bared her teeth. The fur around her snout wrinkled. She was losing patience. The drum beat twice. Kai watched Dakini's paws inch up around her chest and then hover. She remembered to keep her hips still so as not to give her own move away. On the third beat, Dakini punched her paws in the air to make the fox while Kai pulled back the hunter's bowstring. The force of the arrow made Dakini reel backward.

"Two for the human." The crowd gasped.

Dakini staggered to her feet. Kai felt calm and clear.

Clap. Dakini teetered on her hind legs. Kai kept her hands still.

Clap. Dakini's paws swooped out and up at her chest. Kai didn't move.

Clap. Dakini's paws went down as Kai's hands shot up. Glittery stars from her fox blasted Dakini's village chief in the chest and sent her sprawling.

"Three," the scorekeeper said. "The human wins."

The music stopped abruptly. Everything in the meadow went still. Not a single blade of grass moved. Instead of a massive white fox, a stub-tailed red fox lay crumpled on her side. Then the meadow scene cracked apart like a broken mirror and Kai was back in the cavern, which was eerily quiet. The scorekeeper gaped, so shocked that he had yet to move the third black bead over. She had won. She was the winner. *Get the pearl*, she thought. *Get the pearl before they realize what's happened.* As Kai stepped forward to grab the pearl and her magic bowl, the fox that had been Dakini crouched on all fours and growled. Kai froze. Then the fox launched into the air in a rabid red flash.

"Kai, get down," Ren shouted.

Once again, time slowed. Kai dropped flat like a board. As she fell toward the platform, an arrow whizzed over her, so close that she felt the disturbance in the air. The arrow skewered the fox through the heart. The malice in her golden eyes drained out. Then the fox landed with a thud, blood trickling from her chest.

14

Kai lay on the platform and stared into Dakini's eyes as the fox's disdain was replaced by a cloudy stillness. There was a roaring in her ears like the inside of a seashell. *Move*, she told herself. *Run*. Ren had killed their leader, and even though Kai had beaten Dakini at the game, she didn't know what the foxes might do. She stumbled to her feet and grabbed the bowl and the pearl, which she expected to be heavy but which felt almost weightless. It barely fit in her jacket pocket. After leaping down from the ring, she ran through the dumbfounded crowd. Ren was in the back near the tunnel, covering her, bow drawn.

"Fox killer," she heard someone shout. Then more took up the cry. "Fox killer!"

Kai sprinted into the torchlit passage with Ren right behind her. From the cavern came a high-pitched yipping.

Kai ran harder. The bowl and the pearl slapped against her hip bones with each step. Her legs and lungs burned from the effort. The twisting tunnel seemed endless, the rising slant too gradual. As the yipping grew closer, she pumped her arms. Ren passed her and grabbed her hand to give her momentum. When they reached a split, Kai almost chose the wrong branch and nearly tripped when Ren turned down the other one and pulled her with him. She didn't remember the path being this long when they had gone into the burrow. Over the yips she could now hear paws striking the ground in a steady beat. She was gasping for breath. She wasn't used to running this far this fast. Finally they came around a bend and she felt the air change—becoming cooler, less dense. Then she saw the entrance ahead, a lopsided dark blue oval dotted with stars.

"Stay low and get behind the rock," Ren said.

Focused on the foxes, she'd forgotten about General Takagi and his men. She did as he said, scrambling through the hole with her head down and dashing the short distance to the boulder on the left. Arrows clanged against the rock and mountain face, sending down a shower of dirt and gravel. The pearl suddenly glowed in her right pocket, brighter than the full moon. She tried to cover it up with her hands. More arrows clattered as Ren dove across the gap. Shafts of light continued to shoot through the slivers between her fingers. She hunched over the orb, terrified that the light would make them an easy mark. Meanwhile Ren fell to the ground, his face contorting with pain, an arrow sticking out of his calf.

"Ren," she said with alarm.

"I'll be fine," he said with a grimace. He reached down and yanked the arrow out of his leg as the first foxes streamed out of the hole. Kai had no way to defend Ren from the foxes since she'd left her bow and quiver in the burrow. But the foxes didn't come for him. Instead they charged straight ahead. They ran at the soldiers. A volley of arrows knocked the first wave to the ground. Kai knew they had as many lives as they had tails. But it was still unsettling to see a five-tailed fox take an arrow in the head, collapse, convulse, and then rise again with four tails, the arrow left harmlessly on the ground. The same sequence played out over and over, until the fox had only one tail. By then it was close enough to the soldier that it jumped into the man's chest and disappeared. The possessed soldier's face went blank as he dropped his bow and took a few herky-jerky steps. Lurching around the other soldiers, the possessed man almost took an arrow from one of his comrades at close range. Kicking his heels up in the air, he began to dance a jig with a demented grin on his face.

Another soldier shot a fox with eight tails in the chest. That fox was powerful enough that it didn't even fall down. It staggered for a few steps. One tail dissolved. And the arrow clattered to the ground. The soldier's face went white and he backpedaled, tripping over his own feet. He screamed with terror as the fox landed on his chest and disappeared inside him. A moment later, he was on his feet and spinning with his arms open wide like a top. Another possessed soldier lay on his back, shooting arrows at the moon with a giddy laugh. Several soldiers gave up and ran into the trees.

"Keep fighting," she heard General Takagi shout.

Ren loaded his bow. Blood stained the bottom of his pant leg and sweat beaded his forehead. He was in pain and pretending not to be.

"I'll cover you," he said. "Get on Burden and go. I'll catch up."

"I'm not leaving without you," she said.

"I'm going to be slow getting to the horses," he said. "If anything happens to you or to the pearl, then this was all for nothing. We don't know what these foxes are going to do. You need to put as much distance between you and them as you can. I'll be right behind you."

She nodded. She didn't want to leave him. But he was right. The foxes were unpredictable. If she lost the pearl now and he died from this wound—well, she couldn't bear to think about it. As she skirted the clearing, she looked for General Takagi. But in the mad whirl of red fur, she couldn't see him. When she reached the path, she noticed the pearl had stopped glowing. The foxes had come after Ren for shooting one of their own. But once the pearl sensed the soldiers aiming for her, it had summoned the foxes to protect her.

She ran along the edge of the path in the shadows toward the two fox statues. Behind her in the clearing, she could hear howling and singing. She picked out the words to what sounded like a children's song: *On the night of the full moon, it's time to come out. Come out! On the night of the full moon, it's time to play. Play! On the night of the full moon, we dance beneath the stars with joy.*

When she reached the statues, she stopped to look back. Ren was still a good distance away but limping toward her. The foxes seemed to be celebrating their victory. They were standing on their hind legs, paws on each other's shoulders, and doing a line dance around the possessed soldiers, who continued to execute their awkward leaps and pirouettes. She turned to go to the horses. Suddenly the pearl began to glow again in her pocket. But the foxes had won. Maybe she was wrong about how the pearl worked. Somewhere in the dark depths of the forest, Burden nickered. Then a hand clamped over her mouth. An arm grabbed her around the waist and hoisted her off her feet, pinning her arms to her sides.

"Well, little bird," General Takagi said in her ear. "Time to come back to the nest."

She tried to scream and kicked at him with her heels. But she might as well have been kicking an iron door. Out of the corner of her eye, she saw a red blur streak toward her. The foxes were coming.

"So you took the pearl from Dakini," he said. "Impressive. I knew you could be a force on the battlefield. It's too bad, because now I have very different plans for you."

The red blur coalesced into foxes, dozens of them, circling.

"Let her go," Ren shouted.

General Takagi whirled to face him, using her body as a shield. Ren stood about thirty paces away with his bow drawn. Some of the foxes also circled Ren, pacing and growling. They seemed confused, though, maybe because they didn't have a Dakini to give them orders. Kai thrashed her body around in an attempt to signal that General Takagi was the threat, not Ren. But his fingers pressed into her cheekbones so forcefully that she had to stop.

"Ah, yes, the stable boy," General Takagi said. "How wrong Jiro was about you."

"I said let her go." Ren's shooting eye locked on General Takagi's face. His eyebrows and mouth gathered into a scowl.

"And risk hitting her? You won't shoot," General Takagi said.

"I'm not going to miss," Ren said.

Kai tried to telegraph to Ren that he needed to stand down. The foxes would only attack General Takagi as long as Ren didn't appear to be a threat. But all she managed to do was bulge her eyes out and make muffled sounds.

"Lower your bow if you want her to live," General Takagi said.

Ren didn't waver. "Let her go if you want to live."

"We appear to be at a stalemate, then," General Takagi said.

As he spoke, she felt the arm he had around her waist shift. His fingers scrabbled around her hip bone. He was trying to insert his hand inside her jacket. He was going after the pearl, which continued to emit white light. If he managed to get hold of it, she didn't know what would happen. Kai had won it, but did that matter? Maybe the foxes would stop protecting her and protect him instead.

Kai wrenched one arm free and dug her nails into his wrist. The moment she clawed him, red flashes came flying at them from all sides. An arrow whizzed above her head. General Takagi's whole body jolted as he bellowed in her ear. Then she was falling sideways, still entangled in his arms, in a sea of red fur. As they hit the ground, the pearl, no longer ablaze, rolled just beyond her reach. Past the pearl, she watched a fox in midair vanish into Ren's chest. He stumbled backward.

"No," she screamed, pushing herself up to her knees. But it was too late. His eyes went vacant. He dropped his bow on the ground. Lifting his hands in front of his face, he examined each one, curling and uncurling his fingers. Next he lifted and examined each foot. Jumping straight up into the air, he kicked out both legs. When he landed, the leg that had been hit by the arrow buckled. Bending over, he examined the bloody gash on his calf.

Kai grabbed the pearl from the ground and shoved it back into her pocket. "Let him go!" she shouted. But the fox inside Ren made him cackle and windmill his arms. Meanwhile the rest of the foxes around them had gone back to cavorting, standing on their hind legs and dancing around. What good did it do to have the pearl and summon the foxes if she didn't know how to make them do what she wanted?

"Kai," Ren said in a strangled voice as he hopped around on his one good leg and arrows spilled from his quiver. "Kai, you promised."

She felt something barbed and metallic twist around in her heart. She had promised. She should never have done that. Turning around, she looked for General Takagi's bow. He lay flat on his back, blood gushing from bite marks all over his legs. Through a tear in his trousers, she could see straight to his thighbone. The arrow that Ren had shot had lodged in the eye socket of his bandaged eye. Blood seeped in a ring around the shaft. General Takagi was as terrifying in death as he had been in life. Kai picked up his bow from the ground and pulled an arrow from his quiver. Facing Ren, she tried to pull back the bowstring. But the page boy had been right. The bow was built for General Takagi and she didn't have enough muscle to use it. Dropping the bow, she grabbed Ren's instead. As he lurched around, all elbows and knees, she aimed at his chest. What her eyes saw and what her heart knew no longer matched. A person might be happy or sad, angry or calm. But their essence, the way they carried themselves, stayed the same. Ren was no longer Ren. He was the opposite of himself. And even though she knew his body had been taken over, she felt like she was caught in a fever dream. Her hands trembled. Her heart trembled. She pushed down a sob.

"Kai," he choked out.

He was still in there. How could she kill him when the Ren she knew was still inside? He tried to say something else but the fox strangled his words, then made him hop on one leg, flapping his arms like a chicken. Kai steeled her arms and set his chest in her sights. It was the right thing to do, to release him from this giddy prison. All she had to do was straighten her index finger. Such a small, simple movement. But she couldn't do it. She lowered the bow.

"I can't," she said, wiping tears from her cheek that she didn't know had fallen. "I'm sorry."

He gave her a tortured grin as he hopped away, toward the foxes and the soldiers who had formed a procession in the clearing and were dancing up the mountain.

There are times when doing the wrong thing is right. Kai and Kishi's grandmother had not been lucid in her final days and often confused the twins for Mama and Hamako. A day before her grandmother died, Kai had brought her some water. As Kai held the cup to her lips, her grandmother grasped her wrist. "Hamako," she said in an urgent whisper. "The package in my cedar chest is for your brother. Take it now and give it to him. Please." They only saw Uncle Kenji, a fisherman who lived a few hamlets away, when he wanted pearls. He had a terrible gambling problem and Mama had cut him off because he only gambled away what they gave him.

This was the winter before Hamako died, and Kai was

young. But somehow she sensed it was better to give her grandmother peace of mind than to tell her the truth. "You don't need to worry about Kenji," Kai told her. "He's all better now."

Her grandmother relaxed and closed her eyes. "That's good," she said. "He was always a good boy."

That night her grandmother died in her sleep. In that moment, doing the wrong thing felt right. With Ren, she had no good choices, and she was sick about it.

She found Burden and Encumbrance not far from where they'd left them in the forest, snorting and skittish, probably spooked by the scent of the foxes. As she bridled them, her movements felt slow and languid, as if she were underwater. After leading them back along the path to the part of the forest that had been cleared of the laughing fruit, she climbed onto Burden's back. When she took out the compass, she hesitated. She was torn between going home and going to find Basho. Maybe he could exorcise the fox from Ren. But she couldn't risk losing the pearl. She thought she could trust Basho, but she didn't really know. And Ren would be furious if in trying to exorcise the fox she somehow lost the pearl. No, she would go to Benzaiten first. Once Kishi was safely home, she'd ask the Dragon King if she could borrow the compass for just a while longer so that she could find Basho. She'd come back for Ren. That's what she would do.

Using the compass, she carefully steered Burden through the tangled trees. But Encumbrance didn't like being led and kept trying to push ahead. She switched horses, only to find Encumbrance showed her no respect at all. She'd try to make Encumbrance slow down and the horse wouldn't listen. She'd try to make Encumbrance turn and she'd continue to go straight. Ren would say that was her fault, that her commands weren't clear. But it felt like Encumbrance was punishing her, and Kai didn't blame her.

She deserved to be punished. He was not going to forgive her.

Navigating the dark, twisty forest and staying within the area where the fruit had already fallen required all her concentration, and by dawn she was exhausted. She fed the horses and lay down in a patch of tall grass. Now that she was still, the night caught up with her. All she could see when she closed her eyes was Ren. Ren taking aim at General Takagi. Ren pouring her cold tea. Ren teaching her to ride and jogging next to Burden.

He was not going to forgive her. She might as well cut her own heart out.

Kishi, her sweet sister who apologized to the mosquitoes that bit her before she swatted them, would tell her that of course she had to keep Ren alive. Basho would exorcise the fox. And once Ren was free, even if he was still angry, he would be able to choose his own path—go live with the Nomuras and learn the bow-making trade, go to the capital and work in the royal stable, go off with his twin who might even be with him now on Sky Mountain.

He was never going to forgive her. But she owed him that much.

Kai must have drifted off to sleep because the next thing she knew, something was dripping on her face. She jerked awake. Rain was falling, beading the grass. The temperature had dropped and the damp chill hinted at autumn. Sitting up and looking around, she saw the horses had taken cover beneath a tree. Her muscles felt like broken glass when she stood up. The cold air made everything hurt.

Kai tethered Burden to Encumbrance and they headed off, trekking in the rain beneath a muted gray sky the entire day without seeing another soul or passing a familiar landmark. She felt like a ghost, like a shell of a person. Memories that she'd forgotten came back. Fighting with Kishi over a wood doll in a red dress that they both thought was prettier than the identical one in the yellow dress, until they were exhausted and fell asleep in each other's arms. Draping dandelion necklaces and crowns on Papa while he pretended to nap in his hammock. Making the New Year's rice cakes all by themselves for the first time. Kishi had pounded the rice with a mallet while Kai turned the mortar between each swing. Once the rice had turned into a thick warm paste, they turned out the shiny goo onto a floured board. As they pulled off pieces and shaped them into round cakes, Mama grew teary. *Mama, why are you crying?* they asked with exasperation. Mama said she was proud to see them taking over these family traditions and also sad that they were growing up so fast.

Now Kai thought she understood why Mama had cried. All those small moments added up to something big. She wanted to squirrel away every memory of Kishi, every memory of Ren, and keep them safe like freshwater pearls in a jar so that she could take them out one by one when she needed them. So that she didn't lose their color and their shape. That's what she had done with her memories of Hamako, she realized. That's how the spirits of their loved ones gave their protection. They weren't physical ghosts who scared away predators or blocked arrows. Her aunt's spirit lived on inside her, every pearl of memory providing the strength and wisdom she needed to complete this journey.

That night Kai slept hidden beneath the low branches of a pine tree as Ren had taught her. She kept her hand on the pearl in her pocket.

The next morning, she reached a bustling port on a river that likely led to the Saltwater Sea. She paused in the tree line to survey the area. Travelers and goods came on and off the ferryboats that lined a dock. The path she was on ran parallel to the docks and then branched at the other end of the strip. Though she wanted to avoid people, she also wanted to get home as quickly as possible. A detour wasn't appealing. Moving at a trot, she wove through ox-drawn carts, messengers on horseback, a palanquin presumably carrying someone of importance, and other travelers on foot. Nobody glanced at her. It was so much easier to move through the world as a teenage boy, which really seemed unfair. She wanted to make the world a place where she didn't have to hide her true self. At a fork in the path, the compass pointed toward a bridge spanning a broad river. Everyone else went the other way. The palanquin and the many travelers on foot made her think there had to be a pilgrimage site nearby. She was curious to find out where she was, but not enough to ask and call attention to herself.

As she neared the bridge, she gave a wide berth to a beggar hunched at the side of the road. She had just passed him when something metallic clanged. Encumbrance spooked and bucked. Kai flew off her back, managing to twist in the air and take the impact on her shoulder. The shoulder that the arrow had hit. She rocked on the ground and gripped her arm, waiting for the pain to subside. Meanwhile Encumbrance veered off the path and galloped to the edge of the river, pulling Burden with her.

"What is wrong with you?!" Kai shouted at the beggar when she recovered enough to stand. She was about to turn around and go get the horses when she heard raucous laughter. Her heart jumped into her throat. She would never forget that laugh.

"Well, tennyo, we meet again," Doi said. He removed the hood of his ragged cloak, revealing his dirt-smudged face and feverish eyes. In his hand, he held a bell that he must have stolen from a shrine or temple. Kai tensed and put her hand on her bow, Ren's bow, the Dormouse Slayer. But Doi didn't move from the ground. That's when she noticed that his left arm was in a makeshift sling beneath his cloak and that he had a festering wound on his thigh. General Takagi's men had left him for dead, only he hadn't managed to die yet.

"I thought you were the boy," he said. "I guess you got him killed, too."

"He's alive, and at least he's far away from you," she said, angry with Doi for his continued existence, angry with herself for losing Ren.

"Ha," he said, spitting on the ground. "We should have known you were some kind of witch in that wacky feather outfit. We should have let you drown in the lake. But no, Goto had his big plans. Well, here's your chance for revenge, tennyo. Go ahead. You can put an arrow right here between my eyes."

He jabbed his blunt index finger into his forehead. Her grip tightened around the bow. She had learned to shoot so that she'd never be at the mercy of a man like him again. But as much as Doi might deserve it, she couldn't shoot him unprovoked.

"Come on," he said. "You know you want to."

Her mouth went dry. Her hand grazed her quiver, then dropped to her side. He was a steaming pile of ox dung and still she couldn't do it. Mostly because he wanted her to.

"Give me your flask," she said, holding out her hand.

He eyed her warily. "Why?"

"Just give it to me."

He pulled it out of his pocket and tossed it on the ground. "Ain't nothing in it."

"That's why I'm asking," she said, picking up the flask and taking out the stopper. Turning around, she pulled out the magic bowl and asked for sake.

When she handed the flask back, he sniffed the rim. "Is it poison?" he asked hopefully.

"No, just something for the pain," she said.

He took a careful sip. Kai went off the path to the river to get the horses. After leading Encumbrance to the bridge, she was able to climb up on the rail and get on. Her shoulder ached from the fall.

"Tennyo, come back here," Doi shouted. "Tennyo!"

Kai ignored him and rode on. She didn't know if she'd done what she did to be cruel or kind. Maybe a little bit of both.

Not long after they crossed the bridge, Encumbrance started to bob her head as she walked. Soon she was favoring her front right leg, too. Maybe she'd injured herself when she bolted to the river. Kai stopped in a meadow to dismount and examine Encumbrance's front legs. The area below her right knee looked swollen. Kai asked the magic bowl for ice—well, shaved ice with syrup, but ice nonetheless. Using an arrow tip, she ripped off a piece of her tunic sleeve and made an ice pack. Encumbrance wouldn't let her apply the ice pack to her leg, though. She kept hobbling away and Kai kept trying to catch up to her. Worried that all this dodging would make the injury worse, Kai gave up.

Burden, seemingly oblivious, nuzzled her for treats. Kai fed her oats from the bowl and then tried to feed Encumbrance. But the horse turned her head away. *If only Ren were here, he'd know what to do.* She remembered what Ren said about horses having delicate legs, about how a broken bone was a death sentence. Probably Encumbrance had the equivalent of a twisted ankle. Maybe she just needed to rest. But for how long? Kai was desperate to get home. Every day meant another day that Kishi spent with the sea snakes and Ren spent possessed by a fox. But she didn't have another choice. She couldn't force Encumbrance to walk when she was hurt.

To pass the time and to feel less alone, Kai leaned against the trunk of a tree and told the horses the fairy tales that Hamako used to tell. She told them about the old woman who lost a dumpling down a hole in her kitchen floor. When she went to retrieve it, the floor caved in and she fell into another world, where she was captured by an ogre who owned a magic rice paddle. The woman escaped, took the paddle with her, and never had to cook rice for herself again. Kai also told them about the baby boy named Momotaro who was found floating down the river inside a giant peach and grew up to become a great warrior. Burden tossed her mane and pricked her ears forward. She seemed to like that one the best.

Suddenly grief welled up inside Kai. She missed her aunt terribly. Her grandmother's passing had seemed in the natural order of things. She'd lived a long, full life. But her aunt—her vibrant, funny aunt—could not be dead. Kai remembered Papa carrying Hamako's body from the boat to the futon laid out in the family room. Mama brought out a bowl of water and attached a small piece of fabric to the end of a chopstick. Dipping the fabric into the water, Mama had gently wet Hamako's lips. This had been the final test, to make sure she was truly dead.

Wake up. Please, wake up.

Until Kishi hugged her, Kai hadn't realized that she was the one who spoke. Embarrassed, Kai had rushed outside and huddled beneath the oak tree that held up Papa's red hammock. She didn't help Mama and Kishi bathe and dress Hamako. She didn't place their two wood dolls, the ones in the red and yellow dresses, next to Hamako so that they could accompany her to the spirit world. She didn't make the rice cakes or slice the sweet round pears that her aunt loved for the offering table. She didn't set out the raw rice as an offering to the gods. She didn't take part in any of the family duties, as if refusing to accept Hamako's death would somehow bring her back. In a way she'd done the same by running off to rescue Kishi.

Before Kai went to sleep, she tried once more to feed Encumbrance. This time the mare ate a few listless bites of oats, which Kai took to be a hopeful sign. Maybe she'd be well enough to walk in the morning. Kai didn't sleep at all that night. With every rustle in the bushes, she worried that a mountain lion was about to attack Encumbrance, or that Doi had miraculously healed and followed them. When Kai got up at dawn, stiff and sore from the fall, Burden was frolicking in the meadow. But Encumbrance hadn't moved all night. She was as still as a statue, holding her right hoof off the ground. Her head dangled. Her nostrils flared. Her body was drenched in sweat. Kai tried to coax her into eating and drinking, but she refused.

She sat down beneath a tree with her head in her hands. Knowing what Ren would do didn't make her decision any easier. She sat for a long time, her mind heavy and blank, until the sun was high in the sky. Burden came over and nudged her. Encumbrance was still, except for an odd fluttering of her lips. Kai felt a powerful urge to sleep. All she wanted to do was curl up on the ground.

Since she could not stay in this meadow forever, she got to her feet and picked up Ren's bow, which she still didn't consider hers. From about ten paces away, she turned to face Encumbrance. She aimed at the horse's chest and pulled back the bowstring. Then Kai did what she had not been able to do before. She straightened her index finger. Such a small, simple movement. She shot the arrow hard and true, and it lodged deep in Encumbrance's chest. Her legs buckled, and she fell with a thud to her side. Kai should have put a second one in her. That would have been the kind thing to do. But she didn't have the strength. Instead Kai rushed to the mare and held her beautiful head with the white star. With Burden standing solemnly over them, Kai became a bottomless fount of tears. Encumbrance's limbs jerked as the light slowly left her eyes. Kai stayed with her long after she was gone, mourning for the horse, mourning for herself.

15

Everything went quiet for a while. The wind did not blow. The leaves did not fall. The mice and the lizards went to ground. Kai rode Burden toward a rugged mountain where slabs of rock had been stacked precariously, as if by a giant child. When the silence became too much to bear, she told Burden stories. But not made-up stories. She told Burden about her life by the Freshwater Sea and what it was like to dive for pearls and have a twin sister, and it sounded like a fairy tale to her own ears. Burden already knew about Ren. Kai didn't have to tell her about him.

They spent the night at the base of the mountain. The nights were colder now and she didn't know how to make a campfire. But she didn't mind. The cold on the outside was not as cold as what Kai felt on the inside. She cupped her hands and blew into them for warmth. Every so often, she reached inside her pocket and checked for the pearl.

It was misting at dawn as they made their way up the mountain past the balancing rocks. Sweet, reliable Burden moved at a steady pace, yesterday's events seemingly forgotten. As the day wore on, the sky took on a silvery sheen. Once in a while, Kai rolled her right shoulder in its socket, which was still sore from the fall. When they reached the peak, foggy wisps tickled the coast, and her heart swelled at the sight of the Freshwater Sea. Where the coast formed a jagged crescent, she spotted Bamboo Island and traced an invisible line back to shore, to the cluster of dots that had to be Shionoma Village. She couldn't pick out her home from this distance but she knew exactly where it was, two notches down the coast in a cove. As they descended, Kai leaned back, her hips moving in a figure eight to Burden's swaying gait. She breathed deep, unable to get enough of the fresh sea air.

When they reached the bottom, Kai no longer needed to check the compass. They galloped toward the sea, past rice paddies and farm fields, kicking up leaves in the grove of ginkgo trees where she and Kishi had played games of hide-and-seek, passing the rock shaped like a sleeping cat and the woodcutter swinging his axe. Veering off on a path lined with beech and maple trees, they startled three chickens pecking around the grass. The midwife looked up from collecting herbs in her garden, no doubt puzzled by the sight of a horse passing through. When Kai saw the azalea bushes that marked the entrance to her family's yard, her throat tightened. She was home.

Their cottage with the thatched roof looked lonely and quiet, with weeds choking the vegetable garden and the fishing boat sitting far up the beach as if it hadn't been used in some time. The veranda was empty, without a single mussel shell or bucket in sight.

"Mama! Papa!" Kai shouted as she dismounted in the yard and knotted the reins so that Burden wouldn't trip over them.

Mama poked her head out the front door. Covering her mouth with her hand, her eyes widened with shock. Kai had forgotten that she was almost unrecognizable with her hair cut short and dressed in a page boy's uniform.

"Mama, it's me," she said.

"Kai?" She took a few steps out of the house, looking thinner and grayer. Papa followed, squinting as if he'd been shaken from a deep sleep. Kai noticed he no longer had a red crease in his forehead from his too-small straw hat, which made her sad. They were both dressed in white, in mourning colors.

"It really is me," Kai said.

As she threw her arms around Mama, Papa's face crumpled with grief. He hugged them both in his brawny arms.

"We thought you went to be with your sister," Mama said, her voice punctuated by sobs.

"We thought you went into the sea and took your own life," Papa said hoarsely.

"I'm sorry," Kai said, holding them tight. "I'm so sorry. I asked Benzaiten to bring Kishi back. And she said if I brought her the fox goddess's magic pearl, she would exchange it for Kishi's soul. That's where I've been. I went to Sky Mountain and challenged Dakini to a hunt, and I won."

Kai released them and took the pearl out of her pocket. Since leaving Sky Mountain, she hadn't taken the pearl out once. Benzaiten's jewel had been more diamond-like. Dakini's was stunningly perfect and round. In the sunlight, a rainbow prism of colors arced across its luminous white surface. It gave off a bright glow that was mesmerizing, almost alive. Mama touched the pearl with her fingers and jerked her hand back, as if expecting it to be hot.

"Benzaiten will bring Kishi back from the dead?" Papa said, astounded.

"It's a long story," Kai said. She felt weary all of a sudden, as if by holding the pearl it had zapped every bit of her energy. "Can we go inside?"

Kai cradled the pearl against her chest, and her parents each slipped an arm around her shoulders. As they started to walk toward the front door, the sky suddenly went dark. A flash, as if a god had cranked the sun to the brightest level but only for an instant, turned everything bone white. The water, which had been lapping against the shore, grew agitated. A series of waves crashed against the beach, getting larger and larger until a wave broke and pushed their fishing boat from the sand into the shed. Water rushed all the way up to the veranda.

Then the Dragon King burst through the surface, his black-finned mane rippling down his long scaly neck. His webby wings extended and almost blotted out the sky. Her parents clutched her arms as the Dragon King roared and flames streamed from his mouth above the cottage. The smoke stung her eyes and made them all cough. When the smoke cleared, Kai found the Dragon King glowering at her.

"Mama, Papa, this is the Dragon King," she said.

Her parents hurriedly bowed to show their respect. "Welcome, Your Highness," they said.

The Dragon King stretched his scaly neck toward her until she could see the pearl mirrored in his eyes. Entranced by the jewel, he stared at it as steam rose from his nostrils. He blinked his wide amber eyes as if to break himself from its spell. Then he swung his tail out of the water and onto the beach.

Kai wanted so badly to spend the night with her parents, to tell them the whole story from beginning to end, and to sleep in her own bed. But when a dragon taller than a pagoda says it's time to leave, it's hard to summon the courage to ask.

"He's here to take me to Benzaiten," Kai said to her parents, who continued to gape at the Dragon King. "I'll be back as soon as I can. Please take care of my horse for me."

She shoved the pearl into her pocket and climbed up the Dragon King's tail, following the ridge of his spine until she reached the spot between his wings. Feeling forlorn, she waved goodbye to her astonished parents. Without warning, the Dragon King plunged into the sea. The tugging sensation as her ears turned to gills didn't feel quite as strange or scary this time. If only she had gills when she went pearl diving, Mama would never lecture her again.

Be careful what you wish for, valiant pearl diver, or I might turn you into a mermaid, the Dragon King said.

She smiled. The Dragon King had a sense of humor after all.

Or I could turn you into a sea slug, he said.

I meant it as a compliment, she said. *Dragons and gods aren't known for having a sense of humor, much less dragons who are gods.*

All sea creatures laugh at my jokes, he said. *Except for the bakekujira. That's why I banished him in the first place. Now tell me about Dakini and how you took the pearl.*

Kai described the burrow at Sky Mountain and recounted the hunt while the water turned dusky. Schools of eyeless gray fish moved in unison. A dark whiplike creature with a large pointy scoop for a mouth darted past. Tiny luminescent floaters shaped like ghosts with cat ears hovered, then drifted away. Kai wasn't sure which realm these creatures belonged to, human or divine.

I wish I could have seen your fox hunt, the Dragon King said. *You are brave, pearl hunter.*

Kai didn't feel brave, or proud, or triumphant. She just wanted to be with her family and Ren and the horses, all in one place, together.

A pink dot appeared on the horizon. As they grew closer, the dot stretched into a mountain. The mountain soon became a vast palace, with a high dome in the center and six towers, three on each side. Round coral blooms swirled all over the facade in pink, purple, turquoise, and orange. The dome was covered with a different type of coral that resembled webbed gold fans. They passed through a massive gate made of sea stars. Then a round door covered in snail shells spiraled open, admitting them into a grand hall. Kai slid down the Dragon King's tail to the floor, which was inlaid with mother-of-pearl. The interior walls of the palace were also covered in a rainbow of coral. A line of dignified soft-shell turtles bowed.

All hail the Dragon King, they said.

Send a messenger to Benzaiten, he said, his voice lower and more sonorous at this depth. *Ask her to come at once.*

Kai had to swim at a fast clip to keep up with him as they moved down the massive hall toward the dome, where a translucent tube connected the floor to the crown. The tube appeared to be made of glass beads. But when Kai touched the tube with her hand, the surface was not hard, but soft like jelly. Peering up, she saw a giant aqua-blue gemstone embedded at the top of the tube. A second gem in a darker sapphire hue had been set directly beneath it in the floor. Water rushed through the tube with such force that the spray nearly reached the dome. Then the water drained out.

Are those the tide jewels? she asked.

Yes, these are the jewels of ebb and flow, the Dragon King said. *Right now it is high tide. Come. Let us go to the garden until Benzaiten arrives.*

Kai followed the Dragon King through a marbled arch that led to a courtyard garden. Spread out before them was a bed of anemones, frilly underwater flowers in magenta, orange, and white. Winged snails swooped around the flowers. One landed on her wrist, its wings curling toward each other like rose petals. On either side of the anemone bed, seaweed trees twisted upward as far as the eye could see. Kai held on to one of the Dragon King's scales so that she could keep up as he swam over the path that ran between the trees and the anemones. At first she thought the path only appeared to waver because they were underwater. But as they traveled over it, she realized she wasn't seeing a path at all but an army of crabs moving around.

Dragon King, I have another favor to ask, she said. *I'd like to borrow the compass for a while longer. When I left Sky Mountain, I had to leave a friend behind, a friend who helped me get the pearl. A fox possessed him. I know a priest who can perform an exorcism, but I'll need the compass to go back and find him.*

Another quest so soon, the Dragon King said. *Perhaps you are a pearl diver no more.*

Oh, I'll always be a pearl diver, she said quickly. Though she did wonder how it would feel to get up every morning and dive for pearls again. It also occurred to her that her parents would not want her to leave. She hoped they would understand that she couldn't abandon Ren.

A gong sounded and the Dragon King said, *Benzaiten is near.*

Kai felt like a dozen winged snails had suddenly lodged in

her stomach. Even though she had the pearl and they'd made a deal, she was afraid that something might go wrong. She wouldn't stop feeling anxious until Kishi was by her side and they were home. On the other side of the garden, they entered a throne room with sea stars on the walls and bouquets of anemones in large vases around the dais. The Dragon King settled on a giant seagrass cushion with his spiky tail curled around his stumpy legs. Two more cushions made of kelp had been laid out and Kai chose the smaller, human-sized one. The turtles brought out trays of raw fish and seaweed, which they set on low tables. Kai was too nervous to eat. The fish slabs in pretty maroons and pinks leaned against a frilly piece of lettuce. When the lettuce jiggled, she realized it was actually a green sea slug.

The turtles filed into the throne room. *Your Highness, we present to you the goddess Benzaiten.*

Please send her in, the Dragon King said.

Through the arch slithered a large white serpent with obsidian eyes. Stopping in the middle of the throne room, she bobbed her head from side to side. Behind her came a writhing mass of smaller snakes. Kai looked for Kishi and felt a keen cut of despair. What did it mean that Benzaiten hadn't brought her with them?

How now, Benzaiten, the Dragon King said as the sea serpent's form crinkled. Its head shriveled and gray hair sprouted around a white snake tiara. Once Benzaiten had her human head, the molted snakeskin dropped away and she stepped out with eight arms extending from her patchwork dress.

Ryujin, what a pleasant surprise, she said. *You can't imagine what I've been dealing with. This tiresome poet found a poem near a statue of me and he's convinced that I wrote to him. Night and day, he prays for me to appear. He swoons over my penmanship. Does he think that I have time to write poems to mortals? Does he not know that I have acts of nature to reverse and virgin sacrifices to prevent?*

Mortals rarely consider the world beyond themselves, in my experience, the Dragon King said.

He's not even a good poet, she said.

Kai was impatient with their small talk, which she might have enjoyed if she hadn't been so worried about her sister.

A most tiresome matter indeed, the Dragon King said, cocking his scaly head and revealing his sharp teeth. *Noble Benzaiten, I have summoned you because the pearl diver has returned and she has the pearl.*

Benzaiten turned to stare and seemed to be at a loss for words. Going to her cushion, the goddess kneeled and clucked her tongue. *Oh dear,* she murmured. *Oh dear, oh dear.*

Kai felt a spark of fury. After all she had been through, Benzaiten had better keep her end of the bargain. *I did what you told me to do,* she said. *You can get my sister back from the Underworld, can't you?*

Benzaiten's four sets of hands fluttered in the air. *Well, of course I can. It's just—oh dear.*

Kai was frantic. *You don't have her spirit, do you?* she said. *You didn't expect me to survive.*

You wanted hope and I gave it to you, Benzaiten said, raising all eight hands as if to deflect a blow. *Had you died, you would have been reunited with your sister, which was what you wanted.*

To be fair, the Dragon King added, *the odds were not in your favor, valiant though you may be.*

Benzaiten, you promised to trade the pearl for her soul, Kai said, not caring that her thoughts were shrill and angry and that she was speaking to a goddess. *Why isn't she here?*

I did and I will, Benzaiten said. *I don't need her body here in order to reunite it with her spirit. All I need is the pearl.*

The turtle crawled to her with a pillow-lined tray on its back. Kai glanced over at the Dragon King, who nodded. She wasn't sure whether to believe Benzaiten. But they could take the pearl away whether she handed it over or not. Kai pulled the jewel from her pocket and placed it on the tray. When the turtle reached Benzaiten, she held up the pearl in two hands.

All hail the glorious jewel, she said, her eyes gleaming, her face flickering back into snake form for a moment. Then she turned her ancient eyes to Kai. *Are you sure this is what you want?*

Of course, Kai said, puzzled. *Why would I change my mind now?*

Just as you have changed from your journey, so has your sister from hers, Benzaiten said.

What does that mean? Kai asked.

It means that she may retain the memories of her death and crossing over to the spirit realm, Benzaiten said. *Memory can be a terrible burden, especially for humans.*

Getting to the Underworld was supposed to be arduous and scary. The soul endured harsh winds and had to climb a thorn-covered mountain while being followed by ogres wielding clubs. But for a second chance at life, it seemed like a small price to pay.

Yes, I want her back, Kai said.

The goddess rose from the cushion. *As you wish,* she said with a nod.

Benzaiten moved to the center of the throne room. Two white snakes slithered alongside her. When the snakes stopped, their scaly bodies cracked and shriveled. Their female forms appeared, though they kept their serpentine heads. One held a two-sided drum and the other a flute. Benzaiten put her hands into her pockets and pulled out eight bamboo clappers. The desolate cry of the flute soared above the deep drumbeat.

From darkness we enter the world. Into darkness we must return, Benzaiten said, her body swaying and her clappers clicking. *But now, O Lord of the Underworld, we ask you to reverse the path. Bring the dewdrop back to the blade of grass. Bring the petals back to the withered bloom. Bring the light back from the shadows.*

As she spoke, her eight arms rotated around her face and multiplied until there were too many to count. Her black diamond eyes grew larger and more infinite. Dizzy, Kai tried to turn away, to focus on some other point in the room. But Benzaiten's gaze was like iron. She couldn't look away no matter how hard she tried. The inky black eyes expanded until they covered up Benzaiten's spinning arms. Then her two eyes became one. Kai could no longer tell up from down. Her stomach lurched, and she had the sensation of falling into a deep well. Falling, falling, falling. Until everything went black.

Kai heard the ocean first. Waves rustling on the shore. Ebb and flow. So soothing she couldn't open her eyes.

"Kai. Kai."

With supreme effort, she raised her eyelids. She was lying belly-down on the wet sand, her head turned to one side. The sky was a brilliant blue.

"Kai." Kishi shook her shoulder. Bits of seaweed were plastered on her chest and flecked her white diving skirt. Her diving scarf had come off her head and dangled from her hair.

"Kishi," she said, pushing herself up to her knees and flinging her arms around her sister. "Kishi." Kai squeezed her tight, laughing and crying at the same time.

"I thought I was dead," Kishi said with a sob.

"I would never let you die," Kai said.

They hugged each other and rocked back and forth on the beach, taking long jagged breaths. Then they kneeled, facing each other and holding hands.

"Where are we?" Kishi asked. "Is this real or did you die, too? Are we in heaven?"

Kai was so focused on her, on her beautiful twin sister, that she hadn't noticed anything other than sand, sea, and sky. Now she looked around. In the distance, she spotted the burial mound jutting into the water. They were on Bamboo Island. Their rowboat, which she'd left on the beach, was upside down. She must not have pushed it far enough up the beach to avoid high tide. They were lucky it hadn't washed out to sea.

"It's real," Kai said. "We're on Bamboo Island." She wondered how much time had passed in the Dragon King's palace. A few hours? A day?

"What about Mama and Papa?" Kishi asked, her voice quaking. "Where are they?"

"They're home," Kai said, almost adding, "with my horse." She had so much to tell Kishi. "Do you remember what happened? Do you remember the bakekujira?"

Kishi nodded and sniffled. "I never thought I'd see any of the monsters from Hamako's stories. I was on my way back up to the surface when I sensed something behind me. I turned my head and saw a giant cave with teeth. Suddenly it felt like I was caught in a whirlpool. I was sucked inside its mouth and went tumbling down with seaweed and fish. It was violent, that's the only word for it. When I finally stopped moving, I saw Papa swimming below me. I saw you swimming toward me. I tried to swim to you. But I couldn't find the water. It was all around me yet I couldn't get to it.

Then I saw you trying to press your hands against mine, and I heard your voice in my head saying, 'It's not a ghost wall. It's a ghost *whale*.' And after that everything became a dark blur, and I felt incredibly sad because I was never going to get to ask you what that meant."

Kai squeezed her hands. "I followed you," she said. "I went inside the bakekujira to get you. Do you remember?"

"No," Kishi said, her voice trailing off. Her eyes traveled to a place that Kai couldn't go. Her face went pale and her body began to shake. "I'm cold. It's cold, Kai."

"I'll get you home," Kai said, leaping to her feet, energized by having a task to do. She jogged up the beach, picking up the oars and turning over the rowboat. But Kishi hadn't followed. All she had done was fix her headscarf. Kai dragged the boat into the water and sloshed through the surf to bring it closer to her sister.

"Come on, Kishi," Kai said. "Let's go."

Kishi stood up and walked to the water's edge. When the surf threatened to nibble her toes, she backed up and crossed her arms around herself. "I can't," she said, with a look of sheer terror.

Kai was so perplexed that it took several long seconds before she realized Kishi was afraid to step into the sea. "It's all right," she said. "The Dragon King got rid of the ghost whale. I know that sounds like a story that Hamako would tell. But it's true. He really did."

Kishi shook her head again. Then her chin quivered and a big fat tear rolled down her cheek. Kai pushed the boat back onto the beach and took her by the hand. "Get in and then I'll push the boat into the water. You're safe now."

Kishi nodded and climbed inside, pulling her knees into her chest and trying to stay as far away from the sides as possible. While Kishi curled herself into a tight ball, Kai muscled the boat into the sea. Once the water reached her thighs, she climbed into the rowboat and began to row.

"You're not going to believe everything that's happened," Kai said. "I met someone—a boy, I mean. He's brave and kind and smart. His name is Ren. He's on the quiet side. But I think you'll like him once you get to know him. I hope you will anyway, because, well, I do."

Her heart was bursting. She had been strong and brave and capable, and she knew now that there were no good twins and bad twins, just two people who shared the deepest of bonds. But Kishi continued to stare at her feet as if she hadn't heard a single word. Kai stopped rowing and touched her sister's hand. Kishi's eyes were dull and her jaw was slack. *Don't panic,* Kai thought. *It's only natural that Kishi would be scared of the water after what she's been through. She'll get over it.*

"I'm sorry," Kai said. "You've just been through something awful and I'm being selfish again. Do you want to talk about what happened? After the ghost whale, I mean."

"It was—" Her mouth moved but no words came out. A chill that had nothing to do with the temperature ran through Kai. Their lives had diverged for the first time these past few weeks. Kishi was no longer her mirror image inside and out. She now had dark caches of memory that Kai might never know or understand. And Kai wasn't sure if she could put into words all that had happened to her these past two weeks. The scary moments—the looming jaws of the bakeku-jira, almost drowning in the lake after getting shot with an arrow, running away from the fox pack—were not the things that would be hard to talk about. The incredible despair as the light went out of Encumbrance's eyes, the wrenching pain in her heart when she pulled back the bowstring and took aim at Ren, those were the moments that would haunt her forever.

Kai tasted something sharp at the back of her throat, salt mixed with seaweed. *It will get better,* she thought. *Kishi just needs time.*

They both did. But how could Kai leave tomorrow to go find Ren when Kishi was in distress? How could she let Ren live a single day longer tortured by a fox while she tended to her sister? It was an impossible dilemma. A gentle breeze kicked up and she swore she heard Hamako's voice: *Go home. Rest tonight. Be with the family. Tomorrow is a new day.*

Kai picked up the oars. Hamako was right. She had to let go of these questions today and savor this reunion with her sister and her parents. Ren would want her to do that. The question of when to leave could wait until tomorrow. The water was calm, almost glassy, and she quickly rowed the distance between the island and the shore. As the boat reached their cove, Kai looked over her shoulder and caught sight of Papa's red hammock swaying in the breeze and the buckets and baskets teetering in stacks on the veranda. The fishing boat had been returned to its usual spot on the beach and was no longer shoved up against the shed. As the rowboat drifted sideways in the current, she saw her parents walk between the azaleas and up the path toward the cottage. They were not wearing their white mourning clothes. Papa had on his too-small hat, while Mama was back in her special teal robe with the seashell pattern. They both cried out and ran into the water, splashing up to the boat. Mama threw her arms around them both and sobbed. Papa wrapped them all in his protective embrace. Kai hugged them back, glowing with pride that she had been the one to make the family whole again.

But even as she was swept up in this joyous moment, she realized that like the young fisherman Urashima Taro, she'd been wrong. No time had passed at all.

Looking at the yard over Mama's shoulder, Kai saw no sign of Burden. Looking down, she found that she no longer wore the page-boy uniform, but was back in the same outfit she'd put on to hunt for the ghost whale. Touching her hair, she discovered it was no longer short but pulled back in a low ponytail. She didn't have to touch her chest to know that the necklace with the compass was gone. But that no longer mattered, because Ren did not need rescuing, at least not from the fox. Letting go of her family, she shoved her hand up her right sleeve and felt around frantically for the scar.

As her fingers found the rough patch of skin, Kai began to fathom what Benzaiten had meant by the ripple effect of the tossed stone. She had done what she set out to do, and it had come with a cost. There were no more horses. There was only the sea.

Glossary

Ama: Kai and her family are loosely based on the ama, female deep-sea shellfish divers who traditionally passed down their skills and techniques from mother to daughter. The ama date back to at least the eighth century in Japan.

Bakekujira: This vengeful whale skeleton haunts the sea and brings bad luck to those who encounter it.

Baku: This guardian spirit who eats bad dreams has the head of an elephant, the body of a bear, the legs of a tiger, and the tail of an ox.

Basho: The priest's name is an homage to the seventeenth-century haiku master.

Benzaiten: Also called Benten, the water goddess Benzaiten is the only female deity among Japan's Seven Gods of Fortune. She has origins in the Hindu river goddess Sarasvati and was introduced to Japan in the seventh century.

Dakini: Like Benzaiten, the goddess Dakini also originated from Hinduism. In Japanese Buddhism, she is depicted riding a white fox.

The Dragon King: A mythological sea god, the Dragon King, or Ryujin, controls the tides with two magic jewels.

Enma: The lord of the Underworld who judges the souls of the newly dead in Buddhist hell.

Fox fist: Called *kitsune ken* in Japanese, this is a variation of the rock paper scissors hand game.

Honengame: A type of mermaid with a female human head and a turtle body, known for telling prophecies.

Kitsune: Magical foxes capable of human possession and the power to shape-shift.

Momotaro: Found as a baby inside a giant peach, Momotaro defeated a band of demons with help from a monkey, a dog, and a pheasant.

Ninmenju: Laughingstock Forest is based on the ninmenju, a tree with flowers that look like human heads and that will laugh if a person laughs at them first. The flowers wilt and fall off if they laugh too hard.

Princess Hase: This virtuous, obedient princess became the target of her evil stepmother.

Samebito: A type of merman with a shark body and a human head and limbs who was banished from service in the Dragon King's palace.

Tamamo no Mae: This powerful nine-tailed fox shape-shifted into a beautiful woman, bewitched the emperor, and became empress.

Tennyo: A beautiful celestial nymph whose feather gown allows her to travel between heaven and Earth.

Urashima Taro: This young fisherman rescued a sea turtle who turned out to be the Dragon King's daughter. After spending three days with her in the Dragon King's underwater palace, Urashima Taro returned home to discover three hundred years had passed.

Sources

Though *The Pearl Hunter* is set in the fictional Heiwadai Empire, the folklore and fairy tales hail from Japan. This book was informed by and owes a debt of gratitude to Zack Davisson, author of *Yokai Stories* and the hyakumonogatari.com website, and Matthew Meyer, author of *The Fox's Wedding* and the yokai.com website, for the fantastical creatures and folklore; Lafcadio Hearn and Yei Theodora Ozaki, who collected and translated many of the tales found here; and Karen A. Smyers, author of *The Fox and the Jewel*.

Japan in the eleventh century was known as a cultural golden age with a ruling class devoted to beauty in all forms. Many of the period details came from *The Tale of Genji* by Murasaki Shikibu, *The Pillow Book* by Sei Shōnagon, and *The World of the Shining Prince* by Ivan Morris.

Acknowledgments

I started *The Pearl Hunter* in the most solitary of times, in March 2020 when the COVID-19 pandemic shut down New York City. Holed up in our Brooklyn apartment during those eerie first few months, I filled the long hours dreaming up Kai and her journey.

While this book was born in solitude, the creative process has been truly communal.

I'm grateful for my fantastic agent, Victoria Wells Arms, who saw what this book could be and whose warmth, wisdom, and generosity of spirit helped me get there. Thanks also to the HG Literary team for their support.

I enjoyed every minute working with my brilliant editor, Donna Bray, whose keen editorial eye and fine-tuning elevated this book. Many thanks to the talented team at HarperCollins Children's Books, including Mikayla Lawrence for her incredible attention to detail and Molly Fehr for the stunning design. Thanks also to Maxine Vee and Sveta Dorosheva for their gorgeous work.

I never would have made it this far without an amazing group of writer friends. I'm deeply indebted to Beth Ain for her insights and for the great energy and intelligence that she brings to this very hard thing that we are inexplicably called to do. My splinter sisters—Kate Clifford, Laura Gilbert, Leila Mohr, and Lisa Parker—provided close reads, camaraderie, and lots of laughter. Rachel Sherman also gave invaluable feedback in the early stages of this book.

Off the page, thanks to Miki, who sparked my interest in her native Japan; to Chris and Margaret, who passed on their love of books; to Susan, Christian, Janet, Emma, and Ellie for keeping the California sunshine in our lives; and to Howard and Talia most of all.